THE PHYSICIAN'S HELPER

The Caregivers, Volume 3

Rose Fresquez

Published by Rose Fresquez, 2021.

To Joel, Isaiah, Caleb, Abigail and Micah. I love you so much and I'm so blessed to laugh and cry with you every day. Thanks for being my inspiration.

ACKNOWLEDGEMENTS

I want to thank the Lord, my Savior. Without you, Father, there's no point in trying to do anything at all. It's my prayer that I can honor you with my words. I thank you for connecting me with an amazing group of people who helped support me in accomplishing this novel.

To my husband Joel, who works so hard to provide for our family, so that I can stay home and take care of the kids. I'm so blessed that we get to journey through life together.

To my children Isaiah, Caleb, Abigail and Micah, you fill my heart with joy. Thanks for the giggles, laughter and encouragement.

Unending thanks to my editor, Deirdre Lockhart. Your insights and wisdom have helped shape this story.

To my insider team, thanks for always suggesting the coolest ideas.

Jerri Hall, Thanks for your support and encouragement always. You're such an inspiration

To Nicole, Deb, Melissa, Marie, Nancy, Linda, Katherine, Elizabeth and Trudy. You ladies are so amazing for the time you invested to brainstorm, beta read and critique my manuscript. Thank you from the bottom of my heart.

CHAPTER 1

On an unusually slow midafternoon at Olive Medical, Lucas Matthews opened the medical chart of his thirty-five-year-old patient. Having given the chart a cursory glance earlier, he now studied the vitals intently. *Hmm?* He squinted, grateful for the vibrant LED light as he concentrated on the computer displaying the man's blood pressure. Too high for the patient to go under anesthesia.

He straightened in the leather swivel chair, letting out his dread on a sigh. Patients hated having their surgeries postponed. He still had another forty-five minutes before his appointment, but if he was going to deliver unwanted news, he'd better first snag a refreshment. He grabbed his phone from the desk and stuffed it in the pocket of his scrubs before leaving the room.

Lucas had the best job in the hospital, or even in the world. He earned a great paycheck, worked predictable hours, and rarely encountered complications with his procedures.

On his way to the doctors' lounge, he browsed through his emails and texts for anything urgent. An email from the house cleaning company he'd used before. Delete. The next email was from a company selling him insurance. Delete.

By the time he took the elevator to the lounge, he'd deleted six emails. His phone vibrated and displayed his big brother, Adam's contact info.

"I know you're at work, but I promise to keep it quick." Adam spoke as soon as Lucas slid his thumb on the screen. "I'm getting married on June tenth."

He wasn't kidding about getting straight to the point. Lucas sidestepped a couple of doctors to walk toward the hallway.

June tenth, only four weeks away, wasn't enough warning to schedule time off. Plus, he'd need mental preparation to go home. His heart rate picked up, and his grip tightened on the slim phone. At least the late notice gave him a good excuse not to make it to the wedding. "Why am I just finding out about your wedding now?"

"You're the first to know."

His brow tightened. It didn't make sense that he'd find out about his brother's wedding before their parents. He walked down the hall, pausing at a tall window overlooking the Denver skyline. How were the out-of-town members going to make it on such short notice? "Don't you have to send invitations six months ahead?"

"You know how spontaneous I can be."

Way too spontaneous. Lucas tugged at his hair and tried not to think of a similar call he'd gotten from Adam ten years ago.

"Hello?" Adam's voice pulled Lucas back.

On the sidewalk below, pedestrians scurried to their various destinations, oblivious to those around them.

"I'm listening."

"You're the best man." It wasn't a question.

Adam had used his firstborn privilege to his advantage. With their parents giving him handouts early in life, at times he acted entitled to his family's time and money.

"What makes you think that will work out for my schedule?" Bracing one hand on the cool glass as he leaned closer to the window, Lucas tried to keep his tone firm. Someone had to be straightforward with his brother. "Isn't the best man a job for your best friend, anyway?"

"Brothers were born for emergencies."

Wow. As his gut tightened at the flippant words, Lucas closed his eyes until every bit of him felt as placid as the cool glass. What were Adam's motives for choosing him?

Before he could come to the wrong conclusion, Adam spoke in a low, finally serious tone. "I need you. There's loose ends to tie up."

Lucas wasn't one to hold grudges, but Adam could easily think there was still tension between them—a division over his best friend, Brit.

They both fell silent, and it felt like there was nothing else left to say. Yet Lucas better say something to assure Adam they were still family, and he'd put the past where it belonged.

"I'm happy for you, big brother." He meant it.

"Hearing those words means a great deal. Much different from last time."

Right. He knew what Adam meant.

Lucas had been too shaken up by Adam's first engagement—to Brittney, the only girl Lucas ever loved.

He scratched his clean-shaven jaw and stared at the glass as his smudgy handprint began to fade. "I don't even remember what I said."

"You questioned my sanity and called me all sorts of names I don't care to repeat." Adam chuckled through the phone. "Glad we can laugh about it now. Even my girlfriend laughed about it when I told her last month."

Lucas gripped the back of his neck where heat tingled on its way to scorch his ears. After a year of tension between them, they'd reconciled and never talked about Brit since.

Feeling jealous of the girl he could never have—the best friend he'd lost—was pathetic. He'd rather not revisit the past, so he redirected the conversation to Adam's fiancée.

"Tell me more about Olivia." He rubbed his forehead, the tightness easing from his muscles. "Is she okay with a rushed wedding?"

"You remembered her name?"

Lucas's heart swelled at his brother's awe. "You talk about her whenever you call."

A silence passed before Adam spoke. "This time I know she's the one."

With such tenderness in his brother's voice, Lucas believed him. In that case, it didn't matter who could make it—as long as Adam and Olivia showed up to their own wedding. "No need to wait, I guess."

"We both want to get married right away. You'd better start figuring out the best man stuff and all it entails."

Being the best man would mean going home and facing his past. "I don't know.... Work is complicated...." He clamped his lips around the urge to tell Adam about his interview for promotion to Chief Anesthesiologist. He instead told him the thorns he would have to crawl through to find a replacement, but either Adam wasn't listening or he was only thinking about his bride-to-be.

"You always have a plan. You'll figure it out." Adam left no room for Lucas to argue. "You'll need to arrive home two weeks before the wedding."

Lucas threw his head back, staring at the ceiling as if it had the answers. He could easily say no, but then he risked Adam thinking Lucas was still mad at him.

Which meant he had less than two weeks to go home. "You've got to be kidding me."

"We need to get matching suits." Adam continued mentioning all the things they needed to do before the wedding as if Lucas was his wedding planner. "I'll need all the help I can get."

Lucas needed time to process all this. "I haven't agreed to be best man yet—"

"You haven't been home for twenty-some years."

"Ten," Lucas corrected, but saying it out loud made it seem like an eternity. Something chilling and regretful crept through his heart, so intense it overpowered his will to turn Adam down.

Twice Adam had visited Lucas in Denver. Grandma, Mom, and Dad had come with him one Christmas to celebrate with Lucas at his apartment.

It seemed Adam took advantage of the silence to detect Lucas's internal battle. "On second thought, you should stay for two months when you come."

"Any chance you could postpone the wedding to July?" Lucas needed more time to work up the nerve to go home. God willing, should he get the promotion, he'd know by July and be able to get a new schedule going. "What's the rush if you're crazy about each other?"

"You're stalling," Adam scolded. "I wouldn't have pegged you for a chicken. You're afraid to deal with your past...." When Adam trailed on about his admiration for Lucas's confidence while they were younger and how he missed his baby brother, the words rushed out of Lucas's mouth before he could think better.

"I'll be there."

"Good," Adam said, obviously pleased with himself. "Can't wait to see you home."

When he hung up, Lucas's mind started spinning. How was he going to find an anesthesiologist on such short notice? Who could cover for him that long?

He may have to look into stand-ins from out of state or even the country. He stuffed his phone back in his pocket and leaned his forehead against the glass. The clear blue sky above the skyline brought to mind the long summer days in Soda Creek. The flawless brown-skinned girl with a dimple snuck into his mind, the same way she did whenever he thought of home. The tender thoughts vanished when he thought back to the last time he'd seen her.

It was in the fall, two days before he'd planned to fly home and whisk her to the tree house and confess his feelings for her.

As usual, Adam was ahead of things, and since Lucas had kept his feelings for Brit a secret even from his brother, he'd had no right to be upset when Adam called to announce his engagement.

Lucas's heart felt as if it were ripped in two. Without thinking, he'd taken the first flight home and pulled Brit into his arms.

"Please don't marry Adam," he'd begged, his heart racing with panic over losing the love of his life. It hadn't been his place to remind her that she and Adam had no chemistry, but he told her anyway before breathing out the words he'd kept to himself over the years. "I've loved you my whole life.... You're my forever, Brit."

She moved out of his embrace, her brown eyes shiny with tears. "Why are you telling me this now?"

"My timing has always been terrible." Desperate, he cupped her chin, his heart beating against his ribs as he leaned in and kissed her with years of pent-up emotion. For a moment, he thought she kissed him back, so he savored her soft lips on his. But it all had to be in his mind, something that became brutally clear when she shoved him.

"I can't. You're my best friend." Shaking her head, she swatted at the tears coming from the corner of her eyes. "We can't be anything more."

Like any irrational decision went, he'd messed up badly. A shudder went through him the way it did whenever he let himself think of that night.

With his heart heavy over what going home meant, he needed to talk to someone. ASAP.

But when he checked his watch, he didn't have long to get to the operating room and update the patient about changes to the procedure. After returning his phone to his office, he was almost panting when he made it to the OR.

He put his hands under the automatic dispenser on the wall. The cool gel dropped in his hands, and he rubbed them together as he introduced himself and sat on the stool in front of the computer.

When he spun to face the patient, his chest tightened, and he stretched one sentence into a fifteen-minute lecture before drawing a breath.

"With your high blood pressure, you're not fit for anesthesia." He drew in a deep breath, taking in the thick smell of disinfectant. "We'll have to reschedule the procedure."

The man threw his head back to the pillow, staring at the ceiling and touching his shoulder. "I'm sure my blood pressure will be normal in twenty minutes." His chest rose and fell, and his voice emerged gruff. "I need to have the surgery today."

Lucas's heart ached for the man. No doubt he'd had to rearrange his schedule to be here, but he needed to meet the man's gaze as he addressed the risks involved if they proceeded with anesthesia. Really, someone should have stopped the procedure before this. How could the man's blood pressure have slipped past unnoticed? Shoulder surgery wasn't urgent enough to risk going under.

"Listen." Lucas rolled his stool closer to the bed, and the man tipped his head to look at him. "We're doing this for your safety." As an anesthesiologist, he had to be the patient's advocate. "Your brain is used to sensing a certain blood pressure, and the chemicals in the anesthesia will typically bring blood pressure way down...." He went into a detailed explanation about brain reaction to anesthesia. "You could have a stroke."

The patient nodded, his eyes widening. "I'd rather not have a stroke."

Lucas recommended he get an evaluation from the primary care physician to determine the cause of his high blood pressure. Then he rolled the stool back toward the computer, the keyboard clicking as he typed his reasons to postpone the procedure into the patient's chart.

"Any chance I can get the surgery on Monday?"

Lucas glanced away from the computer to look at the patient, who was now staring through the window.

Monday was only three days away. "You will need at least a week. That's if your doctor can get you started on medicine to lower the blood pressure."

His body would need to re-equilibrate his brain, kidneys, and heart. Lucas relayed all that.

"Okay." At least the man understood why his plans had to change.

With a promise to see him possibly in one week, Lucas left the patient's room and returned to the reality of his own life.

The code blue announcements sounded through the intercom as he passed people in the hallway. Apparently, his problems weren't as bad as someone's on their deathbed, waiting for the doctor to determine a life-changing decision.

He rode the elevator to his friend Ryan's office, and after it deposited him on the fourth floor, one of the doctors he'd recently worked with stopped him. He folded his arms over his chest. "What's up, Dr. Krey?"

Her perky brown ponytail swung over one shoulder as the slim woman pursed her red lips. "Julia. Call me Julia."

He knew her first name, but he also knew her motives. His ease in carrying on a conversation with anybody was sometimes misinterpreted—okay, maybe some colleagues deemed him a ladies' man. But he wasn't anymore, not since he'd acquired conviction through his newfound faith.

As for Julia, he used her last name like a face shield to keep things professional and eliminate any complications. He tried to be polite so he didn't make anyone experience the brutal sting of rejection, but good grief, he had his own issues to deal with.

He glanced down the hall. He was only a few feet away from Ryan's office. She must have gotten the hint of his urgency and spoke.

"A few of us are going to Rockley's tonight." She flashed an alluring smile, lifting one penciled eyebrow in question. "Would you like to come?"

She was attractive. The kind he usually asked out to a black-tie event. Months ago, he would've saved Julia the trouble of reaching out to him, but lately, he didn't want to waste his or anyone else's time. Especially not today with Brit consuming his mind.

"Sorry." He gripped the back of his neck. "I have plans."

"On a Thursday?" She stuffed her hands into her white lab coat's pockets.

"My nephew's basketball game." His best friend's kids were practically his niece and nephews—the only kids in his life. But Lucas didn't have to explain himself. With that, he gave a curt nod, his way of wishing her a great day.

"Next time, then?" Her words carried on his back, and he spun around, not intending to give her false promises.

"Have fun," he said instead, ignoring her question.

Once upon a time, he'd taken each day in stride with not much thought, but since he'd turned forty, noncommittal relationships no longer held appeal. He needed stability, but if life came with charts like one's medical history, his would show falling in love wasn't a possibility for him.

Just as he'd hoped, when he knocked once and pushed the half-open door, Ryan's hands were flying over the keyboard, typing surgeon-related notes he usually had to catch up on in between surgeries. He had crazy hours, yet unlike Lucas, he still had a life outside work.

Ryan became a family man when he took legal guardianship of his deceased sister's kids and then married the love of his life.

"Matthews." Ryan slid off the blue light glasses. He set them on the table next to a framed picture of him, his wife, and kids, among their many other pictures on his desk. "You look like you've seen a ghost."

Sort of. "You could say that." Lucas flopped onto the gray sofa, then stood and walked to the tiny refrigerator and back to the door. Great. He couldn't even figure out whether he wanted to sit or stand.

"Your pacing is making me dizzy." Ryan spun his swivel chair to face Lucas. A wrinkle crinkled his brow, and his mouth pinched in a firm line.

Although Lucas had a brother, Ryan, slightly older, knew him better than anybody and had become like his big brother. Even if they didn't look alike, what with Ryan's curly brown hair and lean frame and Lucas's dark-blond hair and muscular build.

"You'd better start talking before I page a psych consult for you."

"Adam's getting married." He snatched the apple from Ryan's desk, biting into it and walking back to flop onto the leather couch.

"You're eating an apple. This is serious stuff."

With his sense of taste gone, Lucas didn't care as he bit into the sticker, chewing and swallowing before finding his voice. "He wants me to be the best man."

Ryan leaned back, his brows drawn as he crossed his arms. "As long as he's not marrying Brittney, we're happy for him, right?"

Lucas nodded.

"You have plenty of time to plan."

Lucas told Ryan the time period. "What if I get the promotion, and they want me to attend training or some sort of meeting?" He'd done an interview two days ago, but he wasn't the only one they'd considered for the role. Even if he was good at what he did, two other credible anesthesiologists were vying for the position.

"Let's not worry about the job right now." Ryan crossed one leg over the other and rocked back in his chair. "Good thing we will be in Soda Creek about the same time."

Lucas had forgotten his friend's vacation was coming up. "I guess that will be good."

"You guess?" Ryan pounded the table playfully. "You can guarantee the kids will be a good distraction if you need an escape from... um, family issues."

He didn't miss the hesitation in Ryan's sentence. By family, Ryan meant Brit, since his friend was well aware of how she'd ruined Lucas for any other woman.

He massaged his forehead, sensing an oncoming headache. A headache caused by nothing other than the woman who was the source of his current problems.

Ryan stood and slapped Lucas on the shoulder. "Going home is a good thing. Sooner or later, you must face your past before you get a grip on your future." *yeah*

If only facing the past was that easy.

Ryan ambled to the fridge and retrieved a black lunch box. "On the bright side, Destiny made us some cookies." He patted the lunch box. "Let's go have lunch."

Lucas had no appetite, but with nothing else to do, he followed Ryan out of his office. Despite not tasting the apple, Lucas devoured the rest of it and tossed the core in the trash can outside the elevator. He had no choice but to return home.

Even if he had no idea where to start, he knew one thing for sure. Since the day Brit cut him out of her life, he'd been searching for what the two of them had, could've had—for someone like her, but he never found that person. Not even close.

CHAPTER 2

Brittney Young tossed her client's clothes in the washer and snapped the lid closed. The fluorescent bulb made it easier to locate the right detergent for her next load.

With Clarice's sensitive skin, Brittney used the fragrance-free detergent for her clothes before closing the soap dispenser and pushing the power button to start.

She let out a yawn. The whirring machine was soothing enough to put her to sleep, but taking a nap would only interfere with her rest tonight.

Clarice's voice carried through the hallway down to the basement as she spoke to her oldest grandson. Brittney had taken Adam's call and handed Clarice the phone before leaving for the laundry room.

Turning to the pile of clothes in the basket on the dryer, she retrieved the crimson T-shirt with the words *Harvard Medical* silkscreened in white. She lifted it to her face and closed her eyes while whiffing the faint masculine scent. Even if it had been several years since her best friend had worn it, she could almost smell his scent whenever she wore the old shirt.

Dwelling in the past was a terrible mistake, but she clung to anything that reminded her of the friendship she'd lost. She lowered the shirt from her face and folded the corners, which was silly since she intended to wear it tonight after her shower. She reached for a blouse and folded it onto the stack.

The quiet afternoons always offered a pleasant time to get housework done. Living on the jobsite had its ups and downs. While she didn't have to hassle with traffic, knowing when to take a break could be challenging. She couldn't complain, though. She had a good life. Taking care of Clarice, the grandmother Brittney never had, was an honor.

"Brittney!"

Brittney tossed the jean shorts on the floor. The carpeted stairs creaked as she took two at a time until she was standing between the kitchen and the living room.

"Are you okay?" she asked, letting out a relieved sigh when Clarice's wide grin met her gaze. Propped in a comfy recliner, Clarice spread her hands wide as if to hug her. Her white hair still held the curls Brittney put in yesterday.

"Adam's getting married." The slippery magazine stack on her side table wobbled as she placed the phone on it. Clarice's eyes held surprise, but the news was no shock to Brittney. Her ex adored his girlfriend.

"In four weeks." Clarice lifted four fingers for emphasis.

Now that was short notice for their families coming into town, but maybe it would be a small ceremony. "That's great news."

"Guess who's the best man?"

Easy answer. Adam's best friend. "Conrad."

"Who?" Clarice adjusted her hearing aid, and Brittney repeated the name.

"Wrong." A glint lit her golden eyes as the older woman rubbed her hands together, an unusual tremor displaying her glee. "Our Luke is coming home."

With the words, something in Brittney's heart caught, and one hand automatically went to her chest. Barely able to stand on her wobbly feet, she leaned against the wall, surprised when she managed a response. "That's good."

"Seven years since he left—"

"Ten," she corrected. Tuesday next week would be ten years to be exact.

Funny she knew the number of days since Lucas left Soda Creek, taking her heart with him. She looked through the kitchen window to the backyard. Her gaze wandered to the tree house on the oak tree. Beyond it, the bright sun shone over the grass extending to the pond and creek running through Clarice's four-acre property.

It had always been hard not to think about Lucas. Especially when everything around her involved him. All the memories of her childhood, the hours they'd spent in the tree house, talking and planning their future. Him as a doctor and her as a caregiver. The long, lazy summers they'd spent riding their bikes, swimming, and skipping rocks in the pond. It all seemed like it was someone else's dream.

"Don't worry." Clarice's words brought her out of her daze. "His trip home will be good for us."

Brittney shrugged, unsure what to say. Even if she and Lucas assured his family they were just friends, Clarice always thought someday their friendship would turn into something more—a couple. As it turned out, Lucas *had* wanted more from their friendship, a line Brittney always worked so hard to never cross.

Lucas had been her best friend and confidant, even before her parents died—if only she'd known then what she knew now. It would've been better to cross the line than not to have her best friend in her life at all.

"Maybe don't go out with the postman yet." The glint in Clarice's eyes flared. "That's if you haven't called him."

Brittney hadn't told Clarice yet, but now was a better time to say it. "I'm really not interested." Not just in the mailman, but in anyone else for that matter. Thanks to Lucas.

She had no idea what she'd done with the man's number, anyway. She'd only let Clarice play matchmaker because Clarice needed to interact with more people than just Brittney. The mailman made Clarice laugh whenever he dropped off mail, and Clarice insisted he stay for lemonade or use their bathroom whenever he needed to.

"We're going shopping." Clarice picked up her cane from the gray carpet. "I need a dress for the wedding, you know."

Brittney would do anything for Clarice, but with such news, she needed a moment to herself. Plus, they'd had a long morning of aerobics, a senior brunch at the recreation center, and Clarice's dental appointment.

"I might lay down." Maybe her hint would get Clarice to nap. Not only did Brittney hate giving direct orders, but also her client wasn't one to order. So hints worked for both of them.

"I know your workday is over." Clarice waved a hand. "But I promise to give you the entire day off tomorrow."

Brittney didn't need a day off, but she also didn't need to see Clarice's blood pressure go up with all the excitement. "We still have four weeks."

Plenty of time for shopping.

Clarice preferred planning her days months ahead, and sometimes she pushed herself to the limit. Brittney's job was to keep her from extending those limits. She made room for Clarice's normal self by giving her space to do her own thing, yet staying close in case she needed help.

Clarice dropped the cane, and it thudded on the soft carpet. "All right... all right, Miss Bossy." Her voice was light. "As long as the only thing I'm doing tomorrow is shopping."

It sounded like a pout, but it was a resolution.

"What if we host your sewing club here, instead?" There were only ten of them, but seven were consistent in their meetings. "There's no need to cancel anything when we have a whole day."

Clarice tapped a finger on her chin as if thinking. "We have to get Luke's room ready."

Which only meant putting blankets and bedsheets on the bed. Whenever Brittney cleaned the house, she dusted all the six bedrooms. But surely... "I'm sure he'd rather stay at his childhood home."

Her heartbeat kicked up speed, and she calmed it with slow, steady breaths as the part of her that wanted him to stay with them struggled against the part that wasn't ready to face him.

"This is his childhood home, too." Clarice gave a firm nod, then trailed on about wanting Lucas to spend all of his spare time with them.

Since Brittney was ten, she'd always had a room at Clarice's house. Just like all Clarice's grandkids did.

Needing to get back to her laundry and into her thoughts, Brittney walked over to Clarice and took the cordless phone back to the charger. "Can I get you anything else?"

Instead of answering, Clarice scanned the floor, then the table, her brows drawn tight. "What did I do with my pencil?"

Brittney glanced at Clarice's ear, where she kept her pencil whenever she took breaks from crossword puzzles, and as she expected, there it was, tucked between her ear and hair. Not wanting Clarice to feel embarrassed about the situation, Brittney played dumb herself.

"Hmm, could it be on your lap or shirt pocket?"

Clarice patted her lap and pocket.

"Or in your hair, something like that."

She patted her hair, then her ear, and grinned, brandishing the pencil at Brittney. "Good grief, I should remember that." Then Clarice reached for one of the magazines from the stack. "This should keep me busy for a while."

"Let me know whenever you're ready for the shower."

"Thank you, sweetheart." She gave her that warm smile. "Go take your break."

Clarice preferred her independence, which had been hard at first when her arthritis got worse at seventy-five and Lucas's mom wanted to hire a live-in caregiver for her.

But after spinal surgery, high-blood-pressure episodes, and two falls down the stairs, Clarice had compromised. "As long as it's Brittney taking care of me and not some stranger in my house."

At the time, Brittney was working with a caregiving company, and they were charging Clarice far too much. In the end, Brittney quit the company and started working solo, for Clarice.

Clarice talked Brittney into moving in, which made sense. Brittney already spent 90 percent of her time at Clarice's house. Since then, she'd worked and stayed with her for eleven years.

Instead of walking downstairs to the laundry room, like she should, she let her feet lead her down the hall, and she almost tripped over Midnight.

"I almost ran you over." She squatted and scratched behind the cat's ears, her black fur a balm to her distraught heart. When Midnight was content with all the rubbing and cuddles, she walked out of Brittney's hands and ambled toward the living room.

On her way to the bedroom, Brittney paused to look at the pictures lining the wall. They were mostly pictures of Clarice's grandkids, Lucas and his siblings, as babies. Then several pictures from when they got older and Brittney joined their family.

She fixated on a picture of her and Lucas, with a football in his hand and his other arm slung around her shoulders. It was taken after a homecoming game. She could almost smell the subtle scent of his spicy cologne mingled with the healthy scent of him. At the end of his games, both basketball and football, she'd always been the first person he hugged as she congratulated him before he went to shower and change in the locker room.

She'd never known an intelligent person who was as good an athlete as Lucas. He could've easily pursued a basketball career if he'd wanted to.

Her gaze wandered to the next picture.

Adam's senior picture. His hair combed back, dark like his dad's, as opposed to Lucas's dark blond. Adam, although he acted spoiled at times, was mellow and laid-back and always had a small circle of friends as opposed to Lucas or their sister. He had similar qualities to Brittney, except for his impulsiveness when it came to relationships.

On the other hand, Lucas, adventurous, wild, and fearless, always had the excitement and thrill in him, and that had kept Brittney feeling more alive. Until she got engaged to Adam.

If Brittney had kept the lie going, she would be Mrs. Adam Matthews now. Her stomach dropped at the reality. She'd made plenty of mistakes, but getting engaged to Adam topped all those.

Their one-week engagement had ended as fast as it started. Now, with the big four-oh behind her and still single, she was starting to accept the reality of the mistakes she'd created.

While it should bother her that her ex had moved on and was getting married, Lucas was the one who occupied her mind. Would he want to stay at his grandma's house? He might, having always valued the place since his grandpa built it with his bare hands. Things would be awkward if he stayed with them.

If only she hadn't gone out with Adam out of sympathy for his breakup. If only she'd known how Lucas felt about her all those years. If only she'd said no to Adam's proposal. Then things would be different.

Shaking her head, she moved away from the photos, but not the memories. She hugged her arms tight around the aching in her chest. If-onlys never worked.

Instead, she'd created temporary friction in the Matthews family.

She dropped her arms and smiled a little, thinking of when she'd given her notice to Clarice. Her usual vim bubbling over, Clarice had swatted her lightly with her crossword puzzles and told her not to act like her life was a movie, but instead face reality. "You think distancing yourself from the family will solve the problems?" She'd shaken that puzzle magazine at her as if the question were merely a clue to one. "Or will it make things worse?"

So Brittney had chosen to stay. Everyone hadn't made as big a deal as she'd thought they would. Except for the one person who mattered the most.

After the heart-melting kiss, Lucas was gone before she even went to bed that night.

He'd stopped talking to her, probably despised her. Once best friends now seemed like strangers because of a choice she'd made—a single choice that had seemed the easiest one at the time, that had turned out to be the final definition of many uncertainties.

She closed her eyes, pushing past the dark memories of the first two years without Lucas. Feeling worthless, hating herself, and overcome with intense guilt, she'd wanted to stay in bed all day and never talk to anyone again.

If she needed one thing more than anything else, it was the miracle of having her friend back in her life. How to start, she had no idea.

CHAPTER 3

A homecoming surprise was exactly what Lucas wanted. His mom called to make plans to pick him up at the airport, who should come and shouldn't, and what kind of food he wanted for his welcome-home party. Already overwhelmed by everything, he decided to keep his arrival time a mystery. "Sometime in the morning," was all he'd told his mom.

No reason to make anyone go out of their way to pick him up when he could take an Uber from the airport.

He'd worked a night shift at St. Anne's charity hospital, where he volunteered once a week during the daytime, or twice if he sacrificed sleep for a random night shift.

As soon as his shift had ended at three a.m., he'd gone straight to the airport and was now in the back of the Camry, stifling yawn after yawn.

The morning spread rays of light across the land as the driver turned from one familiar street to another.

When the car veered onto the wide street lined with pink cherry blossoms, a thrill of excitement, emotion, and memories of home all gushed at him at once. He scarcely dared breathe, taken back to the long days of summer, riding his bike and tossing a football with Brit in the middle of Cherry Court—their quiet street, since Brit and his siblings had been the only kids on the street back then.

They drove past a middle-aged couple walking their dogs. Although Lucas didn't recognize their faces, they waved, and he waved back. He couldn't help smiling. People were still friendly, the way he remembered Soda Creek.

With Lucas's instructions, the driver parked in front of the white picket fence house, his childhood home.

When he stepped out of the car, he thanked the driver before hoisting his luggage out of the back seat. He'd taken care of the tip when he paid for the Uber service online. With a wave to his driver, he walked toward the driveway, then opened the latch to the low gate.

Not surprisingly, the two-story with its gray and white siding was still in excellent condition. His dad loved painting the house every other summer.

Taking the narrow brick path, Lucas walked past mature trees. The faint scent of lilac and honeysuckle blossoms from vines along the fence wafted in the air.

When he climbed the stairs to the front porch, he regretted showing up before seven. What if his parents slept in lately? They'd aged over the years, no doubt, and their jobs weren't as demanding as they used to be.

Setting his suitcase beside the words *Sweet Home* on the welcome mat, he squared his shoulders and glanced at the hanging petunia baskets. Perhaps he should nap on the patio sofa until everyone woke up.

Before he could go flop on the sofa, he lifted the handle of the door, which surprisingly opened. He set the luggage to the side and eased the door closed behind him.

With the smell of coffee and bacon coming from the kitchen, Mom must be awake. Dad would probably be sitting at the dining table with a cup of coffee, reading the newspaper to her while she cooked. Whenever Dad was home, he always liked to stay in close proximity to Mom. cute ☺

Classical music played in the background as Lucas walked through the living room. The clatter of silverware forced him to announce his presence as he approached the wall dividing the kitchen from the living room. "Hello?"

The moment he stepped on the threshold, Mom's jaw dropped, and something fell out of her hands, clattering on the hardwood floor. He assumed it to be a knife, given the half-sliced avocado on the cutting board.

Mom half gasped, and her hand flew to her mouth. "Lucas?"

Her blonde hair was more light and golden along the edges, but she still looked fashionable in her blue sleeveless top. With her hand by her mouth, light caught on the silver and beaded bracelets wrapping her wrist.

"Son?" Dad's deep voice sounded, and Lucas spotted him with a steaming cup of coffee and newspaper sprawled open on the table. More gray than he remembered threaded through his dark hair. But he sat with a straight posture, and his eyes still lit up with his smile.

Lucas gripped the back of his neck, his chest tightening. Why had it taken him this long to come home? "Sorry, I thought I'd show up before—"

Mom was already eating up the space between them and squeezing him in a tight embrace. "Welcome home, honey."

He closed his eyes, leaning into the warm and comforting embrace, the smell of jasmine making him feel like a child again.

When she stepped out of the hug, she touched his cheek, and the morning light hit through the sliding back door, glinting at the mist in her blue eyes. "You look so skinny. Have you been eating at all?"

Lucas stifled a chuckle, fascinated by her concern, as usual. He patted his flat stomach. "Never missed a meal since I left."

"Lucas." Dad had moved from the table and now took Mom's place. He engulfed Lucas in a hug. "Just in time for your mom's hearty breakfast."

Lucas glanced at the stove, where she started flipping eggs, then sticking bread in the toaster. His mouth watered when he saw a plate filled with bacon stacked on paper towels.

Dad asked about his flight and if he knew the kind of plane he'd flown in. Such details didn't interest Lucas, but Dad preferred them. "I flew with Southwest."

"It must be the 737. That's what Southwest uses."

After Mom put the food on the table, she ushered them forward. "Let's have some breakfast."

Prayer wasn't a ritual in his house, unless things had changed over the years. Not wanting to impose his faith on anyone, he bowed his head, trying not to draw attention. In his heart, he thanked God for the food and a safe trip in as little as two seconds.

When Lucas's attention was back to the table, questions crinkled up Dad's brow. He didn't ask—or more likely didn't have time to ask—because Mom brought over a pitcher of orange juice in one hand and milk in the other, then set them on the table.

Lucas ate scrambled eggs, bacon, and sausage. He turned down coffee when Mom offered. "I had an overnight shift, so I'm hoping to go to bed this morning."

"You'll need a nap." Dad's fork clanked against the porcelain when he set it down. "Your mother assumed you would be here by noon. She's hosting a welcome-home gathering this afternoon."

"Shouldn't we be having dinners in honor of the happy couple instead?" Lucas glugged some orange juice. He had yet to meet the bride. He'd only seen her pictures from the text Adam had sent when he'd proposed.

"Adam and Olivia have their wedding. That's a party in itself." Mom poured milk in a glass and put it in front of Lucas. "They'll be here this afternoon. I thought you'd like to meet your future sister-in-law before the wedding."

"That will be nice." With such short notice, could any out-of-town family members even make it? "Who else is coming to the wedding?"

"Your grandma and grandpa Matthews got here yesterday. They're still sleeping."

Lucas found out his sister, Emery, had been home for the last two weeks from her two-year international world tour.

When his parents mentioned the extended family members who'd be in town soon, Lucas was already exhausted for her sake. "Where are all those people staying?"

Mom looked around and to the back glass door where rays of morning light flooded the room. "We have plenty of space." With four spare bedrooms, he assumed his grandparents were already sleeping in one, then his sister in the other. That still left his room and Adam's. Otherwise, he didn't mind staying in a hotel.

"I was hoping you could stay with your grandma." Reaching across the table, Mom rested a hand on his forearm as if tapping into his thoughts. "She would like that."

He almost choked on his eggs. "No way." He reached for his milk to wash down the eggs, then thudded the glass down on the table. Didn't Mom realize how strange things would be if he stayed under the same roof with Brit? "I'll stay in a hotel."

"Don't be ridiculous." Mom waved her fork in his direction. "You haven't been home in ages, and no way are you staying at a hotel."

"You better listen to your mom." Dad glanced at her with tenderness, then winked at him.

"I'll stay at Adam's place, then."

Mom opened her mouth as if to speak, but shrugged instead. "I'm just glad you're home."

"Can I take a nap in my room?" For now, he assumed it was still vacant.

"Yes."

With that resolved, they continued their breakfast while he asked about Mom's jewelry business. She and two of her friends rented a shop in town to sell their handmade crafts. "We take turns running the shop in the winter. But summer gets busy, and we need to kick up our hours."

The conversation shifted to the town when Lucas asked who the mayor was. Dad, having been reelected as mayor several elections in a row, spoke about the town with fondness. He talked about his involvement in the city council, despite his part-time job at the engineering firm he'd worked for since the company moved to Soda Creek several years ago.

After breakfast, Lucas gathered the dishes to load them in the dishwasher, but Mom took them from him. She set them in the sink and gave him a gentle shove toward the stairs. "You'd better go to bed before everyone wakes up."

Dad nodded. "They'll want to hear what you've been up to for the last ten years."

So Lucas hauled his luggage up the stairs, Mom's voice sounding behind him. "Good to have you home."

He paused on the stairs overlooking both levels of the home, the hardwood floors spread out below, and the soft carpet cushioning his steps. His uncertainty over how he'd feel when he got here vanished. Being in his childhood home felt right.

Although he would deny it if someone told him he'd avoided coming home because of Brit, it was the truth. He'd always appreciated his parents for not pestering him about the whys. One year after Brit and Adam's engagement had ended, Lucas couldn't lie to his mom and grandma anymore about his feelings. Like the genius and wise adults they were, they'd already known he'd always liked Brit beyond friendship. If only she'd detected his feelings for her, too, things might have been different.

He didn't have to look at the hallway wall to know there were familiar family pictures. Knowing it would only stir up memories and interfere with his sleep, he squelched the urge to stop and stare.

After making his way to the corner bedroom on the right side down the hall, he paused in the doorway. Ten years later, the room hadn't changed, just as it hadn't through his growing-up years. The same soft blue still painted the walls behind out-of-date movie posters.

With the room too bright, he walked to the window to draw the blinds, but his gaze instantly darted to the window down below—to the house next door, Brit's childhood home.

Their families had shared meals back and forth, and he'd had slumber parties with her. At her house, they'd sleep in the living room, and whenever she came to his house, they'd sleep in the basement with his siblings until Lucas was in seventh grade. Their parents decided they were too old for slumber parties, especially when Adam didn't want to join them. The exception was if Brit could sleep in the spare bedroom.

How many nights had he looked through the window to see if her light was on? Or climbed the tree to get into her room, especially after her mom died and Brit struggled to sleep.

Some nights she'd climb the window to his room through the garage balcony. They would work on puzzles and talk into the wee hours and never run out of conversations.

He yawned. Emotionally and physically spent, he closed the blinds.

The double bed dipped under his weight when he laid down and closed his eyes, craving darkness, but his room alone was full of vibrant memories. All he saw was light through her laughter while she folded his shirts and rearranged clothes in his chest of drawers—separating T-shirts from shorts and calling him disorganized when he shoved a button-down shirt in the drawer instead of hanging it in the closet. He laced his hands behind his head and tried to breathe deep and shove all thoughts aside. How could he ignore her existence now that he was home?

The bedsheets rustled when he turned his head to the side, still keeping his eyes closed, determined to fall asleep. *Oh, Brit.*

She was always the best fantasy, yet she was untouchable. With her having no big brother, Lucas had taken on the job. He was someone she could count on, someone she could turn to. Until his feelings got the best of him. Until he wanted her to be his forever.

Despite everything that happened after the kiss, it was hard to go back to friendship when he wanted more—something they'd never have because she'd always see him as her brother. In the meantime, he needed to be the friend Brit expected him to be—the unconditional friend he'd always promised to be.

CHAPTER 4

B rittney pursed her lips at her reflection in the full-length mirror. The lip gloss went on pinker than she assumed it would look when she'd bought it.

Not for me.

She wiped it off with the back of her hand.

Her brown skin required a specific powder. If she was familiar with makeup, she could figure something out, but she'd never taken the time to learn what cosmetics worked for her skin tone. She had been, however, tempted to buy eye shadow when she took Clarice shopping for her wedding dress.

Staring back at her reflection, she tucked her mint-green top into the flowy bohemian pants. A new purchase she'd splurged on specifically for this day. "It's not because of Lucas that I'm tempted to use makeup." She mumbled the words like she needed to remind herself. She and Lucas were best friends—*had been* best friends—and if by some miracle she got to talk to him, she intended to use their visit for reconciliation.

It wouldn't hurt if they had a redo of the toe-curling kiss.

She was suddenly warm at the memory.

"I don't want kisses from Lucas." She placed both hands on her heated cheeks before spotting Midnight's reflection through the mirror. Curled up on the white duvet cover on her bed, the cat stared at her as if reminding Brittney that she'd brought this mess upon herself.

She spun around and bent to scratch around Midnight's collar. "Did you hear that, munchkin? I can't be thinking of kissing Lucas. I'm only excited because we've missed him, right?"

30

The cat licked Brittney's arm, and she sat on the bed, snuggling Midnight against her chest. She'd been a kitten when Brittney and Lucas found her wandering on Main Street in the middle of the night. It had been during his visit home, during his first year in medical school. "Let's call it Midnight," he'd suggested, since they didn't know her gender yet. "It's a neutral name."

Brittney had been against taking a street cat into the house while it was used to roaming free, but she'd agreed to bring her home when Lucas thought it was worth trying.

"We'll train it to be a house cat. And I'll call every night to give you moral support." And he'd kept his word. They'd spoken almost every night when he was in school, and he would come on weekends to hang out with them.

"I'm ready whenever you are." Clarice's voice rang from down the hall, bouncing off Brittney's door.

Rubbing behind Midnight's ears, Brittney set her back on the bed. "I'd take you with me, but trust me, I'll be out of shape tonight."

She had no idea what to expect from her encounter with Lucas. She hadn't expected him to arrive two full weeks before the wedding.

The frame almost fell off her dresser when she grabbed her handbag. Adjusting the picture of her and Lucas, she reached for the other framed photo of her mom and dad, touching their faces and wishing they were here.

Now would be a good time to call them and ask for some guidance. Her chest tightened, and she forced in deep breaths to loosen it, missing them so badly. It had been several years since their departure from earth, but moments when she needed assurance made her miss them most.

When she met Clarice in the living room, the contents of her purse were scattered on the table as she tossed one item at a time back into it.

"I can't find my camera." She frowned, scanning the floor. "I just had it."

Before Brittney could start searching, she glimpsed the Kodak's silver string sticking out of Clarice's shirt pocket. "Did you check your pants or shirt pockets?"

"Uh..." Clarice frowned, patted her chest, and shook her head when she felt the camera. "How did it even get there?" She slid it into her bag.

"Maybe Midnight's playing pranks on you."

Clarice nodded, the corners of her lips lifting. "Blaming a cat might not be a bad idea."

Brittany chuckled as she helped Clarice replace the contents in her bag.

"Thank you." Clarice jiggled the bag to settle everything in place, looking at Brittney from her face to her outfit. "Don't you look beautiful? One look at you, and my grandson will remember his roots in Soda Creek."

She was reading too much into things. Brittney shook her head, an aching in her chest. "I just want my friend back."

"You two belong together."

If that had been the case, that opportunity had passed. Not needing to say so to Clarice, Brittney focused on complimenting her client. The floral button-down with purple flowers was vibrant and perfect over her loose dark pants.

"You don't look bad yourself." She outstretched her hand for Clarice.

Like most days, Clarice handed Brittney her cane and braced herself on the table, both hands gripping its edge as she pulled up to stand.

On their way to the garage, Brittney retrieved the container with slices of pound cake. Even if dinner was catered, her mom taught her never to go to a gathering empty-handed.

On the fifteen minute drive to Lucas's parents' house, Clarice ticked her fingers with a list of things she wanted him to do while visiting. "Plus, he has to come to the county fair with us." She added that one on her pinkie.

"I'm sure he has more things to do, with the wedding and all."

Clarice folded her hands on her lap. "He got here early to spend more time with us."

No reason to argue, even if Clarice was making assumptions.

As they turned to Cherry Court, Brittney intended to get Clarice to the front door and run back to the car to tinker with her hair and process a few things. But Lucas's family standing and sitting on the front porch derailed her plan when she pulled into the driveway.

Someone was already flinging open the short gate by the time Brittney walked Clarice over.

"Are we late for the party?" Clarice tucked her hand on Brittney's arm as if needing extra support—support she never would have accepted on a regular day. Yep, the wily woman was anchoring Brittney in place.

"You're just in time." Lucas's sister, Emery, flung her arms around Clarice, squealing. "You look beautiful, Nana."

"Hello, my angel of the earth." Clarice ruffled Emery's short blonde hair.

When Emery looked at Brittney, her grin widened, and she clapped, then squeezed her tight. The cane clattered out of Brittney's hand as she hugged Emery back. Brittney had missed Emery's enthusiasm while she was abroad.

Emery eased out of the embrace. "I love your pants."

"Thanks." Brittney warmed at Emery's genuine compliment, handing Clarice her cane.

"You always look fashionable." Emery had her mom's delicate features, and her blue sundress brought out the color of her eyes.

"Grandma!" Adam called cheerfully. With his dark hair combed back the way he usually styled it, he had his short-sleeved shirt tucked into jeans. As he hugged Clarice, the rest of the family and a few family friends were not too far behind him.

While they greeted Clarice, Brittney returned to the car to retrieve their handbags and the cake.

Most faces were familiar—Lucas's extended family she'd met over the years of celebrating Thanksgiving and Christmas with the Matthews.

One of Lucas's aunts took the cake from her. "Thanks for bringing this." She stared through the glass lid, then winked. "I might have to start with dessert."

Laughter warmed Brittney's chest. "I think you can get away with anything at a party."

Cheerful voices carried on as she said hello to everyone while they walked toward the porch. A breeze stirred the sweet fragrance from the purple lilacs in full bloom along the fence, and a robin sang merrily from the tangled branches.

"I need to take everyone's picture."

When Clarice asked for her purse, Adam reached to take it from Brittney. "I'll help you take that."

Olivia, a petite brunette with extremely white teeth, stepped up to Brittney. Ducking her head, Olivia hugged her arms around herself and poked her peep-toed sandal at a beetle, hurrying it along. "They can all be a bit overwhelming, can't they?"

Her eyes wide, the poor girl looked somewhat lost in the boisterous group. Little wonder she navigated to Brittney as another "outsider." She and Brittney had met no more than four times at the Matthews' family dinners, long enough to assure Brittney that Olivia and Adam were perfect for each other.

Brittney slid an arm around the other girl's waist. "I've known them practically my whole life, so they feel like family. They can be

THE PHYSICIAN'S HELPER 35

loud, but they're full of love and so happy to have you as part of their family."

The girl had been blessed with her in-laws, with her fiancé, too. Adam might not be Lucas, but he was a good man who'd never held a grudge against Brittney over their breakup.

She heard his words, delivered with the Matthews boys' half-smile all over again— *"Honestly, you did me a favor. I was afraid to hurt your feelings, but we both know it's for the best."*

THE AFTERNOON SUN WAS sinking, and the temperature turning cooler when some family members took their seats on the porch. Others stood in circles, talking and laughing. Standing with one group, Brittney kept a discreet eye on Clarice, making sure she wasn't overdoing it. At least the woman had finally agreed to take a chair.

"Lucas is such a party pooper," Adam shouted the moment his mom, Sandra, emerged from the front door and walked down the steps. "I can't believe you let him sleep all day when he ditched us for all those years."

"We can't have dinner until he comes out. He's taking a shower." Sandra wagged a finger, then pointed her chin to the table display of food on the porch. "In the meantime, you can have some snacks."

Sandra strode toward Brittney, her warm blue eyes comforting as always when she spread out her arms for a hug. Her dangling earrings brushed Brittney's skin while she pressed a kiss to her cheek. "Hi, sweetheart."

After Brittney eased away, her gaze wandered to the freshly cut lawn and the added twinkle lights strung across the porch. "Everything looks so lovely."

"I'm glad someone noticed." Sandra's voice danced with light humor. "For that reason, I give you permission to go in the house and be the first to eat dinner."

"Oh, it's not fair that she gets special treatment." His voice light, Adam draped his arm on Olivia's shoulders.

"Brittney takes care of Grandma." The charms on Sandra's bracelets chimed when she planted a hand on her hip. "Whenever she comes to my house, I want *her* to be well taken care of."

Brittney's heart warmed. Sandra and her husband, Gary, were like second parents to Brittney, and they'd taken up that role ever since junior high, when Dad had died.

When Sandra mingled with the crowd and Adam started talking to one of his friends, Brittney made easy conversation with Olivia while struggling to keep her gaze from wandering to the front entrance. "Are you excited about the wedding?"

Olivia beamed in Adam's direction. "I'm excited that I'll be waking up every day with Adam next to me. I'm not thrilled to go through all the work before the wedding."

"Let me know if I can be of any help." Besides the bridal shower Brittney was organizing with Sandra, she still offered her number in case there was any other way she could help.

"I'm so grateful that Adam is willing to handle everything." Olivia tucked her phone back in her pocket, after texting Brittney to make sure she got her number right. "We already tasted the cake, but he might need some help. I'll let him know to keep you in mind."

Olivia chattered about her busy schedule at the five-star restaurant where she worked outside Soda Creek. It didn't seem like she'd have a break until two days before her wedding.

Laughter rang through the front yard and when loud cheering and clapping erupted, Brittney's gaze darted to the front door.

Lucas.

Her heart gave a strange catch.

With a defined jawline and broad shoulders that stretched beneath a gray T-shirt, he strolled down the steps. His dark-blond hair was damp as if he'd just emerged from his backyard pool. She didn't need to look at his eyes to know they were deep brown, like the mucky pond in his grandparents' yard. No less handsome than she remembered.

She'd watched him grow from a kid to a teenager with acne, and they'd traded acne creams during that awkward phase. After that, she watched him become a man with a flawless face. His smile always lit up the room, and he always made everyone laugh. It was one of the reasons girls had been so drawn to him in school.

Olivia was saying something, but Brit was having a hard time focusing. She could only see Lucas as he shook hands and hugged his family while they took turns greeting him.

She'd dreamed of the day she would see him again, the boy she'd known almost her whole life, the friend who'd never asked for anything until that night in the tree house when he confessed his love for her. When he'd passionately kissed her, she'd tasted his warm lips briefly, or maybe even kissed him back, before pulling away with the thought of how messy things would be between the two brothers. Everything happened so fast. Regardless, she'd dreamed of and replayed that kiss over and over.

It wouldn't surprise her if Lucas was engaged by now.

Her stomach knotted at the thought of him being with someone else. *But you rejected him, remember?*

She sighed out a heavy breath.

When Lucas turned, his gaze met hers, and her first surprising thought was to throw everyone else out of the way so she could lunge into his arms and finish their embrace with the kiss he'd started ten years ago.

A shiver coursed through her until she felt like she was sitting on a live wire. Why did seeing him ignite such deep and unexpected feelings?

He gave her a half-smile that didn't quite meet his eyes before lifting his hand and mouthing a hi.

She lifted her shaky hand, surprised she could manage to mouth her own hi back. It seemed like they had their own secret language.

"Looks like we might have two weddings." Olivia's voice made her pull her gaze away from Lucas.

"Um... what's that again?" Good grief, what was she talking about before Lucas showed up in the yard?

Olivia shrugged, a knowing glint in her eye. It was probably best for Brittney not to engage in any conversation with anybody for the rest of the night, unless she specifically wanted to make a fool of herself.

She didn't blame Olivia when she walked back to Adam. With her heart pounding in her throat, Brittney wasn't sure where to begin.

But Lucas was only here for a wedding and would leave in no time. Knowing that didn't stop her from wishing they'd spend a day together—as friends, of course.

Yeah, right.

Everyone was still standing outside, hovering around Lucas, who now had his head leaned back, shoulders shaking as he laughed at what his grandma said. It was a good time for Brittney to accept Sandra's offer to get some food from the house.

While in the house, Brittney hurried toward the mouthwatering scents of barbecue and fried food, which was covered with silver lids and lined up on the counter. The short candles flamed beneath the pans. Despite the aroma, no way could she force down a meal tonight.

She walked to the back glass door and slid it open, taking the stairs to the balcony above the garage. There, she sank onto the wicker chair with Lucas's bedroom window to her back. It had always been convenient for her to climb into his room from the balcony, but his parents preferred she go through the front.

The sunset reflected orange on the pool below, a perfect afternoon to get lost in thought.

When she looked at the house next door where she'd grown up, a sense of loss lanced her, the same way it did whenever she came here and glanced over. She'd had to sell it to pay off her dad's medical bills.

She was still grateful to have lived there. Otherwise, she never would've met Lucas and his family. For the longest time, she'd been the only child on Cherry Court, until Lucas's family moved in.

Those were some of the best days—when her only care was to ride a bike and play with her best friend.

CHAPTER 5

Family laughter rang through the front yard, and conversations carried on, centering around Soda Creek. Lucas enjoyed catching up as the topics shifted from Adam's wedding to Emery's travels.

"I want to take another year and volunteer somewhere in Africa." Light danced in Emery's blue eyes. "I figured I could enjoy the scenery while helping the needy."

With her standing next to him, Lucas draped his arm over her shoulders, squeezing her toward him. "I'm so proud of you." He jostled her, meaning it. Being the baby of the family, Emery had grown up surprisingly adventurous. "Do you have an organization in mind?"

"I've done some research, but I'm not yet sure."

Two people came to Lucas' mind. Eric Stone, who had multiple charities, and Brady Sharp.

"I don't think you remember Ryan's friend Brady—"

"The boy who always tucked in his shirts?"

"That would be him." Lucas told her about Brady and his wife's hospital charity in Uganda, and the work they did. "If Uganda is not for you, I'll talk to Eric, since he has orphanages in different parts of the continent."

Emery let out an excited squeal. "I loved Uganda! And I would rather support a new charity. They might need all the help."

He braced his back against the porch support, having fun listening to her plan to use her degree in Social Work, until Grandma Clarice singled him out.

"Lucas, can you stay for a month?" Grandma slid her half-empty plate of food to the side. She'd already asked him earlier, but one of

40

Adam's friends had interfered with the conversation. "You love the Fourth of July. The fireworks these days are much better than the ones from years ago."

Lucas smiled. He'd almost burned down his grandparents' shed while testing some fireworks. Either way, he needed to get back to work after the wedding. "My time is tight."

"Which is why you're staying with your grandma." Mom nestled the rice salad bowl on her lap. "It will be extra time for you to catch up."

"Mom, we've already talked about this."

Not exactly, but as he looked over for Adam to suggest his house, Adam had moved out of earshot, helping pull out a picnic chair for his fiancée under the maple tree in the yard.

As if Grandma Matthews hadn't been listening, she spoke out of the blue. "Where's your wife, Luke?" She adjusted the nasal canal of oxygen in her nose. "Is she coming to the wedding?"

Emery stifled a chuckle, covering her mouth, and Lucas elbowed her in the ribs.

"He's still single, Nana." She smirked, ignoring his warning glare.

"I thought you were married to the black girl."

Dad's mom had met Brit several times, but since her eighty-seventh birthday two years ago, her memory was fading. Before he could formulate a response, his sister chimed in.

"Her name is Brittney. She's somewhere around here." Standing on tiptoe, Emery scanned the porch and the yard scattered with about twenty people. "They're friends, who will get married some-day."

If it were any other day, he'd be plotting a practical joke on his sister for revenge, but he doubted there was a toy snake in the house he could shove in her handbag.

Now that they brought up Brit, where was she? She never came back from the house. Even when he'd gone for his food inside, she was nowhere in sight. No doubt she was avoiding him as much as he wanted to avoid her.

If Brit was avoiding him, why had she looked at him like she wanted to back him into a corner and kiss him senseless? Last he remembered, she didn't want him beyond friendship. A twitch jerked at his jaw, and he rubbed it, bothered by how his heart had raced the moment he saw her.

With her flawless brown skin and dark hair that danced over her shoulders, she was still the most beautiful woman he'd ever met—the only woman he'd never tire of talking to if it wasn't for his dilemma. Seeing her snapped something in him, an urge to reach out and scoop her up in his arms like he used to. It felt like no time had passed between them at all.

Still curious as to why she'd vanished, he used the excuse of gathering the used disposable plates from people's hands. "I'll take these."

When his mom opened her mouth to stop him, he shook his head. "I'm headed inside to check out some desserts."

After tossing the plates in the trash can inside, he scanned the row of dishes on the dessert table. The sliced pound cake caught his attention, the only dessert in a glass food-storage container. Knowing who'd made it, he reached for a slice. It all but melted in his mouth as he thought of the work she'd put into making it.

Now, where could she be?

No way would she be sitting in one of the bedrooms upstairs, so he took the stairs back to the open door of his room. When he spotted the back of her green top outside his window, his feet felt heavy, and he stilled in the doorway. Seated on the wicker chair, she'd propped her chin on her hand as if lost in thought.

Should he go to her? All he needed to do was open the window and climb onto the deck. What would he talk about?

Start by breaking the awkwardness. Not today, though. He gripped the doorframe, a battle raging in his mind. As he glanced down to the house next door, he leaned his head back on the frame and felt his mind drift back to years ago—to the time when their friendship started.

IT WAS EARLY SUMMER after fifth grade when his family moved to Soda Creek. Mom needed to help Grandma Clarice take care of Grandpa. Grandpa, six years older than Grandma, was failing in his health, and Grandma didn't want to hire outside help or move him into a nursing home. Dad resigned from his engineering job in Maine and found another firm outside Soda Creek.

Two days after they'd moved, Mom was pulling noisy toys out of a box and tossing them throughout the living room.

Wanting to go biking, Lucas spoke over four-year-old Emery's screams. "I want to meet some kids in the neighborhood."

Mom stopped rummaging through the box and stood to look at him. Her hair was disheveled from yanking at it in frustration over not finding Emery's favorite doll, and those wrinkles on her forehead must have been caused by Emery's ongoing tantrums. "See if Adam can go with you."

Adam was busy. That rule of hers for them never to be on the street by themselves was dumb. "He's fixing his radio." Mom had bought him the cassette player at the garage sale the day before their move, so he could dismantle it and then put the pieces back together. "Can't I go by myself?"

Maybe he'd even extend his bike ride to Grandma's house. It had been less than ten minutes away when they drove there two days ago. Surely he could find his way.

Emery's screams rose before she lunged into the wall and pounded her head once, then twice. She let out a piercing scream, rubbing her forehead and jumping up and down. "Ouch!"

Mom winced and dashed to Emery, her words bouncing off her back. "Lucas, you can either help me look for your sister's doll or find something to do in your room. I'll go with you later!"

In other words, you're on your own. Whenever Emery got into her whining, she could stay that way for the rest of the day.

"But... I..." Heat burned in his chest as he stammered, throwing his hands up in the air, not that Mom saw his attempted outburst.

"Baby, I'm so sorry." She hoisted Emery on her hip, pushing hair out of her face. "I promise to get you another doll if we don't find your Kirsten."

Lucas rolled his eyes, sticking out his tongue at Emery while Mom wiped fake tears from his sister's face. He loved Emery, but on days like today, he didn't like her at all.

He stomped up the stairs and closed the door when he got to his room.

He reached for a tennis ball in the bin and chucked it at the window, missing the target when it landed at the sill and bounced back to him.

"I hate this place." He caught the ball and sat on his bed, tossing the ball again. This time he aimed for the wall. As much as he wanted to express his anger, smashing a window would get him in trouble.

He'd left a neighborhood full of kids, his friends, to live in exile on a secluded street. He'd not heard any kids' noises or seen any kids walk past whenever he stood on the front porch.

What was with Adam anyway? Who could be content staying in his room all day? While Lucas's toy bin was filled with different kinds of balls, Adam's toy bin was filled with puzzles, broken computers, and radios. Too boring a life for a thirteen-year-old.

Several minutes went by before Emery stopped wailing and the doorbell rang. Voices carried up the stairs. Then muffled footsteps climbed the stairs and stopped outside his room.

The door creaked open, and Mom popped her head in. "There's a kid your age downstairs. You can come and meet..."

Finally! He was up and running past Mom before she could finish. He jumped down the last three stairs, sliding in his socks on the polished hardwood floor before scrambling around the corner to the hall. Wait a minute. He stopped so fast he nearly toppled with the lost momentum.

A girl? His heart sank.

The girl's back was to him. Her skin was brown, and her pigtails bounced as she nodded to whatever the woman with her, likely her mom, was telling her.

He lurched a step back, retreating, but the woman lifted her head. "You must be Lucas." Her kind eyes almost made him smile.

The girl turned. She resembled her mom when she stood up with the woman.

"I'm Marjorie, and this is my daughter, Brittney."

"Oh." What else was a guy supposed to say? "Why couldn't you be a boy? Do you have any brothers? Do you know where the other kids around here are hiding?" None of that seemed right, so he clamped his teeth over his words. He rarely introduced himself to kids.

Unfazed, Brittney stuck out her hand for him to shake. "Nice to meet you."

"Uh..." He pinched her hand with a few fingers. It didn't feel like it had cooties. Still, he yanked his hand away fast just in case. "Nice to meet you, too?"

"Lucas was just looking for someone to play with." Mom's voice sounded from behind him.

Betrayal! He spun to glare at her as she handed Emery a cookie. His sister finally seemed content playing with her toy kitchen.

Mom winked, not getting his not-too-subtle message. "It's your lucky day."

"Brittney was so thrilled when I told her there were kids next door."

Mom walked toward them, and while she spoke with Marjorie, Lucas craned his neck toward the stairs. Bouncing a tennis ball beat playing with a girl if Brittney was anything like Emery. Playing with dolls was not something he was about to do right now.

"We brought you some cookies."

Oops. He fell for it and turned toward the girl's voice. Sucker. Even if he'd devour the cookies later, he had to act uninterested, so she didn't expect him to bake stuff with her. "Thanks. I'll have some later."

"Would you like to play basketball?"

Had she said *basketball?* He blinked at her question, not trusting his hearing.

Head cocked to one side, she looked him over. "We have a hoop in our front yard."

Basketball! This must be the best day of my life. "Let me go get my shoes on."

He scrambled up the stairs two at a time, excitement coursing through him as he slid on his shoes, and returned with a basketball to meet her.

Minutes later, they were in her driveway, bouncing the ball off the concrete. She came up with a game called knockout, and they took turns aiming the ball to get through the net.

It was a while before either of them shot the basket through the hoop, but they were silent until she got the first shot in. "I'm usually better than this."

So was he, but he had to warm up to play with a girl. And he did when Brittney asked about his move and his friends in Maine. "Do you miss them?"

"Yeah." He tossed the ball in the net, and it slid through with ease. "Dad says we'll make new friends here."

"When school starts, you will." She hit the rim. "There's no kids on our street. There's a few kids three blocks away, but Mama doesn't want me to go by myself."

"My mom, too." Maybe they'd go together sometime.

"Don't you have a brother?"

"He's always busy." Lucas took a turn shooting. "What about you?"

She shrugged, her face sad. "I'm an only child. Mama said she can't have any more kids when Dad is always sick."

"Won't he feel better?"

"He had a bad accident, and he's in a wheelchair forever."

Whoa. Sadness sloshed through Lucas, and he stood, pausing the game. He couldn't imagine himself bound in a wheelchair and not able to ride his bike anymore. "Forever?"

Brittney nodded, wiping sweat from her forehead. "He has a disease called quadriplegia."

"That's a big word." Lucas tried to imitate it but almost bit his tongue.

"I've said it a lot of times." She shrugged.

When her mom returned, she called them in for lemonade.

Brittney's skirt swayed as she skipped ahead. "My dad will be happy to meet you."

So was Lucas, when Ronald chatted about cars and wanted to know what kind Lucas had played with when he was younger. Which he'd done, but he hadn't kept track of brands, except telling him some were Hot Wheels.

Apparently, Ronald's wreck during a car race had almost killed him.

They drank lemonade while Marjorie spoon-fed her husband.

Lucas didn't mind when they played checkers. It was his first time playing the game, and it was a good break from basketball. It was a long game since Ronald had limited control over his hand movements but he won and promised to teach Lucas the hidden tricks in checkers next time.

He and Brittney returned to the front yard to play foursquare until Marjorie called them for lunch, and then they played more basketball. He stayed until his mom called for him from the backyard.

When Brittney escorted him, he tucked his basketball under one arm. "That lemonade was so good." The best he'd ever had.

Her feet fell in step with his as she clasped her hands behind her. She was close enough he could smell her hair. It smelled like chocolate.

"Mama taught me how to make it. I squeezed the lemons this morning."

She offered to teach him sometime.

Maybe, but he needed to secure his next playtime.

"Do you like to bike?" Adam wasn't into it.

"I have a bike." Her brown eyes lit up. "Mama doesn't want me to ride alone, but now... now I can use it." She squealed and jumped to him, throwing her arms around him. "I'm so glad we're neighbors."

"Me, too."

"I'll get my chores done early, and I'll come get you."

Wow, he ran from chores, not toward them.

Good thing his enthusiasm surpassed Brittney's, and the next morning when she came knocking at his door, he was dressed and ready to go.

Funny it didn't feel awkward hugging her when she greeted him with an embrace.

The mature trees covered the street with a shady canopy as they rode one block, then two over, doing the same thing the following day, riding the extra two blocks to the playground. The neighborhood was mostly filled with older people who had grown children.

Even at the park, they rarely ran into kids their age, but the one time they did, Lucas and Brittney were content playing with each other.

"Where are all the kids who go to the school?" Lucas asked one day when they rode past the school.

"They don't live in our area."

Weird, then, that the school was in their neighborhood.

Whenever they rode their bikes, Brittney was fascinated by sunflowers and would want to stop and admire any gardens with the big cheery things.

By the second week of their adventures, they rode the seven blocks to Grandma's house, and Grandpa took them fishing at the pond, telling them about his time in Vietnam. Brittney would ask questions, like what kind of food they ate in the Army, and whether he'd learned his building skills there. His ability to build a house and a tree house with his bare hands fascinated her.

"Working with my hands is something I enjoy," Grandpa would say.

As their families became friends that summer, so did Lucas and Brittney's friendship deepen.

One evening, when both families gathered for a barbecue in Lucas's backyard, Brittney gave him a flat piece of cardboard with a drawing. "I made you something."

His heart soared when he looked at the tree and the ladder drawn with a brown marker, the tree house above. Then the expansive yard with stick figures of people he assumed to be kids.

"I'm not the best drawer," she explained, "but I thought it would remind you of the new place you could call home."

How very kind.

At that moment, he knew he wanted Brittney to be a part of his life—always. She was so nice and wonderful. The first friend who'd ever given him a gift when it wasn't his birthday. "I love it." He didn't think twice before wrapping his arms around her in a tight squeeze. He liked the smell of her hair, chocolate mixed with something he couldn't tell, so he asked why it smelled like that.

"Mama uses shea butter in my hair." She touched her long braid. "It keeps my hair from itching, and the cocoa keeps it from getting dry."

He liked it, but when he shifted, he remembered the cardboard in his hand.

"Thank you, Brit...." Now that he called her that several times, keeping her name short sounded better. She looked like a Brit. "Is it okay if I call you Brit?"

"I like that."

And just like that, they spent most of their summer playing basketball, riding bikes, and tossing a football after he'd taught her. Sometimes Adam would play with them, especially in the pool after it was installed in their backyard.

They celebrated the end of summer with Brittney's eleventh birthday on Labor Day Weekend at her house.

Lucas brought her a bouquet of sunflowers he'd asked his mom to buy in addition to the present they'd got her.

Her smile was as radiant as the sunflowers when she took them from him. "You are such a good friend," she'd said, admiring the bouquet. At the end of the day, they both couldn't wait to walk together when school started on Tuesday.

CHAPTER 6

The day following his arrival in Soda Creek, Lucas met Adam at a Men's Wearhouse to try on suits. Adam's two groomsmen had to work and couldn't join them.

"Will you have to bring them back to match our suits?" he asked, stepping out of the changing room and joining Adam by the full-length mirror in the main room.

"As long as you and I match, I don't care." Adam smoothed the collar of his navy suit while inspecting his reflection.

"This is your wedding. You should care."

"If Olivia marries me, that's all that matters." He turned and lifted his hands. "How do I look?"

Adam always dressed up in button-downs for no special occasion, but he looked sharp in the navy coat with a white shirt beneath it. "Like a groom." Lucas adjusted his brother's bow tie. "Be sure to get this right on your wedding day."

"In case you didn't know, that's one of your jobs." Adam slapped Lucas on the shoulder. "You don't look too shabby yourself, by the way."

When they left the bridal shop with their clothes, they stopped for lunch at Crimson—a new burger joint with pool tables and brick decor in the dining area. They ate while discussing Adam's expectations from the best man. Although Lucas had been the best man at Ryan's wedding, he assumed each wedding to be different.

"Why are you taking this like a job interview?" Adam licked the ketchup off his fingers.

"With your spontaneous plans, I need to make sure there are no surprises."

"The only surprise is the wedding." Adam's blue eyes shone bright. "The best surprise in all this is Olivia."

There was no doubt about Adam's love for his fiancée. Lucas shifted on the wooden barstool. Seeing his brother happily in love smoothed some of his lingering hard edges, taking away traces of guilt over how Adam's last engagement had ended. Lucas breathed deeply, letting his muscles relax. He'd do everything he could to see this wedding a success, and he might as well start gathering details to add to the best-man speech.

"You never told me how you two met." He dipped a french fry into ranch dressing and popped it into his mouth. "She's from Wisconsin, right?"

Adam nodded. "She was visiting a friend when her car broke down and she brought it to the shop." The corners of his mouth folded into a smile. "I asked her if she'd brought some cheese from Wisconsin, and she thought I was funny. One thing led to another, and before I knew it, we were going on our first date."

Adam rarely struck up conversations with anyone he'd just met. "I'm proud of you."

As his clean-shaven jaw went tense, Adam rested his hands on the table. Dark stains lingered in the cracks of his callused skin, and old scars spoke of years of combat against sharp mechanical edges. He picked at some grease under his thumbnail. "I wish she didn't have to work long hours."

"Why does she have to work long hours?"

"I told her not to worry about the wedding, but she wants to pay off some debt before the wedding. She feels bad that I'm taking care of everything."

That was reasonable for Olivia not to haul debt into their marriage. But Adam shouldn't have to go through wedding preparations alone while he had family. "I'm sure Mom would love to help with the planning."

Adam closed his eyes before opening them. "I wasted a lot of Dad and Mom's money when I started the business." His tone heavy as if the words were hard to say, Adam met Lucas's gaze. "I'd rather not bother them with my problems anymore."

Right. Dad had even cosigned a loan for Adam, but he'd spent most of the profits to sponsor his girlfriend Shana's boutique, instead of paying back the debt.

"You've really grown up." Lucas reached for his soda and took a sip, surprised by the change in Adam. The soda bubbled in his mouth, and he choked a little—or maybe that was because his throat closed as he thought of that woman who'd stolen from Adam, and then conned funds from Lucas when she dumped his brother.

Brit had called to let him know how discouraged Adam was after the breakup. So, when she offered to take him out to a movie, Lucas didn't think it was a bad idea, since she'd always cared for people that way. Plus, he was in his second year of residency and far from home. Of course, his best friend would step in and do him a favor by being there for Adam.

But one movie night had led to weekly movie nights and dinners, to which Brit kept telling Lucas she didn't have the nerve to turn Adam down.

He'd endured them dating, waiting for her to drop out of whatever she had going on. Unfortunately, she didn't know how he felt—again, his own fault. "You *have* grown," Lucas murmured, reaching for another fry and dipping it in sauce.

"I've learned a lot over the years." Adam's mouth drew into a firm line. "Olivia's parents died while she was young. But I've always had parents and grandparents who spoiled us, and I took it for granted."

Being the middle child, Lucas wasn't pampered as much, but he knew it was hard growing up an orphan. After all, he'd witnessed Brit's aching heart and sleepless nights—maybe she still struggled to sleep after losing both parents early in life.

"I'll do whatever I can to help." He had money and wasn't a big spender, never had been.

"You can help Mom and Brittney. They're hosting Livy's bridal shower."

No way was he interfering with anything Brit was a part of. "I'm sure there are several ways I can help." He shoved his plate with its unfinished burger and fries to the side.

Adam gestured to the glass separating their room from the other. "Let's go play some pool. You still play?"

His brother was always good at the game. There were probably restaurants in Denver that had pool tables, but looking for them hadn't been a priority for Lucas. "Not since I left."

"Man, I already feel sorry for you." Adam wiped his mouth with a napkin and put it on his empty plate before standing. "You're going to get whipped."

The waiter returned with their bill, and Adam reached for his wallet. But Lucas was much faster at sliding his credit card into the leather booklet before handing it back to the server. "Your tip depends on my win at the game."

"Ooh." The young man looked between Lucas and Adam. "How about the winner is responsible for my tip?"

"You're a very smart man." Lucas winked and thanked him when he offered to refill their beverages and bring them to the poolroom.

"I know how else you can help." Balls clattered with that sound nothing else made as Adam used the triangle to rack them up before nodding for Lucas to break.

"How's that?" Lucas shot the cue ball at the center, and a satisfying *thwaack* resounded as a good break sent balls rolling across the felt and the green-striped 14 ball zipping into a pocket. Not a bit rusty. He smirked at his brother.

But Adam was frowning at the window. "Livy wants us to exchange vows. I was never good at romantic stuff." He chalked his stick while Lucas lined up another shot. "That's where you come in."

He couldn't be serious. "That wasn't part of the job description." Vows were personal. "In case you forgot, I have a best-man speech to write. Number 11, that corner pocket."

"That's a tough shot so close to the 5 ball."

No sweat. Lucas bounced the cue ball against the side rail. It rolled along and tapped the red-striped ball, just shy of nudging Adam's solid-orange 5 ball. But the ball slid past the pocket and stopped against the side rail.

Adam smirked. "Gutsy shot, but you should have tried for the 12." He bent over the table, leaning in to reach the cue ball stuck midway. "Number 5, side pocket." The orange spun across the table, landing neatly as planned. "You grew up with me. You don't need to write a story, just say all the heroic stuff I did while we were kids, you know."

Lucas tapped his chin. That might work for Adam, but he wasn't one to show up in front of people unprepared. "What kind of speech would it be if I don't add how you borrowed my motorbike without asking and ended up running it into the lake?" That could stir some laughter. "If you finally fixed it, I'd like to know so I can add that little detail."

Adam rolled his eyes and walked around the table. "Number 1, side pocket. That thing was already so old—I could never find a couple of parts for it. Now that you're home, maybe I'll get it fixed."

Lucas wasn't interested in a motorbike anymore. He only wanted to rile his brother. Where could he get the time to fix his bike, anyway? "Consider my bike a wedding present."

The solid-yellow ball dropped into the opposite side pocket. Now that he'd been granted a turn, Adam would likely clean up all his balls before missing a shot. He straightened and braced his stick against the floor, his face now serious. "Believe it or not, you know me best." He re-chalked the end of his cue. "That's why you're my best man. I also wanted to make sure there's no hurt feelings between us."

They'd already had this conversation. Lucas held the stick on his shoulder and stared into his brother's eyes. "Like I said, you didn't know I had feelings for her."

The server returned with their drinks and set them on the small round table next to them. He then handed Lucas the leather booklet with the receipt and his credit card. Lucas signed for the tip and gave it back to him.

When Lucas tucked his card back in his wallet, Adam was guzzling his Mountain Dew. He stared at Lucas, opened his mouth as if to say something, but set his glass down before they resumed playing.

He shot two more solid balls in silence, other than calling the play, and they made it to the called pocket. Either he was focusing on the game, or something was on his mind. Either way, Brittney was on Lucas's mind since Adam brought her up indirectly. Adam missed his shot on the number 7.

Lucas stepped up. With the table cleaner, two shots were too easy to count, sinking the number 9 and 15. The 10 and 13 took a bit of finesse, but instinct was taking over, his mind elsewhere. *Thwaaak!* The cue struck the 2 ball, sending the solid blue shooting across the table—right into the 12, which spun out and sank in the corner he'd called.

"Why didn't you fight for her?" Lucas asked as he shot his final ball, the pesky number 11 he'd first missed, directly into the pocket. The 8 ball followed into its called pocket. He straightened, surprised by both the win and his choice of topic. He'd never asked Adam why they broke up, but if he claimed to love her, Brit was worth fighting for.

Adam set his stick on the table and leaned against the glass dividing the rooms. "I've always asked the same question about you." He squared his shoulders. "Why didn't you?"

It was Lucas's turn to reach for his drink, taking a long sip of Dr Pepper before responding. Yeah, why didn't he? He almost felt sick thinking about that heavy question he had no answers to.

"I told you about the kiss, almost ten years ago." The rejection stung. It was best to start another round of pool if they were digging into a sensitive subject. So, he grabbed the triangle and gathered up the balls, the permeating odors of fries and nachos adding to his sudden queasiness. "I didn't have a choice."

"Yeah... yeah." Adam broke the balls, sending them scattering, but not sinking any. "You were always well spoken, confident, charming—and you never backed down from anything. It's a shame you backed down when it came to the most important person in your life."

"It's all in the past." Lucas made his shot, slamming into the red, and it bounced off the edge and glided to the middle before he stepped back to let Adam take his turn.

Brit didn't share the same feelings. Otherwise, she would've known he'd always loved her beyond friendship.

"I never told you this before." Adam stared at Lucas, wincing. "I was scared to kiss her. But I finally did the day I proposed."

Lucas stiffened. He didn't want to hear about Adam or anyone else kissing Brit. Even if it wasn't his turn, Lucas aimed his stick to the cue ball.

Adam continued, "It felt as if I was doing something wrong—as if I was kissing my sister."

Lucas stood, letting out a shuddering breath as he met Adam's knowing stare.

"I'm sure your kiss with her didn't feel awkward." After dropping those words, Adam used his cue stick to edge Lucas aside, then lined up a shot.

Standing there, Lucas tightened his grip on his stick, unscrewing it a bit. The only awkwardness from the kiss was the rejection. Otherwise, he might have misinterpreted it as a kiss between two best friends in love with each other.

Did his kiss ruin Brit and Adam's future together?

A ball sank after Adam's shot. Lucas hadn't even noticed which group Adam's shot called for his game. As if reading his mind, Adam shrugged, then called his next shot and bent over the table as if trying to distract Lucas from his discomfort. "Trust me, you saved me from messing things up with you and the family. You're not the only one who called me crazy. Mom accused me of using Brittney as a rebound, Dad told me I needed to grow up, and Grandma literally asked me to come up with five reasons why I was in love with Brittney."

"I'm sure you came up with a long list." Wow. Had his family intervened like that? Lucas hadn't known.

The number 3 ball sank. So Adam was solids. Another ball rocketed across the table, dropping into the corner pocket before Adam straightened and ran a hand over his face. "I was just relieved when she broke things off with me two days after you left town."

He hadn't even seen Adam that night. "How did you know I was in town?"

"Brittney said she kissed you, among the many other things she said."

Lucas's jaw dropped. He closed it with effort, the same effort he used to take in another breath. She'd said *she* kissed *him?*

"When you apologized to me about kissing her, I assumed it was a mutual thing between the two of you."

If only it had been mutual, but no need to dwell in the past. "I've moved on." Sure he had. But a guy could wish.

"I hope you can fix whatever you two had. Orange ball, that corner pocket." Adam bent over his game, ignoring Lucas's comment. "If you don't believe she loves you, why do you think she broke off the engagement?"

"Maybe she's not into Matthews boys."

Adam chuckled, shaking his head. "She's still single, and it's not because she's lacking pursuers. I had a couple of friends she turned down right off...." Adam told him about the mailman. "When I stopped by last week, he was having lunch with them and couldn't keep his eyes off Brittney." He lifted the stick up in the air. "She was oblivious to his interest."

As much as having Brittney still single pleased Lucas, it didn't solve his problem. So he urged Adam to continue the game. Their server stopped by to fill their sodas again. When Lucas glanced through the glass to the restaurant side, he could only see about five customers in nearby booths. In two hours or less, the place would probably have a dinner rush.

They continued for a while, one shot better than the next. Adam took the second game. Lucas conceded with a high five. A couple came into the pool room, greeting Adam and Lucas before claiming the pool table in the far corner.

They played a third, fourth, and fifth game. Lucas won three out of five rounds.

"I wasn't keeping score." He pointed the stick to his brother. "But wait, did I just win or what?"

"That's luck." Adam hung up the stick on the wall. "We have to do another round."

"That's what you said before we did the fifth round," Lucas said, hanging up his stick. "What a sore loser."

"You calling me sore?" Adam shook his head, giving Lucas a high five. "I'm only congratulating you because you're my best man. I'll let you fly with the victory this one time."

"We'll have a redo soon, before the wedding." He could handle it now, more prepared after he'd had a refresher.

"You're going to be busy." Adam reached for his glass and drank the rest of his soda. "That's if you're staying with Grandma."

If he could help it, he'd rather not. "Can I crash at your place?"

Adam winced. "Afraid not. Livy's aunt and uncle will be in town on Tuesday. They're staying at my house." He clapped Lucas on the back. "Just stay at Grandma's. She'll love that."

Did he have a choice at this point? He loved Grams's house, and it made him think of Grandpa. In most of the furniture in the house, he could see Grandpa's handiwork. Despite his good reason for hesitating, he'd rather not disappoint her by not staying with her.

Even though he could walk from his parent's house to Grams's, he had luggage and didn't want to bother Mom by asking her to drive him. "I'll go tomorrow. Do you mind giving me a ride there though?"

"Since I took half a day off today, I have to work until noon tomorrow. After that, I'm at your service."

"Any time after five will be good for me."

That left plenty of time for Lucas to go to church and visit with his parents and the extra family members before going to Grams's house. There wouldn't likely be a way to stall like he did last night. Grams had had a bad headache, and she and Brit had left early, saving him from having to deal with Brit. It was probably time to work things out, apologize, and get back to the friendship he and Brit once had.

CHAPTER 7

The sun was sinking down the horizon when Brittney gathered up the gardening tools and put them in the shade.

Sunday was a bit different from the other days in their routine since Clarice preferred to stay home and rest. They'd still had their morning walk and done exercises before Brittney went grocery shopping for Lucas's favorite foods.

After Clarice's nap, Brittney helped her with a bath. Then, while Clarice baked brownies, Brittney spent the afternoon deep cleaning the house. She'd had to put bedsheets on Lucas's bed and dust his room like she did every time she cleaned the house.

Once she'd finished, she'd clipped the shrubs in the backyard. As she passed the two oaks, she startled, jumping when a squirrel leaped from the tree and fell on the hammock.

With her heart in her throat, she blew out a huff.

One more look at the expansive backyard, and she nodded, satisfied by the sharp edges around the crape myrtle shrubs. Having run out of time, she couldn't mow the lawn. It could wait until tomorrow.

She'd start cutting the grass if she knew what time Lucas would show up. All Clarice said was that he would be home in time for dinner. With such vague timing, Brittney had to move Clarice's bath time to an hour earlier than usual. Clarice wanted to be ready when her grandson arrived.

Good thing Brittney had already set the table on the back porch and the chicken had marinated overnight in the fridge. All she needed to do when Lucas arrived was to light up the grill.

In the house, she took a fast shower and listened to contemporary music on her phone while she dressed. She lingered before her closet, one hand on the soft chiffon of a bronze midi dress. She let her fingers trace a ruffle along its wrapping before she jerked her hand away. If she wore such a thing, Lucas would see through her motives to impress him. He *always* read her motives.

She crossed her arms over her chest and stomped none-too-ladylike to her white dresser. Then she rummaged for a jean skirt and one of Lucas's old T-shirts she wore around the house. She'd been being silly anyway. She needed something she felt comfortable in, and it was perfect for her to man the grill.

When she walked out of her room, she wasn't expecting to hear laughter. Not just laughter, a male voice—all too familiar—stopped her in her tracks. *Lucas is here.*

Beads of sweat formed around her forehead. Lucas had nothing to do with her sweat outbreak. She must have forgotten to turn on the air conditioner.

What was the point of a shower if it couldn't help her with the cool off? Leaning against the wall, she breathed in, then out, as she composed herself before taking the next steps. One foot in front of the other, she emerged into the kitchen and walked to the living room. Clarice's hands were moving as she emphasized whatever she was telling her grandson.

"You are so funny, Grams." Laughter carried in his tone. Midnight was curled up on his lap while Lucas's strong hands stroked her back. Traitor cat! She looked so content, as if she'd forgotten how Lucas abandoned them. "What did you end up—"

Lucas stopped when he lifted his head and his gaze found hers. His smile vanished and his shoulders stiffened. He stood, keeping Midnight nestled in the crook of his arm, then set her down on the sofa without breaking eye contact.

"Here you are," Clarice said, but Brittney was frozen in place, too taken by those brown eyes she'd always gotten lost in.

"Um... Hey." He pocketed his hands in his jean pockets.

Say something. She swallowed. "Uh... How did you get here?"

Not the greeting she'd envisioned, but again, she hadn't figured out a new form of greeting for her best friend. They'd always hugged and been free to talk about anything.

He opened his mouth, then closed it, and pulled his hands out of his pockets.

"Pssst..." He put his hands up, one arm overlapping the other, and the corners of his lips folded into a smile. "I flew."

Brittney couldn't help but smile. "To Grandma's house."

He winked the way he used to, taking her back in time to when they were in sixth grade and would watch *Justice League* on Saturday mornings for their cartoons. She was Wonder Woman, and he was Superman.

She would ask, "If you could fly, where would you go?"

And he would respond, "I'd carry you on my back and take you to my happy place."

"I forgot how you kids speak in codes." Clarice's voice sounded.

Brittney had forgotten someone else was in the room. She tore her gaze off Lucas to acknowledge Clarice.

With a wave of a fragile hand, Clarice ushered Brittney to the sofa. "I was telling Lucas about that day when I dropped my billfold in the mail collection box."

Brittney sat at the end of the sofa, self-conscious and keeping the needed space between her and Lucas as she tried to get into the conversation. "Oh, yeah."

"Grams said you brought her home and went back to wait at the mailbox?" Lucas said, crossing one leg over the other.

Brittney nodded.

He stifled a chuckle, already relaxed, which helped ease some tension off Brittney. "How did you explain yourself for dropping a wallet in the collection box?"

"Good thing he knew me and Clarice." Brittney didn't have to show proof to retrieve Clarice's wallet. "He thought it was funny, but he'd seen unusual things people dropped in mailboxes."

Clarice was wise, and as if she knew the tension needed to be broken, she continued one funny story after another until they were all talking and laughing. Then she shifted the conversation to gardening and quilts. Not what Brittney and Lucas would usually talk about, but for now, it was a start.

"I'm glad Brit is always here to rescue you." Lucas's warm brown gaze grazed her before he looked down at Midnight and rubbed the cat's ear.

She'd always liked how he called her Brit. A welcome glimpse of hope peeked in her heart. If she was still Brit to him, then... maybe he didn't hate her as much as she thought.

"How's work?" It was the first time she'd asked about his job since he'd vanished before finishing his residency.

"Good." He slid his hand away from the cat, then didn't seem to know what to do with it. "Grams says you've been working hard." He looked at her, his voice softer. A silence passed between them as they held each other's gaze, and her breath caught. *This is Lucas, the boy who grew up next door.*

It was as if Clarice wasn't even in the room. When Brittney took her gaze off him to Clarice, she'd unplugged her hearing aids, and they were on the table while she stared at a magazine. Was she even reading, or watching them through the corner of her eyes? Trickster. She was letting them talk. Although small talk wasn't Brit's favorite way to reunite with Lucas, she had no alternative. In response to his comment, she said, "If you consider dusting the house and laundry as work, then you've forgotten who I am."

She didn't mean for that last word to come out the way it did, and his flushed face meant she'd said the wrong thing. Her bare toes curled against the rug as her muscles clenched. How she hated calculating her words with him. The whole thing was new for her.

"You're hard to forget." His lips pressed into a tight line.

Maybe he was still mad at her. Unsure of what to say, she'd best stay silent rather than say something he could misinterpret. She stood. "Can I get you something to drink?" She'd bought him Dr Pepper, his favorite. But with the black T-shirt defining his toned muscles—leaner than she remembered—he probably didn't drink sugary beverages anymore.

"I'll get it." He set Midnight on the couch, kissing her forehead and whispering tender promises to the cat. "I'll be back, okay?"

Aware that Clarice had her hearing aids out, he touched her shoulder and asked if she needed anything.

She seemed to read his lips when she responded by pointing to her water in the insulated mug with a straw. "I have to finish this before I earn my next coffee." She was way too loud, but of course, she couldn't hear herself. She cocked her head toward Brittney. "Unless you want to face her wrath."

"I wouldn't want to do that." His eyes aglow and lips twitching upward, he responded to Clarice but kept his gaze on Brittney. Then he raised a brow, still holding her gaze. "Need anything?"

"You're our guest."

He chuckled. "I also know my way around this house. Any changes I need to know?"

"Everything's still the same." Including his domination over her heart. The thought made her pulse quicken.

It was time to get dinner going, so she followed him into the kitchen. Even though she was standing several inches away from the fridge, waiting for him to retrieve his drink, the space suddenly felt small.

"Thanks for remembering my favorite." He hoisted the Dr Pepper in a salute before popping it open and bringing it to his mouth. She watched his Adam's apple bobble, and she swallowed as if she were the one drinking the soda.

"You always warned me against the corn syrup in this stuff," he said, setting the can on the island. "But it's refreshing sometimes."

"I made an exception. It's a special day." Special two weeks while he was here.

When she reached for the container from the fridge, he stepped to the other side for ice, and she almost plunged the bowl of chicken on him.

They shared excuse me's, and he held the other side of the bowl, making sure she had a steady grip before he let go.

"Thanks." Avoiding eye contact, she walked to the back. She was suddenly having a hot flash, something she should be expecting as she neared forty.

Outside, the breeze teased her hair, and she tipped her face toward it, letting it cool her skin as she stepped on the deck. Then she turned on the grill and assembled one piece of chicken breast at a time.

Smoke billowed, and she breathed in the smell of charcoal, gas, and meat.

She needed to go back inside and grab a clean plate, but that could wait until the chicken was ready. After walking to the outdoor table to adjust the checkered tablecloth and brush off twigs the breeze had dropped, she made her way back to the grill.

"Need any help fixing dinner?"

She jumped at his voice and stared at the empty plate he held in one hand and a plate of asparagus in his other. How had she forgotten about the vegetables for their side dish?

"I got it." She reached for the tongs and turned the chicken. It was still pinkish, not ready to be flipped, but she did anyway. Busying herself was necessary if she wanted to keep any semblance of control over herself with him so near.

"Hmm, lemon garlic chicken." He stepped beside her, setting the plate on the grill's tray. His tantalizing scent, a mix of Lucas and something fancy, replaced the tangy meat smell.

He put out his hand. "May I have the tongs, please?"

She did as asked, and he flipped back the piece she'd turned earlier. "It's always good to know how to cook—"

"So we don't eat ramen noodles every day." She finished the line Clarice used to say whenever she made them cook with her. She'd been almost eleven, Lucas, eleven and a half the first time they'd ridden their bikes to Clarice and her now-deceased husband's house. Clarice was making chicken marinated in lemon juice and garlic when she asked them to put it on the charcoal grill under her supervision.

"Grams taught us well, but it's been a while since I cooked." He turned the knob to kick up the grill's temperature.

The flame rose beneath a couple of pieces, so she took the tongs from him. Their hands brushed, sending a slight jolt of electricity through her arm. *It's just Lucas.*

They'd always held hands, and she'd never been affected. That was after she'd trained her mind that he was off-limits.

"You haven't lost your touch, I see," she said when he turned down the heat.

"I'm burning the chicken already." His warm breath tickled her cheek. "I think you're the only one who hasn't lost your touch. I might need a refresher course."

"You can't be that bad." She clattered the tongs on the metal plate by the grill.

"I haven't cooked since I left Soda Creek."

"You'd better not tell your grandma." She nudged him with her elbow. "Unless you want to be in charge of dinner every night." For the next two weeks, at least, since he was only home temporarily.

"I'm not up for cooking. Let it be our secret." He winked, and her stomach flapped with butterflies.

Should she pretend the last ten years had never happened? As long as he wanted to, she'd better not stir up past emotions. She'd missed him, and perhaps he'd missed her and their friendship, too.

Wanting to push their conversation toward reconciliation by keeping things light, she made easy conversation by asking about his flight.

"I slept the entire time." He told her about the charity hospital where he'd worked the night he flew home. "I help there on nights when I don't have to work at Olive Medical." He stared at the blue jay landing on the tree house as he spoke fondly about work and Ryan Harper's family.

A pang twinged her over Ryan's kids and the special place they had in Lucas's heart—a place *she* once held. The jealousy vanished when she learned they were orphans and Ryan was their legal guardian.

She let out a gasp, her heart squeezing. "It's so tragic to lose both parents at once." At least with her, Dad lived another year after Mom's death.

"They're happy kids." Lucas turned the chicken, then lowered the heat on the grill. "Ryan and Destiny have done a great job."

"It's been ages since I saw Ryan. Does he visit his family?"

"As a matter of fact, they're in town for two weeks. I promised the kids I'd bring them to camp by the pond, but I'll clarify with Grams first."

"Clarice will love that."

"You'll love these kids, too."

If they were anything like he said... "I can't wait to meet them."

With the chicken perfectly browned, he transferred one piece at a time to the top rack before spreading out the asparagus on the bottom and covering the food with the grill lid. "Grams tells me you still visit the resource center once a week?"

"I volunteer on Wednesday afternoons." In honor of her dad, she visited people with disabilities and found it fulfilling. "They're the sweetest people you'll ever meet." Especially those with Down syndrome. "They're so genuine and tenderhearted."

Clarice was so kind, making sure she got extra free time to do something else. Brittney drew in a deep breath. She didn't deserve the bonus pay she was getting for the last year.

"I noticed you gave me a raise," she said when she remembered who was actually her boss. "You didn't have to."

"You're working more than you bargained for." He crossed his arms and leaned against the deck railing. "Grams doesn't want anyone else cutting her lawn, and I wasn't paying you for landscaping services."

Clarice had her way to keep certain things the same, including her yard. "I might have to write a manual someday. 'Clarice's Yard Upkeep.'" She waved a hand toward the manicured shrubbery. "It would help the landscapers if she ever agrees to hire one."

"Speaking of books, you ever finish the quadriplegic caregiver book?"

He remembered! Warmth radiated through her. How sad that it felt like she'd tried to pursue someone else's dream. "I gave up a long time ago." That dream died when he walked out of her life.

With the vegetables ready, he helped set the table while she brought the food and drinks out on the deck.

Once Clarice joined them, Lucas asked if he could pray before they ate. Brittney frowned, surprised by the new guy in their midst as he spoke about gratitude and blessings.

"Amen," he said, then answered Clarice's question about what they were supposed to do. "You repeat amen if you agree with my prayer."

"Amen, it is." Clarice tucked her cloth napkin to her chest. And Brittney echoed the amen.

Their dinner conversation was mostly about Lucas's work, because Clarice wanted to know his schedule and why he couldn't take extra time off after being away from home for so long.

"It's the nature of my job." He cut through the juicy chicken and forked a piece into his mouth. "Hmm." He pointed his fork to his plate, keeping his gaze on Brittney. "This chicken is the best."

"You cooked it." She dabbed a napkin on her mouth.

"He didn't." Clarice's eyes widened. "My grandson still remembers how to cook?"

When he spluttered as if he was ready to deny the compliment, Brittney cut in. "He wouldn't even let me help."

He mouthed the word *liar* at her.

She squished her face, stifling a laugh and almost feeling light since things were off to a great start. On the surface, they were, but they would unravel the core at some point.

As afternoon turned to dusk, she decided not to turn on the porch light, since that would gather bugs over their food. The peppermint candles lined up on the railing offered enough light while keeping mosquitoes at bay.

They stayed at the table, talking and laughing way after dinner and dessert. A lawn mower purred in the distance, orange clouds turned to dark gray, and hope bloomed through her heart with each laugh and his presence in their midst.

Clarice wanted to play a hand of cards when they returned to the house. The fluorescent light above the dining table sent a radiant glow over them, making it easy to see the extra-large numbers on the cards.

Brittney won, and Lucas suggested playing another round. "I was so close to winning."

"Still competitive, I see." He'd never back down on so many games they'd played until he won.

"I played pool with Adam yesterday." He shrugged. "I still have some skills left."

"You're starting to sound like my grandson." Clarice rubbed her hands together while Lucas shuffled.

When Clarice won that round, Lucas threw his head back. "Seriously? We'll have a redo tomorrow." He stood, stretching and yawning.

Determined to stretch the night, Clarice insisted they start the 1000 piece puzzle on the coffee table in the main room. "You've always loved fireworks, Luke. I got this for your visit."

He shook his head. "I think I've had enough losses for the day. I'll take on the puzzle tomorrow."

"I'll let you go to bed if you agree to stay in Soda Creek for another week."

Brow scrunching, he rubbed his stubbled chin. "I forgot how much you like bargains. I wish I could stay, Grams." He then ambled to the living room, lowering down on the carpet and opening the box. "Shouldn't you be sleepy by now, anyway?"

Clarice pushed up to stand from the kitchen and took her cane with her.

Brittney walked behind her to make sure she had her footing. The grandfather clock ticked, and she checked the time. Ten minutes past ten. Almost two hours past Clarice's bedtime.

"You stayed up so late." Brittney reminded her of the time in case she wasn't paying attention.

"I need to spend time with my grandson, you know." Yawning, Clarice stared at the puzzle Lucas was scattering on the soft carpet. "On second thought, I'll go to bed. You two should start the puzzle."

Brittney cringed. Clarice wasn't being very subtle, but Brittney couldn't blame her for trying to help them heal their friendship. So, when Clarice left for bed, Brittney joined Lucas on the floor. He was probably exhausted from the stress of the trip and being home.

"You're up for this?" she asked.

"Let's get a few along the edge." He tossed some flat pieces on the table.

Now that it was just the two of them, her heart was thundering. She strained her eyes and started gathering connecting pieces as he flipped them upright on the table. She connected three, four, and then five pieces.

"That's a good start." He held a piece in his hand. "Is it okay if we continue tomorrow?"

"Of course." She needed to go to bed, too, but with her room next to his, it would be impossible not to listen out for his every shift in the bed. "Good night."

"Good night." He stood, stuffing the piece in his pocket. He probably had no idea he had it, but it would be a long time before they needed the last piece. "Thanks for setting up my room."

He must have taken his luggage there before he joined her on the deck to grill. "Anytime."

She let out a breath as if she'd not been breathing the entire time she'd been around him.

As she connected the puzzle pieces, she listened to the shower turn on and then, minutes later, turn off. Now and then, Clarice's soft snoring whispered from her room.

Brittney stayed until his bedroom door clicked closed before she tiptoed to her room.

There was a lot she didn't know about Lucas over the last ten years... a lot she hoped to relearn. One thing was certain, he was root-ed in Colorado with a job he liked, a charity hospital depending on him, a friend from their childhood, and even kids whose lives he was part of.

But, despite him smiling and laughing, deep down, Lucas wasn't his true self. Everything about tonight was just a surface gloss to get them through the awkwardness. Still, she had to take him in any form she could.

CHAPTER 8

Lucas turned and tossed, his sheets rustling beneath his body. It was way past his bedtime, and he'd thought turning off the lights would make sleep come easier. Wrong. How could he sleep, even if he wasn't staring at Brit's childhood drawings hanging on the wall—artwork she'd given him in middle school when she'd been obsessed with drawing.

His mind was more active than he wanted it to be as memories of the evening played out. Being around Brit—pretending around her, pretending they were back to their normal friendship, pretending he'd never wanted more than friendship from her, pretending the last ten years apart never happened—had drained his energy.

His response of flying to Grandma's house had helped loosen things, taking tension from her shoulders. A memory she'd seemed to remember far too well.

He'd always felt freer and gotten more attention from his grandparents than from Mom and Dad. He understood how Emery had needed more attention, and so had Adam, so Lucas had sought his freedom with his grandparents.

One of the times he and Brit stayed the night here, they'd watched *Justice League* in the morning. She'd asked where he would go if he had the power to fly. He'd given her the same answer.

"I'd carry you to my happy place," he'd said. "How about you?"

"Assuming you're Superman, we'd fly together and find the biggest field of sunflowers there is. I'd make sure we had a picnic, too." Her smile revealed the deepest dimple he'd ever seen. "You never even told me where your happy place is."

"I didn't?" He stood up from the carpet where they'd been laying on their stomachs, elbows on the carpet, heads propped in their hands before the TV. Then he crouched, lowering himself and asking her to climb his back.

Her nose had scrunched, but she'd obeyed. "Why?"

"I get to take you to my happy place."

She wasn't as heavy as he'd thought, which made walking out of the house and to the tree house much easier. Although she'd been there before, he pretended it was her first time in it. "Now this is where I can't risk carrying you, but I'll let you climb first."

When she eased off his back, he let her climb the ladder and followed her up the mighty oak to the house Grandpa had built for him, since he'd asked for a tree house whenever his family came to visit. Grandpa had also built the wooden bed and bench in it. When Lucas's family moved to Soda Creek, Lucas stowed a stereo and a few of his favorite things up there so it could look like a real house.

That day, he had plugged headphones in the radio and handed Brit one side of the earpiece while he had the other, and they listened to music on one of the FM channels.

Later, she told his grandpa how smart he was for building two houses, the main house and the tree house. "Can we add Christmas lights to the tree house?"

"That should be easy." Grandpa's low voice had rumbled from his chest, his eyes like twinkling lights. "I just pulled electricity into the tree house last month."

Lucas flopped onto his back, one hand under his head as he peered at the oak's leafy shadow on his wall. How he wished he could go back to those days when he and Brit were just friends, before his heart got tangled up with her.

His chest hurt, and the pain would continue to grow because they were under the same roof, but distant. The only thing separating him and Brit was the wall—not the one between their bedrooms, but the wall he'd used to create a wedge between their friendship.

He scrubbed a hand over his face, his eyes burning from more than tiredness. Any other time in their history, he'd be up all night talking to her, catching up. But he was here at another time, unexpectedly.

It was all Adam's fault.

Parts of Lucas felt like being mad at his brother, but that wouldn't fix the past. If only blaming someone *could* ease the ache.

Ugh. He flung his legs over the side of the bed and sat up, raking both hands through his hair and pulling on it.

It was going to be a long night. Even if he didn't want to tamper with his phone right before bed, he needed a distraction, so he patted the nightstand for it.

Eleven fifteen flashed across the screen, and he winced at the bright light. He scrolled through the emails in case HR had contacted him to let him know if he got the promotion.

Nothing.

A text message popped up from Ryan's fourteen-year-old nephew, Josh.

A smile lifted the corners of his mouth.

They must have arrived tonight if they were up this late. Unless Ryan's wife was behind the kids staying up, his friend wouldn't let them.

Josh: Zoe and Pete wanted to know when you're taking us camping.

Lucas: Did your parents forget to take your phone from you?

Josh: Destiny talked Uncle into letting us stay up late. What can I tell Pete and Zoe?

Lucas: As long as your uncle is okay with it, I'll confirm with him first.

Josh: Cool.

A week before he left Colorado, Zoe insisted Lucas tell them something he remembered from his childhood home. When he told them about camping in his grandparents' backyard, one thing led to another, and before he knew it, he was committing to taking them camping when they arrived in Soda Creek.

Their grandparents would probably keep them busy, but he'd never hear the end of it if he didn't follow through.

He closed his phone. Tempted to hit the Facebook app, he decided against it and forced himself to go to sleep. It seemed to be a vain attempt, but he must have drifted off at some point, because he woke to a thin ray of light peeking through the vertical blinds.

When he lifted his phone from the nightstand, it was five thirty.

Using the little knowledge he had from a few months of going to church, he thanked God for the three days he'd been home. He wasn't too sure about detailed prayers, but no one else was listening except God.

Tossing the covers, he unzipped his luggage to retrieve his favorite running shorts and pulled them on.

His bedroom hadn't changed much, with Brit's drawings that Grams had framed still intact on the wall. Only the fresh coat of beige paint was different. Brit, no doubt, had painted it. She always liked to keep things crisp and clean.

Curious about what could still be in his dresser, he pulled out the top drawer and inspected his nicely folded T-shirts. The two sleeveless shirts to the left and the other T-shirts to the right. When he slid his arms into one of the muscle tees, it smelled of lavender detergent, no musty smell from being stored in the drawers for so long. Brit, no doubt, had washed his clothes.

After getting his shoes on, he retrieved his wireless AirPods from the luggage and tucked them in his pockets, intending to listen to the Bible reading app as he ran.

In the kitchen, he opened the cabinet where everything was still kept in the same place, the way he remembered. Just like the china cupboard next to the dining table, Grandpa had built ninety percent of the furniture. It was another reason he valued everything in this house.

The scent of lemons, cinnamon, and spices reminded him of his grandparents' house. He breathed in deeply, feeling like he'd stepped back in time as he brewed a pot of coffee. If Brit hadn't changed over the years, she never drank coffee, but Grams drank enough for all of them. He poured himself a cup and downed it while standing, hoping to polish it off and make his exit before anyone woke up.

After rinsing the cup, he set it in the dishwasher. The stove clock showed five fifty-five. Midnight ambled toward him by the back door. He carried her for a quick snuggle, rubbing her ears and whispering, "I'm not leaving yet" before setting her down.

He adjusted the volume on the AirPods and rolled the rubber pieces into his ears.

"'In the beginning, God made the heaven and the Earth.'" The deep voice sounded through the earpiece. Lucas needed to read the Bible as Ryan had encouraged him after he'd made his peace with God, but he'd only read the poetic chapter because it was easy to grasp. Now that he was away from his busy life, starting from the beginning made sense.

He took the narrow path toward the pond, passing over mowed grass, then to the damp tall grass that brushed against his legs. He would cut it when he returned from his run.

Trying not to let his mind wander, he slowed and walked on the boardwalk past the creek running through Grams's property. He climbed a hill, then down further, passing through trees and jumping over another stream further west.

The sun peeked over the horizon and barraged the awakening world with fiery colors, and he almost laughed. What could be a more perfect setting to listen to "day four; the sun, moon and stars were created..."?

It didn't matter that he had no planned destination. He was familiar with all the surrounding areas, but a few things had changed the further he ran. New log cabins and homes nestled between trees—homes that hadn't been there when he was growing up.

Memories of the mountains, the campfire, and the waterfall came crashing back when he passed grazing cows, the privately owned sunflower field he'd snuck Brit into, and the private lake they'd swum in twice. A grin quirked his mouth. Man, the owner had hollered at them the second time they'd gone there!

As he kept running, he headed down into the Rising Valley community with homes not too far apart from each other and nodded at the random people walking and running. He then took a right onto Stride Lane, and with another mile, he was at the park the community built two years after his family moved to Soda Creek, the park where Brit taught him to roller skate.

Apparently, he wasn't the only one up early and running. With more homes and people at this end of town than his grandma's side, he ran past people, young and old, walking their dogs, couples, and solo runners. They offered friendly smiles and waved their greetings.

A woman in a bright pink sports bra jogged toward him, with her smile so wide, she'd end up swallowing the buzzing bugs if she wasn't careful. She slowed her steps, her lips moving as if she was talking to him.

Do I know her?

He drew out a breath, needing to stretch, but that could wait. He reached for his AirPods and turned off the reading. *Rochelle.* Oh, boy.

One of Brit's high school friends, his first girlfriend, sort of—she'd always been more advanced in the romance department than the other kids their age.

"Lucas… look at you." She looked him up and down, breathless from her jogging. "You've… um… still… even more handsome."

"Rochelle." Heat burned the back of his neck at her direct comment. What was he supposed to say or ask, since he'd abruptly ended things with her?

"I got divorced six years ago." She rested her hands on her bare stomach as if drawing attention to it. Her leggings were too tight. How was she able to run in those?

He steered his gaze to the chipmunks scurrying in the unpaved area of the park, a relaxing sight.

"We both wanted different things…." She rambled about her failed marriage as if he was the shrink. So, in other words, she was making herself available. She batted her long eyelashes. "If you hire me for the wedding, it'll be our chance to hang out like old times."

Whoa. Whoa. First, he wasn't interested in old times. Those days were gone because Brit was gone, too. Hire her? Did she think he was a wedding planner? Or did she assume he was in town to get hitched? He shook his head. "I'm not getting married."

"Your brother is."

Right. He now felt like the crazy one for not knowing she was talking about Adam.

"Isn't that why you're in town?" She bit her lower lip. "I put him down for the event center at the resort, and he said he'd make the final decision when you got into town."

Lucas and Brit had worked at Rochelle's family resort one summer. His heart rate, which had started slowing down when he stopped running, kicked up again as his stomach knotted. "So you mean to tell me Adam has no venue?"

The wedding was in twelve days, for crying out loud! Surely a venue was the first thing people reserved for their special day.

She fluffed her loose blonde curls over her shoulders. "Unless they went with the other location, but I need to know by Wednesday so I can open it up for last-minute events."

Great. Lucas wiped at his cool forehead. He had to write a speech, vows maybe. Weren't there terms for best-man contracts and stuff? He'd been Ryan's best man, but he didn't have to do anything beyond giving Ryan a hard time when he planned his bachelor party—a weekend of mountain biking and golfing with their friends.

"I'll talk to him." Now Adam would have to get back to Rochelle by tomorrow, if not tonight.

"He doesn't seem to be in a hurry, but it'll be helpful to know either way."

Despite himself, gratitude for her graciousness loosened his muscles. "Thanks for being patient and holding the venue for him." What business owner would wait so long?

"I only did it for you." She smiled slyly, her comment taking him by surprise when she clasped both hands behind her. "Adam said you're still single."

Adam better find another best man if he was going to tell divorcées about Lucas's status. Not wanting to mislead Rochelle into thinking they were going to start where things ended years ago, he half smiled and gave a curt nod. "Adam will be in touch."

With that, he put back his AirPods and resumed running.

If he was going to be in charge of venues too, he had his work as best man cut out for him. And with that knowledge, he was ready to run back home.

The route led him to Oak Lane to Grams's house. The only off-white stucco with red Spanish tile among the homes spread far apart on the lane. Grandpa had built it with no second story, thinking ahead for when they were older and not wanting to go up and down the stairs all the time.

The leafy oak tree with its lazy tire swing shaded half the front lawn. Just like in Mom's yard, strategically placed shrubs, lavender, and several flowers emanated a sweet scent.

He walked along the red brick pathway, and when he rounded the red shrub, Brit was watering flowers in the planters along the porch. He slowed his steps, stopping to take her in as she tipped the watering can over the next plant.

Dressed in a knee-length navy jumpsuit sporting sunflowers, she'd tied her hair in a ponytail. She crouched and plucked off a leaf, tossing it into the main garden. She was so familiar, perfect in every way, and the sight of her made him nearly dizzy with longing. Despite everything that had happened, he still loved her. He'd sensed a buzz of awareness between them during the grilling last night and their attempt to work on the puzzle.

As if sensing being watched, she paused with a leaf in her hand and stood, setting down the watering can. And just as quickly, he resumed walking and turned off the AirPods when he stood below the front step. May God forgive him for not listening to the last readings.

His thumping heart had to be affiliated with running, not Brit. She was just a friend. He had to train his mind to believe that somehow. With the back of his hand, Lucas wiped sweat from his forehead. "You've done a great job with the garden."

A shy smile curved her mouth, making his heart melt. "Clarice loves to spend time in the flower garden." She gestured at the trimmed rose bushes and further to the daisies. "You must have slept well, if you went for a run."

Not at all. "Yeah. You?"

"Good." Her slightly puffy eyelids could be from something other than a lack of sleep. "Ready for some breakfast?"

With the sun blazing, it seemed much later in the day. "What time is it?" he asked instead of pulling out his phone to check.

"Close to nine."

Early enough, but too late for Grams to have breakfast. "You shouldn't wait for me. It's too late—"

"Clarice ate." She answered his unfinished comment.

"You've always been a brunch fan." He smiled, certain she hadn't eaten yet.

She shrugged. "You've got that right."

After running for so many hours, he was grimy and needed to shower before sitting at the dining table. But while still sweaty, he might as well get the extra work done. "You should eat something, though. It might be a while before I finish cutting grass."

She glanced at the blue sky. "It's too hot. I was planning to cut it this evening."

"You heard Grams last night. While I'm here, I get to help you with housework or, in this case, yard work."

He could hire someone, but Grams never wanted anyone to mow her lawn. She'd always had an exception for family... only people she'd taught how her grass should be cut. Otherwise, she threatened to do the job herself. With his absence, Brit ended up with all the extra work. Precisely why he'd raised her pay.

"At least eat an apple and drink some water first." She rubbed her hands on her jumper, leaving a damp smear as she turned toward the door. "I'll get you some sunscreen."

Always the caretaker of everyone. He hadn't even considered sunblock. "Thanks. I assume the lawn mower is still in the same place?"

"Exactly the same." Glancing over her shoulder, she smiled a familiar smile that warmed his heart and made him feel at home.

When he got to the shed for the lawn mower, everything, including Grandpa's workbench, was still in the same place with tools hanging up in their respective places.

No wonder Brit and Grams got along so well. They had similar habits of keeping things the same. He'd missed home, missed his family, and oh, so much, he'd missed Brit.

BRITTNEY'S HANDS STILLED as she peered out the kitchen window at Lucas cutting the lawn. He'd looked as athletic as ever when he sprinted up to the porch after his run. He probably hadn't been sick in all the time they'd been apart. She could only remember him being truly sick once in their growing-up years. On Valentine's Day of sixth grade, he'd stayed home with chicken pox. After he hadn't come to school for three days, she'd missed him so much, especially during Physical Education.

Mrs. Lee, unfortunately, always chose the athletic kids to pick their partners. Lucky for Brittney, Lucas was one of the best at most of the games they played, and she was the first one he chose to be on his team—every single time.

Her circle of friends wasn't nearly as wide as his was, and although she had her friend, Dalia, Brittney was more comfortable with Lucas. After all, they spent nearly every free moment together, playing, riding bikes, or walking to school.

So, three days without him left her with something big missing in her life.

That evening after making heart-shaped cookies with Mama, Brittney asked if she could go and see Lucas.

"You're only taking cookies to his house and back." Mama helped her slide the cookies from the tray to a cooling rack. "I can't have you getting chicken pox."

Most kids in the class already had their share of chicken pox, except for Brittney and apparently Lucas. If she was going to get it someday, she didn't understand why Mama wanted to stall it off. Besides, it was *Valentine's Day.* Her best friend shouldn't be cooped up all alone in his room on a holiday when the whole class told others they cared about them.

Brittney clutched the food-coloring dye and dribbled teeny bits into the frosting she'd made, mixing up just the right ruby-red color. "Please, Mama. I need to take his valentine cards from school and tell him what we're learning." She mostly wanted to give him a valentine gift *and* take the cookies to his room. "I'll just stay at the door of his room."

But Mama was shaking her head. Brittney's clutch on the dye tightened, but she closed its lid and covered the frosting, setting it aside for when the cookies cooled. Then she scooted out of the house without arguing. If Mama didn't let her, she'd ask Mrs. Matthews. At their front door, Brittney explained that she was making cookies she needed to take to him herself, but she'd stay outside his door.

"Lucas will love some cookies, sweetheart. I'm sure they'll cheer him up, but I don't want you to get chicken pox." Mrs. Matthews gave her a tender smile. "Please bring the cookies over when you have them ready and thank you for your thoughtfulness. Trust me, since you haven't had it yet, it wouldn't be a good idea for you to be around Lucas for a few days."

That didn't make sense. If she got the chicken pox from Lucas, then she'd get done with it.

She returned home with slumped shoulders, and Mama helped Daddy with his bath. Brittney returned to the kitchen and added red frosting to four of the cookies before splashing them with blue sprinkles.

She had no choice but to sneak into Lucas's room later that night.

Lucas had shown her the secret entrance to his room one evening while they sat on the garage deck. Several times Brittney preferred getting to his room through the deck, but Mr. Matthews saw her using the window and told her to always use the front door.

She obeyed most of the time, but around Lucas, she almost had a different mind.

At ten p.m., Mama tucked Brittney in as she usually did after getting Daddy settled in bed.

Brittney looked at Lucas's room, the way she did each night before she fell asleep. Although the main light was turned off, a sliver from his lamp promised he was still awake, since he liked to sleep in the dark.

For some reason, tonight the porch light wasn't on. So she rummaged for the flashlight in her drawer.

She'd already stashed the cookies in her backpack but had forgotten to get her water bottle with the milk from the fridge. She could go back to the kitchen. But what if Mama came out and asked what she was looking for? That would make her late for her plans.

As quiet as a church mouse, she opened her window and lowered herself to the tree, then climbed down a branch and thudded to the grass. She was at Lucas's house in no time, taking the stairs to the garage deck and tapping at his window. "Lucas... it's me." She spoke with a hushed voice.

"Brit?"

Lucas turned on the porch light after opening the window. Red spots and scabs covered his face. Dark shadows lurked under his eyes, but those eyes lit up when he smiled. His tousled hair glowed in the porch light. "You're here."

"I missed you." And, oh, how joy filled her heart at the sight of him!

"I missed you, too."

"I thought you would like some cookies." She handed him her backpack, and he put it in the room while she pulled up to climb. His firm hands held her back, stopping her from landing awkwardly.

As soon as she was inside, she launched into him, throwing her arms around him and inhaling the clean scent of him, so familiar and comforting. He squeezed her back in a tight hug.

"Do you know how happy I am to see you?"

She stepped out of the embrace just as thrilled to be here. "Tell me about it."

"I'm so bored, locked up in this room all day... but wait." He scooted backward, frowning at her. "I don't want you to get sick."

"You've been inside too long." She walked toward his bed and straightened the covers, then reached for her backpack and sat at the end of the bed. "You're starting to sound like our parents."

After unzipping her bag, she handed him the plastic cookie container. "Sorry I couldn't get you milk." He always liked to drink it with his cookies. "It was either that or risk not seeing you."

"I'll blame the chicken pox if I choke."

She grinned, always loving his sense of humor.

When he joined her on the bed, he snapped open the lid and pulled out the first cookie and offered it to her. "Want some?"

"I already ate."

He took the first bite, and the cookie muffled his words. "What have I missed at school?"

"John and Linda were caught kissing in the music closet."

He chuckled softly, almost choking on his cookie. "No way." He criss crossed his legs on the bed, and she did the same. "Who found them?"

"Mrs. Creed," she whispered to remind him to keep his voice hushed so they didn't wake up his parents. They might both be in great trouble if she got caught sneaking into his room. She told him about the valentine notes, and what kids traded love notes she'd read while passing them to their rightful owners.

She leaned back on her hands, loving how relaxed she felt around him. He was the best friend and brother she never had. "By the way, your friend Ryan told me to tell you to ask your parents if you can join his baseball team."

"Did he say where?"

"In his neighborhood, I think."

"I'll join if you join with me."

"It's probably a boys-only team."

He shrugged. "We can find a different team that has girls and boys."

Wow. He always wanted her on his team. She ducked her head, letting out her smile before a more serious thought interrupted. "It might be hard for my mom to drive me there."

With Daddy needing constant care, Mama rarely drove anywhere other than the grocery store, or taking Daddy to the hospital.

"My parents can always take us."

Baseball sounded fun. Thanks to Lucas, who'd taught her how to play all sorts of sports their first summer.

When he finished eating, Brittney handed him a bag of his valentine cards from the kids who'd wanted her to deliver them to him.

They lay side by side on their stomachs, her feet swinging as they read his notes and cards beneath the lamp on the stand.

Brittney pulled out the next note and read.

Lucas, you're the most handsome boy in class. I like you.
Do you like me?
Check the box and pass it to me in class.
◻Yes
◻No?
Yours lovingly,
Tilly.

"Who's Tilly?" He eyed the card over her shoulder as if it might hold a clue.

"The cute girl with red hair." Brittney flicked the card. "She sits behind you."

"Oh." Shrugging, he pulled out another card. Taped to it was a Hershey's chocolate bar, and he ripped it open, broke it in half, and handed half to her while he ate the other.

She read the card through a mouthful.

Lucas, will you be my handsome Romeo? I have the Romeo and Juliet movie at my house. When can you come and watch with me?

Kisses... kisses,

Rochelle.

"Who's Rochelle?"

Seriously? Brittney smacked his shoulder. She'd talked to him about Rochelle a few times. How could he not remember her? "The only girl who wears makeup in class."

He didn't respond as he dug through the bag, tossing out the cards in search of chocolates.

"I thought you didn't have an appetite." Wasn't he supposed to be sick? Now he wanted more candy after scarfing down the cookies?

"Other than itching, I don't feel sick anymore. I'm supposed to be secluded."

Since he wasn't interested in reading any more cards, Brittney sat up and got her bag. "Speaking of valentines, I got your present."

She retrieved the most hideous plush toy and handed it to him.

He sat up. His eyes widened, and he frowned. "What is this?"

"A lobster, I think." She had no idea. "Wait until you hear what it says."

So she pressed it, turning down the volume button. The toy's wide eyes popped out, its pincers snapped, and its fake sharp teeth moved. "I've got you in my claws forever.... You're my best friend, and I'll never let go!"

Lucas smiled, putting a hand over his mouth when the toy wagged its head to one side then to the other. "This is the ugliest thing I've ever seen." His eyes gleamed. She hadn't been sure he'd find it as funny as she had, but she got her answer when he waved it in front of her. "I love it. Crabs don't have pointed teeth or giant eyes, but this... is so nice."

His shoulders fell, and he shook his head. "I didn't get you a present."

He was her present even though he didn't know it. "You don't have to get me anything."

"I drew you a card, though. It's downstairs."

"I'll get it when you feel better."

He leaned in toward her and nudged her with his shoulder. "You're the best friend anyone could ever have."

Her heart was happy and warm with his words. Having Lucas was the best thing that had ever happened to her, too. She wrapped her arms around him for a hug.

"I love you, Brit."

It wasn't the first time he'd said those words—to her or his family—and she'd told him so before. It was easy when she said back, "I love you, too."

He eased out of the hug and kissed her on the lips, very briefly but puzzling. Different.

Her parents always kissed her on the cheek, and Lucas must have sensed her confusion when he answered her unspoken question.

"It's a best friends' kiss." He smiled carefreely.

She'd never heard of that before, and she doubted she would want to ask Mama if she'd ever heard of a best friends' kiss.

Instead of inquiring what it meant, she said good night. She wasn't sure how to react or what to think about the kiss, but when she saw him four days later on Monday, he acted like nothing between them had changed.

Even when he snuck into her room two weeks later when she got chicken pox. He brought her the valentine card he'd made for her, and a single sunflower he'd plucked from someone's yard. They talked and laughed the way they normally did.

In the spring, they played baseball on his friend Ryan Harper's team, and most of the time Lucas's family drove them there. As they teased each other and played after school, Brittney dismissed that kiss, even though, deep down, she still considered it her first kiss.

CHAPTER 9

Brittney squeezed water from the rag and wiped the marble counters and sink, ridding any water residue. Besides the blender and cup she'd used for Clarice's smoothie, there weren't dishes for her to clean, but Brittney needed to keep herself busy in the kitchen. It had nothing to do with her need to sneak peeks at Lucas while he cut the grass.

TV noise from the living room drowned out the lawn mower's rumble. She didn't have to look to know Clarice's gaze was more attuned to the quilt she was stitching than the game show.

With one cup of coffee left in the pot, Brittney dumped the dark-brown liquid in the sink and started a fresh pot for Clarice to refill her third cup. Brittney used to argue about the amount of coffee Clarice drank, but since coffee didn't affect the woman's sleep anymore or appear to increase her blood pressure, why deprive her of one of the few things she enjoyed?

As long as she drank thirty-two ounces of water a day to even out the coffee intake that could dehydrate her.

When Brittney had woken up to a coffee pot brewing, she'd known Lucas made it. Clarice hadn't left her room to start the day. Not only had she slept in, but she also normally took her mornings at a slow pace.

After another hour of not seeing him emerge, Brittney guessed he'd gone for a run rather than back to sleep. He'd always loved taking morning runs.

Thinking of him brought her attention to the humming lawn mower. She couldn't help but look back through the window.

The typically hot June day was expected to reach the nineties by midafternoon. For the first time that morning, she was glad about her decision to postpone Clarice's morning walk to the evening. By the time Clarice had finished her breakfast, it was already nine and too hot to make their half-mile walk around the lane.

The basket of lemons on the corner counter sparked an idea as Brittney glanced at Lucas cutting the grass. He turned off the lawn mower and wiped a hand across his forehead.

She should ignore the sun and go help him finish the remaining section of the yard. Or she could make lemonade and take it to him.

Go... Don't go...

Hmm... He was a friend, and she used to take care of him. Why shouldn't she still do the same?

Before she could talk herself out of the idea, she swung open the cabinet and reached for the glass pitcher and strainer. After snagging three lemons from the basket, she rinsed them and sliced them in half. The lemony smell permeated the kitchen when she started squeezing the juice into the strainer.

Her gaze darted back to the window just as Lucas pulled his shirt over his head and tossed it onto a nearby oak branch. She stepped back, blinking as the lemons fell out of her hand and thudded into the porcelain sink.

Guilt caught in her throat as she stood motionless staring at her friend's toned muscles.

It's just Lucas. A friend. The brother she never had.

It was wrong to gawk at him while he didn't know—wrong to feel anything unsisterly. She had the mind to blame Lucas for his confession years ago.

She shook her head to clear it.

It's just Lucas... *Lucas.*

Surely, repeating his name would return her senses.

She'd seen him without a shirt more than once as they played beach volleyball or swam in lakes, ponds, and his parent's pool. She hadn't been affected—or maybe she'd been a little distracted—but she'd ignored him because he was off-limits. She closed her eyes and searched deep inside herself for resolve. But the pull of him was impossible to resist after that kiss—the heated kiss that crawled into her mind every so often and left her yearning and longing for him to look at her and cup her chin the way he did that night.

"Dear, that fresh coffee smells good! Could you bring me a cup?"

Yikes! She jumped out of her stupor. How long had she been standing there, gaping at Lucas and losing herself in a kiss she'd thrown away long ago? Shaking her head, Brittney poured a full cup and carried it to Clarice, setting it on the magazine table. "I'm headed out to take Lucas a drink."

"He will love that." Clarice put down the quilt on the couch a few inches from her. Even with her hearing aid on, she always spoke louder than the TV volume. "I'm sure he could use some company, too."

The lawn mower was whirring again. He probably wouldn't want to stop for a break, now that he'd resumed cutting.

When she returned to the kitchen, she picked up the lemons from the sink and resumed squeezing and filtering the seeds. She then added water, sugar, ginger ale, and ice.

She assembled the lemonade pitcher, a glass, and a spray bottle on the serving tray and walked across the backyard, her confidence thinning with each step. When Lucas looked in her direction, she nearly froze in place. Bringing lemonade was a terrible idea!

He turned off the lawn mower, and his toothy grin as he walked closer sent her heart into a rapid pace. He wiped his forehead, then brushed his hand on his shorts. "I get to have some of your lemonade?"

She kept her gaze on his rumpled hair, fighting the urge to look at his bare chest. "It's the least I could do after you took over my work."

"My work, too." As if sensing her discomfort, he crossed to the tree where he'd hung his sleeveless shirt and shrugged it on.

She looked away and then back again, her gaze following the line of muscles in his arms while something in her stomach dropped.

He took the spray bottle and splashed his hair. "This feels good." He squirted the bottle at her shirt. The water seeping through to her skin was refreshing, given her sudden rise in body temperature.

If it hadn't been for his confession years ago, she'd be spraying him back. Even so, she still fought the urge to turn this into a water fight. Maybe she would later. "You're lucky I have both hands carrying the tray."

"Is that so?" Amusement gleamed in his eyes.

When he set the spray bottle down and took the glass, she poured his juice from the pitcher, almost filling the glass to the rim.

"Thanks." He tipped his head toward the shaded maple tree where it stood alone as if the oaks didn't welcome it. "You wanna stay while I take a break?"

She more than wanted to, and she didn't have any reason not to. So she followed him, setting the tray on the flat grass before sitting across from him. Moist grass tickled her legs as she laughed at him guzzling lemonade. Some things never changed. "I should just let you drink from the pitcher."

"Might be a good idea." He waved the empty glass. "But I'd rather take slow sips while we talk."

Talk. Hope bloomed through her. He wanted to talk.

Things were getting better. "Good thing I have some time." She lifted the pitcher, and he put out his glass for a refill. "I'll finish the grass while you drink the rest of your lemonade."

"You're not cutting that grass on my watch... not today." He took a sip of his drink, making sounds of enjoyment, and handed her the half-empty glass. "I know you didn't have any before you brought it to me. Tell me this is not the best lemonade you've ever had."

She put up her hand. "I don't need any."

She used to like it as a child, but after years of drinking it, she couldn't care less. Despite her response, he held the glass out for her, so she ended up taking a sip and giving it back to him.

"It's hard to know if it's best since I never drink lemonade anywhere else to compare."

At the far corner of the lawn, a cluster of tall sunflower stalks hadn't bloomed yet. They probably wouldn't survive. She was rarely successful at getting her favorite flowers to grow. She'd tossed the seeds along the edge, with hopes to imitate a field. Someday, she'd succeed.

Oh! Lucas was staring at her through the rim of his glass. She ducked her head. "Where did you run this morning?"

"All over the place." He shrugged. "Can you believe I ran past the sunflower field and the lake?"

"You did?" Her head snapped up, memory tugging up a smile. He'd snuck her into that place. "You went a long way."

"I ran to Granby Park, too."

She rarely went to that park since it was closer to town. The only time she did was when she was revisiting memories of their time skating. With it more crowded than it used to be, he'd probably seen some of the kids they'd gone to school with. "Did you run into any people you know?"

"I saw Rochelle."

Of all people, he had to run into Rochelle. Something tightened up inside her. "I think she only became my friend so she could get to you." Had she kept the jealous twinge out of her tone? Hopefully. But, seriously, Rochelle had always been obsessed with Lucas. How had she gotten Brit to plead with him to go out with her? Now that Rochelle was divorced, she'd no doubt secured a date with Lucas. "I bet she was thrilled to see you."

"You could say that." He poured the rest of the lemonade into his glass. "Adam used my name when he reserved the resort." He told her how off-guard he'd been to learn his brother may not have a venue.

Even if Adam was spontaneous at times, she hadn't expected him to be unprepared for his wedding. "That explains why in the e-vite they said they'd announce the venue in the second email." Which she hadn't received yet. Could he truly have no plans with the wedding so close?

"I'm not sure what he keeps telling Olivia, but she trusts him to have everything under control." Shaking his head, Lucas handed Brittney the half glass of lemonade.

Not wanting any, she urged him to finish the rest.

Olivia had been transparent about the loans she wanted to pay off and not drag into her marriage. Working hard, she'd entrusted things to Adam, but she definitely cared about her wedding.

"If it comes to the worst-case scenario, they can have the wedding here." Actually, having it on Clarice's four nicely landscaped acres with their rolling lawn, trimmed shrubs, and vibrant flowers wasn't a bad idea. "Your mom would do a great job stringing all the cool lights—just like she beads her necklaces—and turning this place into a summer magic wonderland."

Lucas agreed the backyard could be a perfect venue, then told her Adam's hesitation to have the family take his burdens. He clattered the glass on the tray, then stretched his legs out, leaning back on his hands as he tipped his head toward the maple. "If they haven't booked a venue, I'll need training for this best-man job." He stared at two squirrels fighting—or were they playing?—in the branches. "I'll go to his work garage this afternoon. If I'm going to organize a wedding, the sooner I know, the better."

"We both know that finding a venue is not the best man's job." But Lucas always went above and beyond for his loved ones. When it came to helping Adam, though, he used to be firmer and call him out on his manipulative tactics. Brit was tempted to remind Lucas to let Adam deal with his own wedding. Even knowing his brother's usual tactics, Lucas was still willing to help. Was this part of her transformed Lucas? The prayers, and now yielding to all his brother's demands.

"I'd be happy to help, just let me know," she said instead.

His gaze left the squirrels, settling on her. "I hear you and Mom are putting on a bridal shower."

She nodded.

"With that and Grams's errands, plus the senior aerobics you teach at the rec center, your hands are full. I don't want to add more work to your schedule."

"I get off at two." She taught aerobics in the late mornings three times a week. Plus she left Clarice for a few hours on her day off to volunteer at the disability center. "I'd love to help." Regardless of his limited time in Soda Creek, they could reconnect somehow. She braved a smile. "We were always a great team?"

Too bad it sounded more like a question than a statement. What was she hoping for? Him to remember she'd been his best friend? She'd always wanted to be his best friend, and they'd lost so much these last years....

As her gaze hooked with his, she couldn't bring herself to look away. A sense of awareness simmered between them, and her mouth went dry. On second thought, she needed the lemonade, but it was all gone. Did he still feel the same pull of attraction, the attraction she felt, or was it just her imagination?

She got her answer when he pressed his lips into a firm line, sad, in fact.

"We were a great team indeed." He stood and reached for her hand. "Thanks for the lemonade."

Maybe that was regret in his low tone. But what was he regretting? The team they'd never be?

"Anytime."

"Maybe you can give me a ride to Adam's garage? I don't have a car, and I've never been to his new workplace."

"You can't fly there?" She nudged him with her shoulder.

His tanned face crinkled with a smile. "I only said I'd fly to my happy place."

It was hard to resist a smile, and she beamed, her heart light. It almost felt like they'd gotten back to normal, yet they needed to go deeper to retrieve the transparency they'd had before everything fell apart.

It was only Monday. They had fourteen more days before he left town. Maybe tomorrow would be a better day to dig into their past.

CHAPTER 10

Just before four, Grams and Brit dropped Lucas off at the auto shop where Adam worked. "Don't wait on me for dinner." He'd spend the entire night out if that's what it took for Adam to decide on the venue. And he'd make sure Adam took him seriously. Something he may not have been able to do through a phone call.

"Brittney planned the menu with all your favorites." Grams gestured to Brit in the driver's seat. "We'll have dinner saved for you whenever you get home."

Brit craned her neck, turning to look at him behind her as she squished her face as if embarrassed by Grams's confession. "It's not all your favorites. I bought whatever was on sale."

She was a nurturer at heart, and Grams was right. Brit would go out of her way to prepare all his favorite things, as a friend, of course. He'd come to terms with that reality. It didn't eliminate the feelings he'd buried beneath the surface, but he was a big boy.

"I like sales." He winked at her.

As much as he loved eating whatever Brit was preparing, he had no idea what to expect tonight and didn't want them waiting on him. What if Adam couldn't even get off work and Lucas was left to go look at a venue by himself? He sure hoped his brother had booked the other venue, at least. When he stepped out, he leaned toward Brit's door, so close he could smell her cocoa-and vanilla-like conditioner. "While I'm here, I don't expect you guys to change your schedule for me. Grams gave me a key in case I get back late."

Brit had nightly rituals of triple-checking locks and checking security lights before going to bed. She'd started that after her mom was shot in a gas-station holdup.

100

"Stay out of trouble you two." He wished them a good evening and walked toward the warehouse-shaped building.

"Tell Adam I said hello," Grams shouted behind Lucas's back.

At the entrance, a familiar face behind the counter greeted him with a quizzical brow.

Darren. Tall and husky, with brown hair due for a haircut. He'd been a grade ahead of Lucas, and their encounter outside of school didn't carry the best memory. Not for Darren, at least, since Lucas smashed a rock into the guy's parents' window, thoughts he'd rather not reminisce about at the moment.

"Lucas..."

Lucas shook his head, returning from his daze. "Darren?" He gave a curt nod. "You work here?"

"This is my garage." That explained why his T-shirt wasn't grease stained. He eyed Lucas. "What brings you to town?"

Strange he didn't know his employee was getting married. But since he was Adam's boss, Lucas put on a cordial smile. "My brother's wedding."

"I didn't know about it until two weeks ago." Darren hung up car keys on one of the hooks lined with several other keys. "That's why I keep forgetting."

No wonder Adam was strapped for time. If his boss just learned about the wedding, how was he supposed to find Adam's replacement on such short notice?

"Is it possible for me to see Adam?"

"Tell me you're married to that girl."

Huh? What was the guy talking about?

"My parents made me work all summer to pay for that window. I'll feel better knowing someone had a happy ending in all this."

Well, he never got the happy ending, and he'd rather not talk about Brit. So he shrugged, redirecting the conversation. "Sorry." He hadn't been back then. He'd been more focused on rescuing Brit. "I can pay you back." Now, he could afford to.

"Thanks for the offer. I just wanted to see if you remembered."

He remembered every battle and the consequences he'd gotten into for protecting Brit. From being kicked off the football team for one season to school suspensions.

"Sorry again. I was young and now I'm old." And wiser, he hoped.

"We're all good, man." Darren opened the door to the garage, ushering Lucas through and reminding him they were shorthanded.

A rush of odors surrounded Lucas—grease, solder, metal, and chemicals he couldn't identify, marking the place as theirs the way an animal marked its territory.

Adam was lying on the concrete underneath the car, his gaze intent on whatever he was twisting with the screwdriver.

"Adam, look who's looking for you." Darren tossed Lucas a pair of gloves. "While catching up with him, feel free to make yourself useful with a tool or something."

Lucas caught the grimy things. "You don't want me touching any of your clients' cars."

Darren was already leaving, emphasizing any work Lucas could pitch in would be helpful.

Adam rolled from under the car and grinned. He stood, wiping his blackened hands on the cloth he'd retrieved from a pocket of his stained overalls. "You got bored with the town already?"

"I'm gonna have a lawyer look at my contract," Lucas teased, staring at the three other tireless cars in the garage. "I think you might be exploiting your best man."

"Let me guess. You're already done writing vows." Laughter carried in Adam's voice.

"Whoa." Lucas raised his hands. "I thought you were kidding when you brought up the vows. Do you seriously want a guy with no love life writing your vows?"

Adam pumped his hand in a fist. "Exactly. You're the one who aced and got all those awards, even in Literature for a science nerd." He wiped perspiration from his forehead. "When you write my vows, perhaps you'll be passionate about finding that love life."

Adam lived like he was in a movie. "You didn't tell me about the part where I'm planning your wedding venue. Please tell me you have a venue secured somewhere."

"Oh, that... yeah." Wincing, Adam rubbed his jaw. "I forgot to bring up that detail.... How did you find out?"

"Rochelle. I ran into her this morning."

Adam chuckled as he walked to the refrigerator. "She still has a thing for you." He pulled out a Pepsi and asked if Lucas wanted it, then shut the door when Lucas shook his head. "You should've seen the gleam in her eyes when I told her you're my best man. She offered to secure the resort for me until one week before the wedding, just because of you."

Couldn't Adam see that was a big problem in itself? "If you already have a venue picked out, she needs to know by tonight." And that should close that chapter of Lucas's life with Rochelle.

"Livy liked Rochelle's venue the best. That's the only reason I haven't canceled it." Adam popped open the soda as he trailed off about the alternative. "The outdoor cabin had a nonrefundable reservation fee. I couldn't care less where we get married, but I think girls want all the fairy-tale stuff."

Apparently, the resort was twice the price of the cabin. As he rattled on, it sounded like Adam would go for the resort if money wasn't a hindrance.

Lucas had some money to spare, money he rarely spent on big purchases since he had everything he needed.

"I'll get the venue. Consider it my wedding present to you."

"No. No, like you said, I've had plenty of handouts, and I'd rather not drain everyone's pockets just so I can get married."

"You're not taking my money." Adam had always preferred the beach over the mountains. "I'm offering, and if I'm the best man, I'd rather we go for a beach wedding."

"I—"

"What do you say we call Rochelle?" Lucas cut him off. "Commit to her venue and cancel the cabin."

"We'll lose the two hundred."

"Consider it a donation to the cabin venue."

Adam needed to make his bride happy by giving her the wedding she deserved. That's what Lucas would do in his brother's position.

Adam leaned his head back on the wall. "I'll pitch in."

"Use that money to take your bride on a quality honeymoon." Surely, Adam *had* made plans for a honeymoon.

Adam grabbed his phone from his locker along the wall and called Rochelle. His smile stretched wide as he spoke. "We're in."

He nodded. "Uh-huh?" he responded to whatever Rochelle asked. "Thanks for reserving the place for us."

Adam rubbed his hands together after hanging up and putting the phone back in the locker. "Wait until Livy hears about this." He slapped Lucas on the back. "Rochelle is working late. She wants us to meet her at the resort at six thirty."

Why would they need to go to the resort?

Adam, likely noticing Lucas's frown, answered his unspoken question. "We need to sign the contract and choose a caterer."

Lucas hadn't expected things to take place in one night, but with so little time left... "She probably wants us to secure the place with a payment this time."

"Probably." Adam tilted the can to his mouth to take another sip. "Can you stay until I get off?"

Besides having dinner with Grams and Brit, Lucas didn't have a commitment. "Sure." He surveyed the cars. "Why are you the only one working?"

"Two mechanics called in sick today, and one of them gets here much earlier than I do. So I get to work late."

While Adam worked under the car, he swooned and gushed about Olivia and asked for suggestions on songs he could add to their wedding playlist. "Olivia has already chosen her songs and wants me to come up with at least five songs."

"You'd better text Olivia each night," Lucas said. "Perhaps you two can figure something out."

Lucas stood, alternating with squatting as he passed the tools whenever Adam asked for any. Adam showed such confidence as he worked, as if he were a surgeon and the cars, his patients. Too bad he'd lost his business.

"You know you could have your business again."

Adam snorted a laugh. "I can barely pull off a wedding, let alone business start-ups."

"You don't need start-up costs, not when you have clients." Lucas stood, rubbing his hands together, but it'd take more than that to get rid of the grease smudge on his finger. "You could buy a farmhouse and fix cars in your garage at your own home."

"No kidding." Adam rolled out from under the car. "That's why I need you around. You always have genius ideas."

"Guess who was left to fend for himself while you and Em took up Dad's and Mom's attention?" Lucas had felt like that as a child. Although he'd known his parents loved him, at times he'd felt over-looked. "I had nothing to do but plot ideas."

"Explains why you became the family Einstein. It's a good thing. Look how you've turned out to be the most responsible one of us."

It was his turn to laugh mirthlessly. As for responsibility, he needed to figure out a better definition for it. Based on his bumpy relationships, he acted anything but responsible. Otherwise, he would've fought for Brit, especially after she'd ended things with Adam. In fact, he should never have let her go out with him in the first place.

But he'd always stood aside and tried not to mind while those who were louder and more demanding got what they wanted. His jaw twitched, and he tried to push the unwelcome past from his mind. His identity wasn't defined by his past or birth order, but as a child of God with a purpose.

When Adam got off work, they drove together to his house for him to shower and change. Gone were the greasy overalls, now replaced with a button-down plaid he'd tucked into khakis.

"You clean up nice." Lucas brushed imaginary dust from his brother's shirt, then gestured to his own polo over jeans. "You make me feel so underdressed."

Adam, who'd always liked to dress up formally, shook his head. "You always hated suits, ties, and tucking in your shirt."

What Lucas didn't tell Adam was that he looked forward to dressing up for the charity events and parties for work.

"How are things with Brit?" Adam swung open the door and motioned for Lucas to exit first.

"Good. We've talked." Basic stuff. But he didn't offer details, and Adam didn't pry.

When they met Rochelle at the resort's office, Lucas handed her his credit card for a full payment. He then signed the liability forms and contract before she pulled out a menu for them to look at.

Beyond the window, seagulls swooped along the beach. The undulating palm branches made him long to sprawl underneath and watch the waves lap the sand.

"I hadn't realized our contracted caterers are booked out for the whole summer." Rochelle's voice brought him back to the present. She was tapping a manicured finger on her pink-colored lips. "Even our backup catering company is booked that weekend, but they recommended a starter group. I called, and they're willing to meet with you tomorrow. They'll have some of their food for you to sample."

"Tomorrow after six sounds great."

Adam put the menu back on the table and eyed Lucas. Just as he thought his job was done with venues, his brother added another item to the job description. "Is it okay if you come to add some input?"

Lucas could think of ten things to do with Grams, but since he hadn't arranged anything with her, he couldn't say no. He was the best man, after all. "Sure."

"Great!" Rochelle tucked the menu into one of the folders on her desk. "Due to limited parking at her place, I'll pick you guys up. You're staying together, right?"

"He's staying at Grandma's."

"How's she doing?" Rochelle leaned forward as if she chatted with Grams often. "I run into Brittney now and then, but it's not long enough for us to chat."

"She's good." No need to talk about Grams's arthritis and how that caused her feet to swell.

In answer to her earlier question of where to pick them up, Lucas said, "Just get us from Adam's place." He didn't want Rochelle making herself comfortable at Grams's house over the next few days. That could easily take his problems from bad to worse.

After clarifying pickup times, Lucas scraped his chair back across the tile and stood. "Thanks again."

"Yeah, thanks, Rochelle." Adam pushed his chair back as well.

"Anything for Lucas." She flashed a seductive smile. Oh boy! She was beautiful, by all means. Attractive. Yes. But she didn't have that effect or pull on Lucas. How could he put an end to this without affecting Adam's wedding arrangements?

He'd have to think hard and pray. Yikes! He already had Brit to deal with, and he could only handle one complication at a time.

THE HOUSE WAS QUIET when Lucas got home. He locked the door and turned off the floor lamp in the living room. Brit must've left it on for him so he didn't enter a dark house.

Instead of turning on the hallway light, he pulled out his phone and used the flashlight app as he ambled through the hallway, passing Brit's room, which had always been the guest room when he was younger.

After touching all those tools in the garage earlier today, he took a fast shower before changing into his pajama shorts and getting into bed.

As he closed his eyes, he thanked God for a constructive day, pausing when he heard a door creaking open and muffled footsteps padding down the hallway. He wasn't surprised Brit was checking each lock and window to make sure it was in place after he'd come home.

When he woke up the next day, he took a more precise run than yesterday and was back before anyone other than Midnight was awake. After he filled her containers with food and water, he headed downstairs to clean out the cat litter. He scrunched his nose at the stench he carried outside to the trash can. He'd forgotten how cat litter stunk.

It was almost seven when Brit woke and fixed waffles and bacon while he cut up fruit and blended protein powder with a banana and almond butter. By the time Grams joined them, they had the food set on the table. While they ate, Grams talked about the county fair that weekend and the booth where her quilt club would be showcasing their work.

"When's this event again?" he asked.

"Starts Thursday and ends Sunday." Brit snatched the piece of bacon from his plate.

Needing to bring an element of play with Brit, he said, "Is this how she deprives her guests, by stealing their food?" He pointed to her sitting next to him and stared at Grams sipping her steaming coffee.

"He did it first." Brit kicked his shin under the table. "Stole my waffle."

She'd only eaten one bite and started devouring her fruit. She'd never been a breakfast eater. He raised both hands. "I didn't want food to go to waste."

"Looks like I'm going to play judge after we eat, doesn't it?" Amusement jittered in Grams's hoarse voice. "As long as you come with us to the fair on Thursday, Friday, or Saturday, I might give you a fair judgment."

"You want to ride a carousel, right?"

She'd said as much yesterday when she brought up the fair. She nodded.

Brit was smiling. "I'll take pictures."

"Let's plan to go on Thursday, then." As long as Adam didn't have any more surprise jobs.

"How did everything go last night?" Brit slid the fruit bowl toward Grams.

"We got the venue." Folding his arms on the table, he told them about the resort and the backup caterer they'd be meeting that evening. "Do you mind giving me a ride to Adam's place again?"

"What time do you need to be there?"

"At five or whenever it's convenient. And you'd better not wait on me for dinner."

Grams jerked her head up. "You're going to miss dinner two nights in a row? Surely, you can't stay later than eight."

He doubted he'd be gone longer than seven. But that would still be too late for them to wait on him, and he told them so.

SEVERAL HOURS LATER, Lucas, Adam, and Rochelle sat in a restaurant on Main Street, munching salads. Lucas moved the fork in his salad, fighting the urge to reach for and check his phone. Were Grams and Brit expecting him back for dinner?

They'd met with the caterer at a private residence. Rochelle had forgotten to let them know how far the place was, and she'd rear-ended someone, which added an extra hour to their trip while they waited for the police to get there. They'd eventually made it and tested three food options—chicken parmigiana, crusted salmon with pasta, and a gourmet-sounding name he didn't care to remember.

They'd agreed the food was bland and not suited for the wedding. Lucas almost felt like paying for them to take the needed catering lessons so he could hire them since they were just starting a business. But that didn't seem realistic.

Rochelle claimed she was starving, and since Lucas and Adam were at her mercy, they'd agreed to join her at the modern-looking café on Main Street.

"I never even asked why your fiancée couldn't join us for the testing." Rochelle forked the remains of her arugula and lifted it to her mouth.

"She had to cover for the manager. She was disappointed not to be here."

"What a bummer."

"Yep, it's life." The bright lights cast the thin, firm line on Adam's mouth into focus before he sipped his Pepsi.

Not wanting his brother to be uncomfortable, Lucas leaned forward. "That's why I'm here to help."

Rochelle put her napkin on her plate. Lucas had long given up on the salad, and Adam wasn't into what he thought of as rabbit food. But, since it was the only meal the restaurant served, like Lucas, Adam felt the need to wash away the caterer's awful unflavored food.

"Two handsome men are taking care of a wedding." Rochelle folded her hands on the table. "Isn't she the lucky one?"

"So am I," Adam added with a gentle nod.

When the server collected their plates, Lucas reached for his wallet, but Rochelle touched his arm. "My treat. I invited you guys here."

Regardless, it wasn't gentlemanly to let her pay. "You held my brother's reservation. The least I can do is pay for your salad."

She smiled warmly, her hand still on his arm. "How can I say no?"

When Adam excused himself to the bathroom, Lucas peered over at the three people seated at the tall bistro table in the corner and tried to sit still despite Rochelle's intense stare.

"Ever heard the term, second time's the charm or, in our case, third time?"

His jaw twitched when he turned to stare at her. She was biting her lower lip alluringly.

This was awkward. What was taking Adam so long? Was now a good time to put an end to this, or should he wait until Adam's wedding was over?

He peeked toward where Adam had vanished, then back to Rochelle, who was leaning forward awaiting his response.

"Listen... I..." He now understood the sting of rejection. Something he hadn't known as a teenager. How could he be polite while ending her plans? He gripped the back of his neck. "It's not you—" Ouch! How cliché that sounded. "You're beautiful and smart...."

Her face flushed, and she shook her head, tucking a strand of her blonde curls behind her ear as he continued. "You deserve to be with someone who will cherish you and love you the way you should be loved."

Her brows creased, so he might as well be honest. "I'm in love with someone." Even if that someone would never love him back, that was the truth.

"Oh." She fanned herself, leaning back, not looking ready to accept his confession. "I assumed you were dating someone, but you're not married yet." She rambled on about his handsomeness and her hope that he would try to give them another chance while in town.

The waiter returned with his credit card, and Adam also returned shortly. Lucas shot up to stand, retrieving his phone from his jeans pocket and blinking when he saw the time. Ten thirty? "We should probably get going." What else could he say?

"Come on." She blinked up at him with big eyes. "You can't tell me you're going to bed this early."

Adam let out a yawn to back Lucas up. "Grandma is asleep by now."

Before Rochelle stood, she scribbled something on the napkin, but Lucas started walking with Adam behind him.

"She's persistent," Adam whispered, but she was already joining them as they approached the door. Lucas held it for her and Adam to exit first. The girl behind the counter shouted her thanks to them as Lucas closed the door.

At the car, Rochelle insisted Lucas sit in the front. "It would be pathetic to drive two handsome men and have none sit next to me."

"Let's drop off Lucas first." Adam saved him, even as he slid into the back seat, leaving the front for Lucas. "Then he doesn't have to stay out late and wake Grandma."

As Lucas buckled himself in, Rochelle dabbed a napkin to her lips and handed it to him. "If you change your mind about dating, there's my number."

Not intending to be rude, he glanced at the napkin, the parking lot lights revealing the pink print of her lips.

"Let me know if you need help finding caterers." She fired the engine.

Did he want her to help him? Yes. But that meant spending more time with her.

He turned to Adam in the back seat. "Adam's got this." When Adam shook his head, Lucas gave him a glare, not that he could see in the dim light as they pulled onto the street. "Right, big bro?"

Come on, Adam. Don't do this to me.

"Right." Adam's response wasn't convincing, but Lucas would deal with him whenever he spoke to him about writing his vows.

For now, Rochelle didn't offer any more help and turned on pop music. It had been a long day. He leaned his head back, tempted to close his heavy eyelids, and counted down the minutes until he could get home and get to bed.

CHAPTER 11

Brittney tapped her knee, her stomach dropping with each ticking of the grandfather clock. She'd learned to ignore it over the years, but it seemed way louder tonight.

She eyed it for what seemed like the umpteenth time. Ten fifty-five, and still no sign of Lucas. She went to the bay window, where she could see the road without the plants blocking her view. Peeking through the curtain, she was met by an empty street, lit from the front porch.

Ugh. She clenched her teeth as she closed the drapes too fast. Why was she all worked up? There was a reason, all right. Lucas had stayed out late two nights in a row. Although Brittney had eaten with Clarice, she'd barely tasted the short ribs—not when Lucas was out with Rochelle, sampling wedding food. An unwelcome image flashed in her mind, an image of Rochelle feeding him or using her seductive tactics to lure him into a two-week fling.

Brittney loosened her jaw. Why had she introduced Rochelle to Lucas? Seriously, why? She'd been a fool to think that if Lucas had a girl as gorgeous as Rochelle, it would keep herself from falling for her best friend.

She lowered herself to the carpet and tinkered with the puzzle. She and Lucas had worked on it after breakfast while Clarice told them the history behind the city park and the first fireworks show in Soda Creek.

She added the piece with a white pole to the gazebo, then reached for another piece with a splash of fireworks. With her mind still a jumble and her nerves too tense to concentrate, she just flipped a tiny piece with a lamp in its corner back and forth in her hand.

At a car door closing, she tossed the piece to the table and dashed for the window, peeking through the drapes. Her stomach clenched when Rochelle's silhouette wrapped her arms around Lucas.

A shudder coursed through Brittney. She was going to throw up.

Suddenly dizzy, she stepped away from the window, flopping on Clarice's recliner and burying her face in her hands.

She'd stayed up waiting for him last night, but as soon as she'd heard the car, she'd run to her room and pretended to be asleep as she listened to him shower. Then, way after she was sure he'd fallenasleep, she'd gone back to double-check the locks.

The least he could do was call and let them know he was running late. *He's an adult, for crying out loud.*

Good thing she didn't have his number, or she might've texted him and made a fool of herself.

When the front door opened, she glanced up and caught the ghost of a smile on his face. Her jealousy turned to anger, igniting a fire inside her, a flame she needed to turn off. He must have caught the heat in her eyes as his smile vanished.

"I forgot I'm on curfew." Amusement loaded his tone as if Rochelle had lit up his mood. Did he have to look so handsome, that rusty polo lighting up his brown eyes?

"You know how I like to lock up everything before I go to bed." She stood and walked around him to turn the lock—just to empha-size her reason for staying up.

"I have the key to let myself in and lock up too." He shrugged, napkin dangling in his hand. "Like I did last night, but you ended up double-checking after I went to bed."

Her cheeks heated. How'd he hear her last night?

"I like to do it." She crossed to the kitchen and turned on the light for no other reason than to avoid his suspicious gaze. She had to avoid staring into his eyes. Otherwise, he'd see through her. And she needed something to divert things from this... this *rage*. "How did the food testing go?"

"It was good." He followed her, and with nothing else to busy herself with, she found herself jerking open the fridge.

"I bet Rochelle enjoyed catching up with you after all these years." Whew. She was doing a great job composing herself. She grabbed the first thing she could from the fridge and closed it a little too hard.

"We had lots of food options, but it was disgusting. Since Rochelle was hungry, she offered to take us out to dinner."

"And it surprises you that she took you out?"

"Why did you pull out mustard from the refrigerator?" Lucas set the napkin on the counter and freed the bottle from her death grip.

"I'm organizing." In case he hadn't noticed. She tried to yank the bottle out of his hand, but he raised it higher, his shirt getting slightly untucked. And without thinking, she tiptoed on her feet. So did he, his gaze meeting hers, and her throat dried. "The fridge is already organized."

Smart aleck! Her feet hit the cool tile as she folded her arms. Her gaze darted to the napkin on the island counter. Was that lipstick? She blinked and caught the inked telephone number and Rochelle's name. The burning rose in her chest, and she had several new names for Rochelle, names she'd never call her to her face. She needed to go to her room, but Lucas was staring at her with a quizzical brow.

"Why do I get the impression you're bothered by the time I spent with Rochelle?"

Couldn't he pretend not to read her mind? Even though she'd blown her chance with him that night, the idea of him moving on with someone else—especially Rochelle—terrified her. Afraid to meet his gaze, she leaned back against the long counter and kept her eyes fixated on the china cabinet across from them. "Why should I be bothered? You're an adult who can do whatever you want."

He moved closer, cupping her chin until she stared at him. "You're not jealous of Rochelle, are you?"

Her heart was thumping against her ribs. Why was it so hard not to stare at his lips? *Look into his eyes—that's better.* Her lips parted to protest, but with his smirk, she had no way of denying what he already saw in her eyes.

He arched a brow, and having him know her so well irked. She brushed his hand off her chin and scurried toward the hallway. That's what her mind wanted to do, but her feet led her back to the living room.

Accusing him was better than the real issue. "You should've called to let us know you wouldn't be home for dinner."

"I told you guys to keep doing what you do. Pretend I'm not even here."

After being away for so long, he thought she could *pretend* he wasn't here? "That might be easy for you, but not for everyone else." She was pacing, her arms fighting the urge to restack Clarice's magazines or rearrange the plates in the china cabinet. "That's what we've done the last ten years—pretend you don't exist. Is that what you still want?"

"I don't think this is about me calling for dinner." His voice calm, he leaned against the wall dividing the kitchen and the living room. "If I remember, you didn't want me that way. I don't get why you care who I have dinner with."

Was this how he was going to play it? Okay, so be it. She planted her hand on her hip and looked at him squarely, several words brewing in her mind—words she'd wanted to tell him when he cut her out of his life. "You can't be serious."

"Humor me." His face darkened as if he braced himself, ready for the attack.

There was no sense in holding back. She stood in front of the small bookshelf and threw her hands up. "You've been gone for ten years, probably charmed all sorts of women, something you're good at—"

He winced. "Is that what you think I am? A player?"

Her mind registered what she'd said. She crossed her arms, biting inside her cheek. "Not exactly what I meant."

But still, he had no right to take off the way he had.

"You had no right to kiss me and take off without giving me time to process... leaving me behind with a mess to clean." She gasped at her honesty, heat rising as her heart clenched. It was hard not to think of those first six months after she'd broken off with Adam, her fear and panic over what his family thought of her. She'd needed someone to talk to, but the only person to tell something that big was Lucas. And. He. Wasn't. Around.

"You don't..." The words were coming out of her mouth too fast. Before she knew it, she was sobbing and shaking in front of him, pointing a finger and accusing him of messing up her love life. Because, even if she'd wanted to move on after Adam, she'd never gotten past Lucas's kiss.

"Oh, now I'm the villain of your story? Is th–that so!" He walked away from her, tugging at his front hair. "I can't b–believe it." His words were choppy. No doubt he was angry since he was stammering. He only stammered when he was mad. She hadn't seen him this upset since that day he'd shattered a window to get her out of her crush's house.

When he spun to look at her, his eyes held a tightness, his words firm and sharp. "You're an adult, Brittney. You need to grow up. When are you going to stand up and say no for once?"

He'd used Brittney, instead of Brit. He turned his back to her, then paced.

"You went out with Silas because you felt sorry for his breakup, went out with Troy because you felt bad about his injury." He huffed. "Don't you see a pattern here? Then Adam—because he was sad. One movie led to two... to a date and another!"

His rising voice rang through the room. He slammed his fist into the air. "Would it have been so hard for you to turn down his proposal?"

Her legs were shaking, more so when he looked back at her, staring down at her with such... condemnation.

"If I didn't show up, would you have married him?"

His accusing tone jarred through her, more insulting since he was right. Truth was—she had no idea, but she may have married him rather than hurt his feelings.

Lucas shook his head. His fury subsided as he stood there avoiding her gaze. "Of course, you would've." He shuddered a breath. "Who was I to assume I knew you?"

She sucked in a quick breath. Her arms crept protectively around her middle. That stung more than anything. Even if he didn't think he knew her... "You were my best friend." The words choked past the tight ball of tears in her throat. "Do you know how it's been these last years without you? When I couldn't call to tell you I got an award for Caregiver of the Year? How hurtful it was to listen to Clarice talk to you, laughing on through the phone, yet I couldn't ever talk to you?"

He sank to the floor, dangling his hands over his knees.

"I made a fool of myself with your family." A fool she was, and she was aware of that. Still, she'd hoped she'd learned a few things during her twelve months of therapy. "I caused a rift in the family." One he was well aware of. Clarice had been open about the tension between Adam and Lucas during that first year after the breakup.

"I... needed... my friend," she ground out, resigned and torn from her outburst.

"So did I," Lucas whispered, his gaze intent on the fireplace mantle. His mind seemed distant, and she longed to sit next to him, to apologize for lashing out.

After several silent seconds with him not looking her way, she decided she'd said enough and marched to her room, wiping at the tears still lingering on her cheeks.

When she sank onto her bed, she slapped her forehead before squinting through the shadows. Her mind went to work processing the words she'd said, the words he'd said.

You need to grow up!
You need to grow up!
You need to grow up!

The refrain wouldn't stop even after she pressed her hands to her ears.

Did she act like a teenager because of her choices?

Oh, Mama, will things ever be the same with Lucas and me? If only her mom were here, or her dear friend, Dalia, but she'd moved to Poland for her husband's job several years ago.

Pathetic! Yes, that's how she felt. She didn't even have a single friend her age—someone who understood the agony of her loneliness.

In therapy, the Christian counselor had talked about overcoming anxiety by relying on a higher power. She'd encouraged prayer as the best resource to get Brittney through each passing day. Who was God to Brittney? Did God know who she was?

She'd had many questions, but then the counselor relocated to another city, sixty miles away, before she could ask. That had been the end of her counseling sessions.

Come to think of it, was she the reason the counselor left?

Another ball formed in her throat as more tears threatened to take over. She needed to change out of her clothes. But her body was so weak, and she was drained with the last bit of hope for their friendship vanishing.

She lay motionless, listening for Lucas's footsteps to pass her room. Several hours later, he opened and closed his door, then took a shower.

She could use the shower in her room, but she had no idea if she could move the next inch to get to it.

They'd had fights so many times, but Lucas always stayed and talked things through before the day ended or early the next day. Maybe, just maybe, things would be okay when she woke up.

CHAPTER 12

Now that he'd spoken his mind, he should feel better about himself, yet Lucas felt anything but.

With each roll to his stomach, then to his back, and to the side, he could hear Brit's bed creak or her covers rustle. Or it could just be him imagining her crying.

Her trembling lips when she poured out her heart had been a breaking moment and a reminder to him to shut up.

His chest hurt, and his temples twitched as if he'd be having to offset a headache. He was too worked up to sleep while the words of their argument rang loud and clear in his mind.

Had she always thought he was a player? Is that why she'd never wanted him? No, surely not. Brit knew him better than that, since he'd spent ninety percent of his time with her before he left for college.

Yes, maybe after her rejection he'd bounced around trying for a woman who was like her, someone to replace her. He snorted. What a vain attempt!

As soon as morning light streamed through the window, he was up and changing into shorts and then out the door. Without second-guessing himself, he jogged the five miles to his childhood home, not caring that his room was occupied.

He was acting like a child, but after last night, he needed to create some space between him and Brit.

Why would she be jealous? She didn't want him, yet she didn't want anyone else to be with him. Isn't that what he wanted from her, too? For her to be his, not anyone else's?

He strained his eyes on the community sidewalks, waving at the few people he jogged past.

Hanging out with my family is better. He could've gone to Ryan's, but he was with his family, and Lucas wouldn't rob him of that time.

When he got to his childhood home, Mom was in the kitchen, a knife tapping on the cutting board as she sliced bread into cubes. But Dad, unusually, wasn't in his regular spot at the table while she cooked.

"Morning, Mom."

She startled, stopping halfway from slicing a piece of French bread. "Oh. Hi, honey." She smiled. "Everything okay?"

"I missed my mom and wanted to say hello." Her earring brushed his chin when he bent and kissed her cheek. "Where's Dad?"

"City Hall. He has a committee meeting at seven. You missed him by minutes." She resumed dicing the bread. "Having a good time at your grandma's?"

"I'm getting a hotel tonight." He yawned, washing his hands in the sink and drying them with one of the kitchen towels on the hook. "The bed's uncomfortable." Even if it wasn't his childhood bed, he'd slept in it when he visited Grandma, but never had a problem.

"I've never heard you complain before." She stopped cutting and eyed him, a skeptical eyebrow rising. "Anything you want to talk about?"

"Yeah." He took a stainless whisk from the bowl of eggy liquid and whipped it. "What are you cooking?"

"French toast casserole. But you know that's not what I mean."

With her knowing gaze on him, he kept his hands moving with the whisk, eggs she'd already beaten and added milk to, now that he stared closely to see white streaks in the mix.

"What time does everyone wake up?" Maybe he could change the topic as far from himself as possible.

"I'd be sleeping in today if it wasn't my day to run the gift shop."

Sleep sounded good, but someone already occupied his bed. Going back to Grams was not an option, but helping his mom might be a better alternative. It would also give him time to plot his next move. Sleep deprivation could cause him to make irrational decisions.

"I'm available today if you need my help at the shop."

"I'd love that." Nudging him aside, she took the egg batter and poured it over the bread in the baking pan. "You were always my favorite kid—you know that?"

"That's what you tell Adam and Emery."

Her warm laughter rushed over him. "Again, you're the smart one, too. Always thinking outside the box."

"Okay... okay." He tossed the whisk in the sink. "I'll let Adam and Emery know I'm the family favorite. Can we put that in writing and hang the plaque in the family room? It might boost my confidence."

Mom's shoulders shook as she laughed. "I sure missed your sense of humor."

When he yawned again, he swung open the cupboard with the plates, then another with cups. Unlike Grams's house where everything was in the same place, Mom always rearranged and changed things in her kitchen. "Where do you hide the coffee?"

"Someone didn't get any sleep last night." She walked to the corner cabinet, retrieved a bag of ground coffee from the top shelf, and handed it to him.

As he fixed coffee, she put the French toast casserole into the oven and told him what it was like having all the guests in the house.

"I eat my breakfast with your dad before everyone wakes up, but it's always nice to spend time with family."

Family. He should feel embarrassed for not initiating family time over the years. But he was here now.

When the coffee pot beeped, he poured himself a cup, then poured one for her. He updated her about Adam's wedding as he walked to sit at the table. "We got a venue last night."

"Adam sent an email last night." She followed him. "I was starting to get worried. Whenever I asked your brother, he told me he had it under control."

"He sure does." Lucas sipped his coffee, not wanting to get her involved, since Adam wanted it that way. No need to tell her they may end up having fast food for the event, unless one of Rochelle's venue caterers had a cancellation.

"So, what happened between you and Brittney?" Both hands wrapped around her mug, Mom braced her elbows on the table and sipped her coffee.

"What makes you think anything happened?"

She narrowed her gaze. "I'm your mother."

He curled his fingers around the mug, savoring its warmth. Honestly, lying to Mom was useless. "She got upset with me. I got home late." She'd used plenty of excuses for her outburst, but he knew what really got to her. "Rochelle brought me home."

"Wait. Rochelle from high school?" Mom's brows scrunched together.

"She's in charge of the wedding venue." He shrugged before she could come to any conclusions. Then he told her about Adam's venue options and did his best to explain without uttering his financial contribution before concluding with last night's events.

"I just hate when I have big fights with Brit." He hated conflict—period. People considered him a happy person, but they didn't understand how any kind of argument drained him.

"Fights are good." She reached across the table and laced their fingers together, giving his hand a squeeze. "You two argued a lot, but by the next day, you were talking and giggling like nothing ever happened."

"Those were the days." His chest hurting, his hand limp under her grip, he stared at the cookbooks lined above the kitchen counter shelf. He missed that, missed Brit.

"You two were so adorable." She tightened her hold on his hand. "I loved listening to your giggles, especially that night when you had chicken pox and she snuck into your room."

All those years he'd thought they snuck in each other's rooms without Mom's knowledge. "You mean you heard us?"

Eyes twinkling, she nodded.

How did she remember all the little details about her three kids? She hadn't been big on discipline or tight rules like Dad or Brit's mom. "Why didn't you come and say something or threaten to ground me?"

Sliding her hand from his, she tapped the table with her fingers. "I thought about it, but I loved hearing you giggle. I never heard you laugh as much as you did when you were with Brittney." She smiled as if lost back in time. "Especially that night. You'd been sick, and I thought if I got after Brittney, she might be terrified. Besides, by that point, it was too late to stop her from getting the chickenpox if she was already in your room."

"What did Marjorie say when you told her?" Their moms had become the best of friends.

Mom winced. "She was too structured, and I didn't want to get Brittney in trouble, not after she'd made you laugh."

Lucas leaned back, laughing. "You were so bad."

"I always felt like you got the least of my attention because you were independent. Anyway, I still didn't want to go too hard on you."

Sinking back against his chair, he cocked his head and studied her as her confession confirmed what he'd observed during his elementary years. Kinda felt good to know she'd known it too, and he couldn't blame her. His siblings *had* been more demanding, leaving her no choice.

"But you turned out wonderful." She reached over to touch his cheek. "So it's a win-win."

Mom then reminded him of her confidence in his ability to make things right with his best friend. Funny, she remembered their fights more than he did. Yes, he and Brit had disagreed, had arguments, especially when she'd stayed with them after her dad died, but he barely remembered their fights because they'd never stayed mad at each other long.

"I'm sure you know what to do," Mom added, pulling him out of his thoughts.

Compelled to share some of Brit's frustrations, the words she'd uttered during their argument, he swirled his coffee, peering at the churning liquid even as bile churned in his stomach. "I wasn't there for her." He ran his hand on the rim of the half-filled cup. "I left her to deal with everything." After he'd kissed her, not giving her time to think and make up her mind. His heart constricted. She'd always had two friends, besides the elderly people she spent most of her time with, including Grams. Her closest friend had left the country, and Rochelle wasn't someone she could confide in, could count on. Had she talked to anyone about the dilemma?

"Was it hard for her?" He cleared the lump in his throat. "I mean after she broke off with Adam?"

"She seemed to shut down after that, but I think she's doing better." Mom touched his shoulder. "She apologized to me and Dad, and we told her it wasn't necessary."

Lucas might have behaved differently if Brit had chosen someone else rather than Adam, but it still didn't justify his mistake. He rubbed his forehead and leaned back, almost sick over the way he'd reacted. "I changed my phone." Not that Mom didn't know. "I never called her, even though I was responsible for ruining things." He should've trusted her to decide whether Adam was good for her or not.

"You can't change the past." Mom fiddled with the beads on her three-strand necklace. "There's a future at your fingertips. Today is a new day with new opportunities."

For the sake of their friendship, he needed to start over. "I hope I haven't done much damage."

"Just my two cents—don't stay in a hotel." She sipped the coffee, wincing, probably because it was cold. "It will look like you're running away again."

His mouth quirked. "Isn't that what I do best?"

She shook her head. "Give Brit a surprise ending, if you've painted yourself as a runner."

"Thanks, Mom."

"I'm almost one hundred and one percent sure she likes you beyond friendship. Otherwise, your going out with Rochelle or anyone else shouldn't have bothered her."

If he was going to start over, he needed to do so as a friend—and nothing more. He would move heaven on earth to be with her, but this time, she'd have to initiate things. "I'm going to need God's help."

"Speaking of God"—Mom slid her cup to the side—"I noticed you close your eyes before you eat. Does God have anything to do with that?"

His shoulders loosened, and he gave her a sheepish shrug. "I'm still new at all this, but I'm learning I'm not as intelligent as I thought." He'd always done things with confidence, in his prideful way somehow. "I have to be accountable to God for my actions." He had no idea why he railed on about all sorts of things. "I always found satisfaction in other things and places." Trying to replace Brit. But at the end of the day, he was empty.

He hoped that someday he could share his life with someone who loved him as much as he loved her. Just like his parents, who, after being married forty-plus years, still adored each other, loved spending time together. *Is that too much for me to ask from You, God?*

He continued, "Brit is my friend, and I wouldn't want anyone to treat her the way I did." Nor the way he handled the whole situation as if he was a spoiled brat. "You raised me to be better than this."

Pressing a hand to her heart, Mom scooted over, then hugged him tight. "That's my boy," she whispered against his hair.

The oven timer went off, the scent of cinnamon and vanilla already tempting him.

Mom took his face between her hands, squeezing it, then kissed his forehead. "I'm so proud of you. I know everything is going to work out." Then she stood, taking their mugs. "I want to hear more about this God of yours."

As she opened the oven, Lucas stood, thrilled to talk about how he came to rely on God. "We have a whole day together."

CHAPTER 13

Brittney lay on her stomach on the hammock as she reread the same paragraph she'd read for the last forty minutes or so. Her mind racked for what the first two chapters of the book were about.

Starting over was practical if she wanted to grasp the story, but going back to the beginning would mean wasting the time she'd spent in the first two chapters. She'd started the book two months ago, but barely had time to read back to back. Whenever she got time to read, it felt like she needed to restart.

She tried reading out loud, the only way that always worked to block her mind from wandering. But doing so brought one person to mind—Lucas.

Whenever they'd studied together or read a book for a class assignment, he couldn't tolerate her loud reading. So he'd end up telling her the summary.

Most times, he'd have read the book before their joint reading.

While he grasped things so quickly, she'd had to work hard to earn her grades. He didn't have to study to pull off an A.

Thankfully, today had been her day to work at the disability center. That helped her not dwell on personal issues while real people were dealing with real-life problems.

Normally she would get chores done at this time of the day, but after dropping off Clarice at the quilters' guild, she retreated to the hammock with her book.

What was wrong with her? Why had she let herself give in to an outburst last night? She was supposed to reconcile with Lucas. Instead, she'd chased him away with accusations.

Good thing Clarice was a deep sleeper and never kept her hearing aid on while sleeping, or the ruckus would've woken her.

Brittney had heard Lucas's every movement, groans and mumblings from his room, until his muffled footsteps walked through the hallway early that morning. Clarice assumed he was busy planning the wedding, and Brittney agreed with her, although his disappearance had everything to do with her.

They'd always fixed things whenever they were upset with each other, but those days of fixing things were gone. Or, at least, Lucas was gone. He was different, and that was the problem.

The breeze rustled the open pages, turning them all the way back to the first chapter. Leaving her no choice but to start the story all over.

The scenario reminded her of her life. It felt like she'd skipped one step after another—her relationship with Lucas could use a do-over.

Lucas was in love with her, or at least he had been. That's what he'd pointed out last night when he told her she had no right to be jealous of him.

In the last ten years, she'd had time to think about that night and his confession. She'd wondered how long he had been in love with her, and as she searched the deep recesses of her heart, she'd seen the signs had been there all along.

Yes, she'd had the same feelings at one point and blamed it on her teenage hormones. He was always cheerful, polite, taking care of her, and doing anything for her. It was easy for her to feel the pull of attraction.

As a heartthrob, Lucas could have dated any girl he wanted, but he'd always told her he didn't have time to date. Yet he always had time for her.

That's why she'd fixed him up with Rochelle, who was bugging Brittney to set her up with Lucas. Plus, Brittney had thought having him go out with someone else would help her not think of him in a romantic way.

If only she'd seen the signs of how deep Lucas's love was for her, things would be different.

She should have known. She tucked her book away and flipped onto her back, staring up at the gnarled oak branches above her as the hammock rocked. Lucas had been her proverbial knight in shining armor when she'd needed him. She should have seen how much she meant to him then....

Silas had come into her life at the beginning of her sophomore year. As a junior in sophomore math, he'd been assigned to her desk. Being a rule follower, Brittney never had a stable desk partner. The teachers preferred putting talkative kids next to her since they knew she wouldn't be a distraction—that was, until Silas.

During his second week in one of the classes, he'd leaned toward her. "I've heard that you're the coolest kid in class," he whispered, his warm breath tickling her ear. It was hard to focus on Mr. Schneider's lesson about proportion and variation.

"That's not true."

"Is that so?" He craned his neck and ran a hand through his thick dark hair, his grey eyes dancing, and she'd found herself lost in them.

With him so confident and handsome, her stomach filled with butterflies. For a second, she'd forgotten she was in class until Mr. Schneider shouted her name.

Brittney jumped, startling and dropping the textbook her elbow was resting on.

"Looks like you and Silas have a class of your own."

"I just—"

She stopped mid sentence when Silas took her hand from under the table and wrapped it in his, squeezing it. Her jaw stayed open. She'd forgotten what she was going to say.

When the teacher gave them the assignment, due the next day, they had no idea what setting up proportions meant in the assignment.

"I'm counting on you." Silas grinned, and her heart melted. "I have no clue what he just said."

"I can help." *What?* How was she going to help when she didn't know what she was doing? But Lucas could help. He was in the senior math class and one of the top students.

"Awesome. I can come to your house tonight so we can work on it."

"My house is—"

"Rochelle knows where you live."

Oh yes, he was Rochelle's big brother. But first, she needed a lesson with Lucas. "Maybe come after dinner."

On the drive home, she'd confided her dilemma and need for his intelligent brain.

"You're always telling me to stay away from troublemakers." Lucas took her hand and linked it with his. "You do not want to be anywhere near Silas. He just broke up with Trinity and—"

"That's why I should help him." He didn't seem too bothered by the breakup, but maybe Brittney could be there to console him.

"Are you going to teach me or not?" she pleaded when Lucas's jaw tightened.

"I'll help you as long as I stay in the room with you when he comes."

Seriously? Her shoulders slumped. "You really know how to ruin a party."

Although she hated the idea of Lucas hovering around, it was much better than her not knowing the answers as she'd promised Silas.

Even though Lucas stayed with them that evening, Silas asked her to the homecoming dance a week later, and she went to Lucas's house to talk about the dance.

"I didn't want you to be by yourself," she told Lucas as they sat in his bedroom window side by side, talking about the fall dance. "I asked Rochelle to go with you."

He rolled his eyes. "I told you I don't want to go out with her."

"She keeps asking me about you. Now that I'm going with her brother, ask her to the dance."

Lucas draped his arm over her shoulders and squeezed her toward him. "This is one of the most annoying things you've asked me to do."

"Please, for me?"

As she looked into his eyes, deep brown, so warm and familiar, he bumped his head against hers. "Only this time."

She leaned her head to rest on his shoulder, grateful for him. "You're so nice."

"Anything for you, Brit." His voice was quieter, almost sad, but she understood his annoyance. Although she wasn't as smart or strong as he was, she'd do anything for him, too.

Her tone and thoughts of Lucas changed in the spring when he shattered the window at Silas's friend Darren's house, so he could get her out of there. Silas had invited her there, promising several kids would be there. But, when she got there, there were only two other girls, and each one was paired with a guy. It felt wrong since it was just the kids with no parents at the house.

With pop music playing in the background, Darren vanished into another room with his girlfriend. The other couple sat beneath the dim light, kissing in a kitchen corner.

Brittney bounced her knee, more uncomfortable when Silas attempted to rub her hand in his. Why was she uncomfortable with his touch? Her heart was beating in panic, rather than anticipation.

She'd never kissed a boy before, except for the best friends' kiss she had with Lucas. She should've asked Lucas to show her how to kiss before she showed up. "We better get going before Darren's parents get home."

Silas laughed huskily. With the light in the main room so dim, she couldn't see his face well. "I forgot to tell you, babe. Tonight it's a teens-only party."

"Why?" She stood, her blood boiling and heart racing. "Why didn't you tell me?"

She started walking toward the door, but Silas pulled her back to him, toppling her into his chest.

"I need to go!"

"I thought we'd have our first kiss tonight."

He'd tried for a kiss the last two times, but she'd brushed him off. Did she want to kiss him? Not here, and not tonight. "Next time, maybe."

He stared into her eyes as if thinking, groaning and loosening his hold on her. "That's what you said last time, and the time before that."

A crash shattered the kitchen window, and Silas dropped Brittney's hand. She stood there, her heart in her throat. Shards of glass splattered everywhere. Her knees were shaking. She should have listened to Lucas when he tried to talk her out of coming.

Silas whispered something about someone breaking into the house, and Darren and his girlfriend came scurrying from wherever they'd been.

"Brit! Brit!"

Lucas? As she walked to the kitchen, a thud sounded. Someone turned on a light. It sure was Lucas.

Relief surged through her that it wasn't a robbery, but Lucas could be in trouble for breaking someone's window.

"What in the world?" Darren glared at Lucas.

Lucas ignored Darren's glare and stood, then stared up and down at Brittney. "Are you okay?"

He was supposed to be hanging out with Rochelle at the movies. "What are you doing here?"

"I'm here to take you home."

"I'll take her home." Silas put a protective arm around her shoulders.

"You just broke my window." Darren stood in front of Lucas and widened his stance, arms folded across his chest. "You're going to pay—"

Lucas looked Darren square in the eyes. "I'll tell your parents you had the door locked and I knocked—but no one let me in."

"Hey, hello." Silas snorted. "Because you're not invited!"

Brittney tried to wiggle out of his hold, but he pulled her back.

"You'd better not tell my parents." Darren jabbed a finger at Lucas's chest.

Lucas stepped around him, marching to her. "We're leaving."

"I'm on a date." The least she could do was let Silas drive her home, since she'd turned him down for a kiss again.

Lucas snorted and took her hand, yanking her out of Silas's hold. "I don't care. It's time to leave."

When Silas reached for Brittney, Lucas hissed, "D—don't... don't ever"—he stammered the way he only did when angry—"don't come near her again." He balled his hand into a fist, ready to strike should Silas make a move.

"Lucas." Brittney's voice shook, her stomach twisting up. What was wrong with him? First breaking a window, and now this. "Calm down."

She wiggled her hand out of his.

"She's my girlfriend!" he shouted at Silas while taking a hold of her hand again. "In case she forgot to tell you this."

He was going mad.

Brittney slapped his hand away and crossed both arms over her chest, but before she could speak, he was lifting her off the ground and hoisting her on his shoulder. As he marched toward the door and twisted the lock open, she was kicking and punching him on the back, screaming for him to put her down. But he ignored her until they got to the car and he put her down.

"Get in the car!" he commanded, taking deep breaths as he waited for her to make up her mind.

She was so mad at him, but the fire in his eyes mirrored the heat in her own.

"I'm not going anywhere with you." Thanks to him, Silas wouldn't give her a ride back.

"Brittney, get in the car right now!" He pointed his finger to the Jeep, gritting his teeth.

With the porch light shining on his Jeep, she could see Rochelle in the front seat, rubbing her temples. At least someone else was in the car. Brittney got in the back seat and slammed the door.

The driver-side door slammed when Lucas got in and fired the engine.

"You left your girlfriend in the car? Is that what you consider a date?" she sneered to get back at him for embarrassing her.

He ignored her and drove off.

"You embarrassed me. Why did you do that?" Her blood was boiling, but she wasn't even good at arguments, except when it came to Lucas.

"Why don't you ask your *friend* to, um, tell you what her brother was planning to do to you?"

"You shouldn't have broken that window." Rochelle flipped down the visor before her, eyeing herself in the mirror, and rubbed a lipstick smear from the side of her mouth.

What was Silas going to do to her? Her heart rate kicking up for a new reason, Brittney crawled from her seat and inched closer to Rochelle in the front. "What does Lucas mean?"

Rochelle flipped the mirror back and waved a hand as she resettled in her seat. "You'll have to ask Silas yourself."

The vehicle skittered to a halt on the country road, and Lucas pulled to the side. Brittney couldn't see him in the dark, except for his shadow through the headlights illuminating the road ahead. "Brittney is not going anywhere near that loser." He then cupped Rochelle's chin to make sure she was looking at him. "Tell Brittney what your brother planned to do to her." His deeper voice boomed through the car. "Tell her!"

Rochelle just shook her head, completely annoyed. "Brittney is grown up. You shouldn't have to baby her all the time."

Lucas gripped the steering wheel, then tugged at the hair on his forehead before resuming the drive.

He never got mad, not this mad.

Rochelle was quiet, and so was Brittney. What did Silas have in store for her? A kiss? Maybe worse, if Lucas was that mad.

When Lucas dropped Rochelle off at her house, she bounced from her seat, then paused, one hand on the door, one on the roof of the Jeep. "Can we go to the movies tomorrow?"

"I don't want to go out. You and I are done."

She sucked in a sharp breath. "You're breaking up with me?"

He chuckled, the sound harsh, nothing like when he and Brittney laughed together. "I don't remember asking you to be my girlfriend."

"I broke up with you first." She swung the door, slamming it shut.

After a brief silence, Brittney said, "You shouldn't have broken up with her."

"I told you I didn't want to go out with her, but you—" He punched the center of the steering wheel, and the horn squealed its protest. "While I was busy, you were almost..." He cringed. "I can find my own girlfriend from now on."

He didn't talk anymore, and she stayed silent until he dropped her off at her house.

She struggled to sleep that night as she thought about the events and what Silas was planning to do to her. She buried her head in the pillow, agitated for being so naive.

What would she have done if Lucas hadn't shown up when he did? Would Silas have forced her to have sex with him? She shivered, rubbing at goose bumps.

When she woke up the next morning, it was still dark outside. Still, she cooked lots of waffles, Lucas's favorite. They were enough to feed her mom and dad and Lucas's family.

She put several in the biggest Tupperware they had in the house, and when Mama woke, she told her about last night's events.

Mama squeezed her tight in her warm embrace and touched her cheek. "I knew it wasn't just yours and Lucas's fight." Mama admitted how she'd not bought Brittney's excuse last night when she'd pried into why she was upset. "That Lucas is the brother you never had."

"I'm taking some breakfast to his family."

Mama said she was so proud of her, and when she got to Lucas's house, Mrs. Matthews smiled at her while she took the container. "What a sweetheart you are."

"Thank you."

"Lucas is still in his room, probably asleep, but I'm sure he won't mind if you wake him up."

The retriever bounded toward Brittney, and she lowered herself. The dog licked her face. "Who's a good boy!" She rubbed Baxter's back and hunted up his leash to take him for a walk around the block while she gave Lucas time to wake up.

When she returned, Lucas and his siblings were still sleeping, or at least she didn't see anyone besides the parents, Mr. Matthews drinking his coffee as he read the paper to his wife next to him. So she slipped up to Lucas's room and let herself in. He lay across his bed, breathing heavily, his bare chest rising and falling in perfect rhythm.

She sat on the carpet next to his head where she could stare at him. He looked so peaceful and sweet. Her heart constricted. His hand had a few scratches, and on his forearm, blood marked where he'd hurt himself going through the shattered window last night.

What would she do without him?

He slowly opened his eyes, ran a hand over them, and looked at her. He blinked once, then twice. "Have you been staring at me while I slept?"

She nodded, stifling a chuckle.

"You're such a creep." His voice was light, not mad anymore.

"Makes two of us." She tousled his hair, so cute all rumpled and soft in her hands. If they weren't best friends, he'd make the perfect boyfriend. He was the most handsome boy in school. Funny, smart, and confident. "You're my boyfriend, huh?"

He rolled his eyes. "Why are you up so early?"

"When did you start snoring?" Two could play this game.

He sat up and stretched out his hands, talking over a yawn. "I don't snore."

"Yes, you do."

"No. I don't."

She stood, rummaging through his messy shirt drawer and tossing him one. She organized his drawers twice a week, but he kept mixing all the colors together.

"I brought you waffles."

He eased the shirt over his head, further rumpling his hair. "When did you make them?"

"This morning." She plopped next to him and reached for his hand, clasping it in hers, the warmth enveloping her. "I... About last night... Thanks for coming after me. For rescuing me."

He winked. "I think you owe me today's chore duties."

"I do your chores every Saturday." She lifted his hand. "Not sure what you mean by owing you."

He had that sweet boy grin. "As long as you stop hanging out with Silas, then we're good."

He'd been her knight in shining armor last night, and she would do anything for him. "Deal. I'll also sell all your football fundraiser cards this season."

"You did that last year, and I was hoping you could teach me your sales skills this year so you don't have to do it next time."

She was friends with several parents of the disabled patients where Dad went for therapy, and they'd loved the idea of supporting her friend's football team.

"I'll be happy to."

When she said it, Lucas raised their interlaced fingers to his lips, planting a kiss on hers. "Let's go eat those waffles."

CHAPTER 14

The sun was fading, the temperature dropping, but perfect after the sunny day. Despite the three cups of coffee he'd drunk that morning, Lucas's eyes felt heavy as he pulled the Sorrento up in Grams's driveway.

Mom had let him borrow her car for his time in Soda Creek. He'd agreed on one condition—she'd call him when she needed a ride to her jewelry shop or running errands. But she'd insisted she could use Dad's car since he'd be off all next week.

The house was quiet when he walked in. No Brit or Grams, and the usually blaring TV remained silent. Where was everyone? He walked on the spotless carpet, breathing in the clean scent of disinfectant.

Hmm, what day was it? Right, Wednesday. Brit volunteered at the disability center. Perhaps Grams had gone with her today.

Even if it was almost five, he intended to use this time to nap until the ladies of the house returned. Now that he knew what he was supposed to do, a burden had been lifted off his shoulders.

As he walked to the kitchen for a glass of water, Midnight emerged from the hallway and sauntered toward him.

He crouched and gave her a gentle backrub, just the way she liked. The cat curled as if telling him she was ready for him to pay for all the rubs she'd missed from him.

"I know...I know." Lucas spoke to the cat, her fur soft under his palm. "I'll give you as many rubs as you want, but I'm going to need a nap here soon."

With that, he stood and grabbed a glass from the cabinet, pushing the water button on the stainless steel fridge. As he sipped his water, his gaze wandered through the window to the backyard. His breath caught at the sight of Brit on the woven hammock between the two oak trees. Was she reading? It wasn't a surprise that she still preferred an actual book over an electronic reader.

With her index finger tapping her chin, she was doing more thinking than reading. She always read aloud, but since her lips weren't moving, she could be using the book as an escape from her thoughts.

He set the glass down, curiosity pulling his feet to the back door and toward her. Since she didn't hear his feet whispering through the grass, she must be lost in thought.

"If you read the way I remember, then I already feel for the characters in your book."

She took her eyes from the book, a ghost of a smile appearing on her face as she sat up. Her bare toes touched the grass, and she closed the book, revealing a mythical creature on the cover.

"You were always a terrible reading companion." She tsked. "Very distracting."

Whenever they'd lay down to read, she'd end up reading out loud, and being an avid reader, he'd read the night before they met to study. He still enjoyed listening to her reading, especially when she added dramatic effects.

"I'll accept that accusation with dignity." The woven canvas dipped beneath his weight when he sat in the center next to her.

His palms were sweating as if he'd just run a marathon. But it wasn't about him. He'd sworn to protect her and be there for her always. He cleared his throat to utter something he should have ages ago.

"I'm sorry," he whispered, reaching out and taking her familiar hand in his. The warmth of it instantly made him feel better. For the first time since he returned, he let himself relax as he entwined his fingers with hers. Everything was going to be okay, eventually. "I should've been there for you when you needed me. I shouldn't have crossed that line in our friendship, shouldn't have left town the way I did, and mostly, I should have stayed in touch."

She let out a shudder. "Why didn't you stay in touch?" Lines pinched between her eyes, her lips set in a pained line, and her question seemed loaded with so many unspoken ones she wanted to ask at once.

With no sense in lying to her at this point, he'd better tell her the first reason for his silence. Heat burned his cheeks. "I didn't know how to go back to that place in our friendship." He squeezed her hand. "I wasn't used to being rejected. I just didn't know how to react."

"I understand." She was being way too easy on him. She shouldn't be after he'd acted that way.

"I... meant to call." That was the other part of his story. He'd dialed her phone several times, but he could never get himself to press the call button. "I just didn't know what to say. I messed up when I kissed you against your will."

"Not exactly against my will." Her voice came in a whisper.

Had she *wanted* him to kiss her? As he remembered it, he'd initiated the kiss, and she'd kissed him briefly before holding back. Again, it wasn't about their love life, but their friendship right now, so he told her how he'd missed her.

"There were many times when I had my firsts..." He told her about his first solo anesthesia in the OR, the award for best anesthesiologist during the second year in his career. "Always, the first person I thought of telling was you, but as the days went on, it became harder for me to talk to you."

When he looked at her, she was staring at him, her eyes shiny with tears, which bothered him immensely. He pulled her into him, and when she tipped her head to rest on his shoulder, he kissed her hair. Its familiar scent, vanilla and cocoa, was the scent of home, but the hopelessness of the situation made him ache. "I'm so sorry." That's all he could say. "I don't even have an excuse."

"I tried to call after two weeks...." She sniffled. "But..."

He'd switched his cell phone after leaving Soda Creek.

"I was a jerk, and nobody should be that way to a friend."

"I didn't... I'm sorry for lashing out last night." She peered at him with those sweet light-brown eyes, and a powerful sense of awareness left him breathless. She ducked her head, keeping her gaze on her turquoise-painted toenails. "I'm not a teenager anymore, and I should try to keep my feelings under control."

He was supposed to be the one person she should be herself around. "You shouldn't have to control your feelings around me. I always want you to be you."

As she lifted her head and their gazes met, the pull of attraction gripped him worse than in the past. His gaze dragged down to her throat. The pulse at her neck was racing. Did she feel the same?

He needed to sleep. He was starting to imagine things.

"If I remember, I once told you I'd love you unconditionally."

She nodded.

"I meant it. We may have grown apart by not seeing one another, but never has a day passed when I didn't think about you, wondering how you're doing."

"Me too."

Dwelling on the past would lead them nowhere, except to a dark place of sadness, but it was the past they needed to fix while he was in town.

"What was it like... after things ended between you and Adam?"

"Hard." She swung her feet. "The hardest part was me hurting him the way his ex-girlfriend had done."

"You're nothing like Shana." She'd only been using Adam for money.

"In a way, I felt like her."

Lucas cringed, hating it when Brittney crushed herself that way.

"I lied to Adam about my feelings, but I also learned a lot from that." She looked down at their entwined hands. "Sometimes you think you're protecting someone's feelings, but you end up hurting them and those around you in return."

Lucas thought of what Adam told him about Grandma's, Mom's, and Dad's reactions. "My family knows firsthand that you're compassionate, kind, and dedicated to everyone else's best interest."

They must have known she was only trying to comfort Adam, but that didn't explain why she agreed to his proposal. After saying yes, at what point had she realized she was lying to herself? That her kindness was hurting them both?

He squeezed her hand. "Why did you break up with him?"

She lifted her head off his shoulder, her brow creased. "You already know I wasn't honest."

Not really. He'd known why she agreed to go out with him, but he'd assumed they'd fallen in love along the way.

"I was glad you showed up. It helped me think of what I was about to do. You stopped me from making the worst mistake." She wriggled her feet, watching them skim the grass. "I might have married him in hopes we could learn to fall in love, I guess."

Lucas cringed, but that was Brit. She'd rather be uncomfortable and go out of her way to make everyone happy. He let out a breath, but he couldn't let out all the frustration.

"Remember how we used to talk about sparks?"

He cocked his head at her, taken by surprise. "Yeah?"

"You said I'd know when it's the right guy." She swung her feet, rocking the hammock. "I just never found that guy."

Maybe because he's right in front of you? "It's not too late." Was the correct response.

"Do you also remember when I asked you about hanging out with Troy?"

All too well. The summer after their sophomore year, Troy had broken his leg. He spent several days hanging out at Lucas's house since his parents were out of town for work. And—like any sane guy—he'd fallen for Brit.

When Lucas returned from a weeklong football camp, he couldn't wait to see Brit. He'd showered quickly, intending to go to her house right after. He'd just gotten dressed when she knocked and let herself into his room, seeming just as anxious to see him as he was to see her.

His heart soared at the sight of her. Man, she'd looked all grown up with her hair cascading down on her shoulders, and when she smiled, showing those dimples, his heart almost stopped. He felt whole, just glad to be home... to be with her again.

That must have been the first real time he'd known she was the only woman he wanted in his life, the love of his life.

The hammock swaying lazily, Brit squeezed his hand, urging him to answer her question.

He cleared his throat. "It was a Saturday afternoon." The day she always washed her hair. "You were wearing a pink dress with white polka dots." When he'd swooped her up in his arms, he'd nuzzled her neck and breathed in her luscious scent of shea butter conditioner.

"Your hair smelled like vanilla, chocolate, and..." He swallowed hard, a longing sweeping over him, desiring to go back and confess his feelings for her again, but that was then.

His heart fluttered when she smiled. "You even remember what I was wearing?"

It was an understatement. It terrified him, too. "It's easy for me to remember everything about you.... You're my best friend. Why wouldn't I remember?"

A silence passed between them until she nudged his shoulder with hers. "I still believe you have a photographic memory."

"I guess." She could tell herself whatever she wanted to believe, and he could only agree, knowing if he said anything different it could move things from bad to worse.

"You wanted to learn how to kiss." Heat burned his cheeks at the memory of making an arrangement for her practice kiss.

She was fidgeting with the hem of her shorts, and no way was he going to look at her now—not if he wanted to erase thoughts of kissing her.

"That was my second kiss—first real kiss, I'd say."

He never remembered her talking about her first kiss. Had she kept that from him? As if she could read his mind, she answered his internal question. "The first kiss was the best friends' kiss."

She remembered? She'd been telling him who kissed who, and he'd missed seeing her for three long days. Seeing her that night, knowing she'd taken the risk of getting sick so she could see him, being overjoyed by her presence, had spurred all sorts of emotions and led him to kiss her. He must have loved her as more than friends even then.

But again, today was not the time to talk about childhood kisses. Not when she only wanted him as a friend.

Composing himself, he drew in a deep breath. "Why did you break off the engagement?"

He'd learned she'd broken up a month after he left town, but he'd never had a desire to find out why.

"When you showed up that night, it was a wake-up call for me."

Was he the reason she'd been bold enough to call things off? "Another question I never got the chance to ask, why did you accept the proposal?" Somehow, he kept his tone light, since he was just curious.

He understood why she went on the first date. Adam had been dumped, and she'd been afraid to let him down. Lucas had to endure whenever he called and she told him about those evening dates she'd called outings.

"He proposed in front of your family and his colleagues in a private restaurant room." She shuddered. "How was I supposed to say no? It doesn't matter. I ended up wasting his time."

It must have taken all her fragile boldness to call off the engagement. "How did you feel before working up the nerve to end things?"

Ducking her head, she bit her lip. "I felt like I was dying inside. But then when you left"—her fingers tightened on his as she breathed the words—"I had to go to counseling. No one in your family knows, but I went through a depression of some sort."

An ache pierced his heart, his jaw twitching. "Oh, Brit." He tucked a strand of her hair behind her ear, a habit of his whenever he'd comfort her. He then unclasped their hands and curled his arm around her waist. "I'm the worst friend you could ever have."

If she still considered him a friend.

"I could've been a better friend, too, should have forced myself to get your new number from Clarice, but I didn't."

He asked about her counselor, how long she'd struggled through depression. Had she recovered? Did she stay in touch with her other friend Dalia?

And she shared freely, including the ups and downs of her last ten years. "It helped when Adam was relieved about the breakup."

Apparently, she'd always felt guilty when she went out with Adam and she'd struggled to kiss him, which she'd abstained from doing until the day of the proposal.

Lucas laughed. "He said it felt as if he was kissing his sister."

She scrunched her nose. "I felt weird, but..." She shrugged. "I'm glad we're talking."

"Me, too." Then he remembered the house being vacant. "Where's Grams?"

"Her quilt club is choosing quilts to display at tomorrow's fair."

"Yeah, that's tomorrow. I promised to go with her." He had so much work to do, but spending time with loved ones was more important, like Mom said. "I still need to find food for the wedding. That caterer..." He cringed just thinking of the food.

"It was that bad, huh?"

He nodded.

"I'll tag along for the fair and help you find caterers. There's lots of food vendors to choose from."

"As long as we can test their food first."

"That's what I'm thinking."

"We were always a great team." He winked, and she eased out of his embrace and stood.

"Clean slate?"

Silently, he stared at her outstretched hand as he thought of that first day she came with her mom to his house. He accepted her hand and shook it. "I'm Lucas Matthews, the new kid on the block."

She beamed from ear to ear. "Brittney Young, the girl next door."

"Nice to meet you."

Brittney's laughter danced through the evening. She clasped his hand tighter. "I want to show you something before we pick up Clarice."

"Really?" he said, remembering the earrings he'd bought from his mom's shop. He retrieved the small velvet bag. "I have something for you too."

She unclasped his hand and opened the drawstring to shake the little doodads into her palm. A sunflower grew around one side of each heart-shaped earring. She pressed them to her heart. "They're beautiful!"

His chest puffed. "Hard not to think of you when I see sunflowers." He scooped them from her palm and touched her cheek, his insides warming. "May I?"

She shivered when he touched her ear and slid the stud into the tiny hole, clasping the back with the nut. He did the same thing to the other ear. He couldn't help but keep his hands lingering on her ear more than necessary. "All done."

"Thanks." Her word was breathy, and he gripped her hand in his, the way he used to, as the friend he intended to be.

As the sun dipped low over the pond, his heart felt light while their feet padded over the grass and back to her room. He sat on the edge of the bed, atop a soft white duvet cover, while she rummaged through her spacious closet.

Unlike his room, hers was one of the two master bedrooms. It used to be the guest bedroom, but as he looked around, it looked like Brit's, with all her personalized things. The photo of her parents on the white dresser and another photo of him and her right next to it made him feel like she'd never stopped being his friend, not even for a moment.

"All right." She emerged from the closet with a big box wrapped with shipping tape. Then she reached for her car keys from the bowl on her dresser and sliced through the tape. When she set it in the middle of the bed, she sat across from him.

It was addressed to his older Colorado home.

"I was going to ship this a year after I ended things with Adam, but things..."

Lucas gave her an assuring nod. "We're starting over, remember?"

She lifted both legs to the bed, crisscrossing her feet. "I gathered all these pictures and things from our past. It helped me through my dark days." Her hands, resting on the box, twitched. "It brought back memories of how far I've come and how you'd always been my constant. I may have taken you for granted—"

"It takes two." He reached across the box to touch her cheek. "I took you for granted too."

She blew out a breath and slid her hand into the box. "You left this."

When she retrieved the familiar, ugly plush animal, a grin lifted his face. It was his favorite childhood toy.

"Oh, my world! Lobster." Taking it, he assessed it, then pressed the button.

"I've got you in my claws forever.... You're my best friend, and I'll never let go!"

They both laughed at the toy's squeaky sound as they revisited memories of that night. Then he told her about Mom knowing she'd snuck into his room.

"You're kidding!"

"I told her she was a terrible parent for not grounding us."

Lucas pulled out a brand-new puzzle in a box, a Soda Creek T-shirt—they'd both won one at the balloon shoot from the last fair he'd gone to with her.

"Headphones, too?" He put the headset over his head to his ears.

"You always loved your headphones," she said. "But these are probably outdated."

"I'll get them fixed if they are." He nestled them down on the covers and dug back into the box.

She picked up a square fabric with three CDs in the plastic case. "These are some of the songs we'd recorded for each other, and some of our favorites too."

He'd preferred leaving his special things at home, so he didn't lose any in case he moved from one apartment to another.

"I wanted you to remember how far we've come."

Too awed to speak, he stared at her reflection through the CD surface.

"I still have the songs on the computer, in case the CDs don't work anymore."

Nodding, he mouthed, "Thanks."

His favorite part of the package was the photos in an album from when they'd met all the way through high school. Several were taken at Grams's, house since she always had her camera handy. He flipped the album page. In the next photo, they were both damp with their clothes clinging to their skins.

"I can't believe I let you talk me into swimming in that lake." Her tone carried a smile. "I don't know what the man would've done if he'd caught up with us."

Lucas shrugged. "One of these days, I'll apologize."

Brit snorted. "Not sure when you'll do that when you're leaving."

Maybe he'd stop by the man's farm soon. Not just to apologize, but also to ask for a formal visit to his farm and lake.

Oh... A pink tongue lolling to one side, Baxter grinned at them from the next page. Lucas let out a low breath, one finger tracing the golden retriever's image. Brit reached over and covered his hand with hers, giving him a comforting squeeze. The picture was taken on Christmas morning. He'd gone to Brit's house to show her his present from Dad and Mom, and Brit's mom took a picture of him, Baxter, and Brit, in front of their Christmas tree.

"It's sad that he got hit."

Somehow, the sorrow catching in her tone comforted him. The six years he'd had Baxter hadn't been enough. "He was such a loyal dog."

"I always thought it was sweet how he'd walk us to the bus," Brit said, bringing to mind their middle school and then high school years when they went to a school further away from their neighborhood.

"Those were some of the best days." He looked at Brit, her eyes soft, and as they held each other's gaze, his stomach flipped. Man! How long could he pretend he was here as a friend? He broke eye contact and flipped to the next page.

Somehow, he kept going through their past. With the woman who'd always been a part of his life. The woman he'd thought to move past—except she was here, in front of him, and planting seeds of something.

Was it friendship or more? That question in itself carried weight on his heart. He wasn't ready to find out the answer. He'd been ready once before, and that hadn't turned out so well.

CHAPTER 15

It was almost the end of summer before they started their junior year in high school. After Brit ended things with Silas last fall, she seemed drawn to one of Lucas's friends.

Troy had broken his leg when he fell from a tree while his parents were on a cruise. Although Troy had a nanny to watch him, he spent his summer days hanging out by the pool at Lucas's house. All Lucas's friends liked coming to his house because of the pool.

Brit was the only girl among the friends in his life. Like the nurturer she was, she felt bad when they swam and Troy remained on a lounge chair watching since he didn't have a waterproof cast. Brit gave of herself, from keeping Troy company to helping Mom get them food and drinks, and Troy savored Brit's attention, causing Lucas to wonder if his friend deliberately whined about his discomfort for more attention.

As long as they hung out with each other at his house, Lucas didn't have anything to worry about. While most of his friends were starting to have girlfriends, he felt drawn to Brit. Unfortunately, he'd not warned Troy off Brit like he'd done with his other friends, and while Lucas went to football camp, Troy stayed behind.

Lucas couldn't stop thinking about Brit and asking her out for the homecoming dance. It was still early to talk about homecoming, but once school started, the dance would be the next big event in early October.

During a break on the field, Lucas discussed Brit with his other best friend, Ryan Harper. "She treats me like I'm her brother."

Ryan ran a hand through his wavy brown hair. "You better tell her how you feel as soon as we get home tomorrow."

"But she's interested in Troy."

"He hasn't even taken her to a movie." Ryan picked up his helmet when the coach blew the whistle. "She's at your house all the time. She'll most likely go for you over Troy."

Lucas clung to Ryan's words. After getting home the next afternoon, he showered and changed. His heart was racing when he glanced through his window at Brit's room. *Is she home?* "I'm in love with you, and I'd like you to go to the dance with—"

A knock sounded on the door, and he jumped. Did anyone hear him?

"Are you talking to yourself?" It was just Adam. "Mom wanted me to let you know we're going to the movies."

Lucas frowned. "Now?" How could he tell his family he wanted to spend the afternoon with Brit?

"Mom invited Brittney, too." Adam shrugged as if reading Lucas's mind.

He'd have to put off his practiced speech until later.

As if she'd been conjured up, Brittney knocked on his open door and stepped into the room.

"Lucas!" She lunged into him. As if they were the only people in the room, he lifted her off the ground and squeezed her tight.

"Brit!" Oh, how his heart was so full whenever she was around! He'd missed her so much. He buried his nose into her hair before setting her down.

"I have so much to tell you." Her long hair bounced off her back when she finally glanced at Adam as if just recognizing his presence. "I missed you, too, but I just saw you yesterday."

Adam lifted his hand and reminded them not to be long. "Movie starts in an hour, I think."

The room suddenly felt warm. Was it because of Lucas's plan to confess his feelings?

Brit clasped her hands in front of her. "I don't know where to start." She walked toward the window, and her polka-dot dress encased her newly acquired curves. She'd changed a lot, grown like the young woman she should be. "You smell good. Is that a new perfume?"

Guys didn't call it perfume, but whatever.

"Yes." Why was she acting strange? "You're okay?"

She put her hands on her chest and started letting out several dramatic breaths. "Can we go to the tree house after the movie?"

Lucas frowned. "Why?"

"To say hello to your grandma."

Grams wouldn't be at the *tree house*. What was up with Brit? He touched her shoulder to stop her from pacing and cupped her face so she'd look at him. "You're up to something. Spit it out."

She pulled out of his arms and covered her face. "I want you to teach me how to kiss."

Heat surged through him as he jerked further away from her. It was his turn to pace. "What?! Why?" He couldn't even look at her face, which must have made it easier for her to explain.

"Troy wants us to meet tomorrow, and I think he's going to ask me to the homecoming dance?" She winced. "What if he wants to kiss me and... I don't know how to?"

His stomach dropped. She was excited about Troy and wanted to learn to kiss. Did she have any idea how Lucas felt? If she did, she wouldn't be asking *him* to teach *her* how to kiss.

He peered through the window, the sun still high in the sky. *Kiss.* Maybe... maybe this was his chance to show her he wasn't the brother she took him to be.

"Please tell me you'll do it? Please?"

Lucas turned around as she squeezed her face. He tossed his hands in a consenting gesture. "I'll do it."

"For real?" Her radiant smile caused his heart to pick up a faster pace.

"Sure."

That would turn some of his fantasies into reality.

During the movie, he shifted in his seat. Even as he stared at the screen, he had no idea what was playing.

Brittney smacked his shoulder, her warm lips whispering into his ear as she reminded him they were in the theater.

How could she be so calm about this whole... *task*? She definitely saw him as a brother if she wasn't affected by his nearness the way she affected him.

As soon as they got home and Mom suggested dinner, Lucas told her he and Brit planned to eat at Grams's. Grams always had plenty of food in her refrigerator, so they didn't have to announce their arrival when they biked to her house.

Despite his crowded mind, he didn't want to act strange around Grams. So he said he was going to race Brit to the tree house, and she followed, beating him there. The sky's vivid orange clouds were fading, leaving it slightly dark. He turned on the switch.

"Have you done this before?" Brit folded her hands. "Did Rochelle kiss you or you kiss her?"

He didn't want to explain that Rochelle's unexpected kiss had caught him off-guard during the fall dance. Before he could overthink, he put his hand on Brittney's shoulder like he'd seen in movies.

"Depends on where you will be when he kisses you, but if you're standing..." He tucked a strand of her hair that had escaped out of the braid and put it behind her ear.

She shut her eyes and whispered breathlessly, "I think I'll keep my eyes closed."

The fact that she wasn't looking at him... the fact that her round lips were shaky, tempting... His mouth suddenly dry, he pulled her toward him and covered her lips with his.

Hers were so soft, so warm, and although her mouth was moving awkwardly at first, it felt like he was dreaming. Brit paused, her body shaking—probably unsure of what to do, but he didn't give her room to talk or pull away.

His hand moved around her waist. It fit just perfectly. The awkwardness was short-lived and he felt his body melt when she kissed him back. He never wanted to kiss anyone else ever but her.

"Lucas." At Grams's voice, they tore apart. "Brittney, come have some dinner!"

"Be right there, Grams!" he responded, his eyes not leaving Brit's.

She took a deep breath, fanned herself, and smiled shyly. "Where did you learn to kiss, anyway?"

"In my dreams, I might have kissed you," he said as if joking, yet it was the truth. "Do you need another lesson?"

She nodded, then shook her head. "That was my... a great lesson."

With his heart racing, he hugged her and felt her racing heart too, as he kissed the top of her head. He wanted her to be happy, and if Troy made her happy, so be it. But he didn't want her kissing Troy.

"Will you go to the dance with me?" The words flew out of his mouth without his thinking.

She stepped out of his embrace, her eyes dancing. "I thought about going with you, but you didn't ask."

His brows drew together. She'd thought about going with him? But wasn't she wanting Troy to go with her?

"Why... Why were you thinking about going with me?"

She playfully punched him in the chest. "You're refusing to ask anyone out, and I didn't want you brooding."

His heart was full to the brim when he touched her soft cheek, lingering. "What will you tell Troy when he asks you?"

"My sad friend asked me first."

He couldn't help but take advantage of the moment and plant a soft kiss on her lips.

"A best friends' kiss," he said before whisking her out of the tree house. "Let's go have dinner."

"LET'S GO START DINNER."

The words jarred him as if Grams had spoken from below the tree house. Lucas shook his head, the memories so fresh. He'd believed Brit would be his then.

"I need to check the ribs I have marinating." She slid the album closed and pushed to her feet. "Come with me?" She headed from the room without waiting, and he followed her, as he always had.

Later, after they'd said good night to Grams, Lucas wasn't ready to go to bed, and he intended to keep Brit up as well. He ran downstairs and rummaged through the basement closet where they used to keep extra blankets, grateful to find just what he needed.

When he returned with the basket stuffed with a picnic blanket, a quilt, and a pillow, he found Brit kneeling on the carpet working on the puzzle.

"Not ready to sleep?" he asked. After the sleepless night they both had, they should be in bed.

She looked up, her brown eyes dancing under the soft lamplight as she eyed the basket.

"I was hoping you could help me work on this puzzle. We have to get it done before you... go back." She hesitated with those last words as if they were hard to utter.

"I had something else in mind." He hefted his basket and nodded toward the shorts she'd put on with his T-shirt after showering. "You'll need to change into your pants, though."

"And what exactly do you have in mind?" Her dimples deepened as her lips pulled back in that smile that always seemed to claim her whole face.

"A moonlight stroll to the pond."

"I'd like that." She stood, putting the puzzle piece back on the table.

In less than ten minutes, they walked into the warm night, light from the half-moon illuminating their path. The frogs called out extra loud tonight, their voices filling the silent night's lullaby.

As they approached the pond, he spread out the blanket, arranged the pillow, and ushered her to sit. He lowered himself next to her, and they both outstretched their legs. "Tell me about your caregiver award."

"We walked here for me to talk about my award?"

He took her hand in his. "I have so much catching up to do in such a short period of time."

Then he lifted the corner of the quilt for her to take one side to cover her feet, and he did the same.

"In that case, then"—she braced her hands behind herself, tilting her face to take in the whole expanse of starry sky—"let's make tonight count."

She talked about her favorite charities and her volunteer work teaching aerobics at the recreation center. "The award was one of those July Fourth events when the mayor comes and talks."

"The mayor gave you the award?"

She nodded and tucked loose hair behind her ears, not seeming interested in talking about her recognition.

"Let me guess, you got voted by your fans at the recreation center and the disability center and—"

"It's not that big a deal. I mean, you do more work than I do every day, preparing thousands of people for surgeries."

"I see what you're getting at here." He bumped his shoulder to hers, aware that she'd diverted the attention to him. But he'd brought her here to catch up on what he'd missed in her life. "Tell me about your book."

She released his hand to wrap her arms over the sweatshirt she was wearing. "That was something we used to talk about together." It was her dream to write the book. Whenever Lucas called her, they'd discuss what scenes and personal sidenotes she could add.

"How far did you get?"

"I finished the draft and did some research...."

As she talked about the topics in her book, he intended to read it. A weight pressed on him when she confided the manuscript was still on her computer. "You should publish that book soon."

But she was shaking her head. "I don't know...." She didn't seem sure of herself, but even if he hadn't read through it, he knew she was capable. Not just because she'd grown up with a disabled dad, but also because Brit wasn't one to tamper with something if she wasn't knowledgeable in the field. He'd have to reach out to an agent on her behalf whenever he returned to Denver.

With the half-moon reflecting on the pond, the frogs croaking in the distance, the breeze rustling in the oaks, they talked about random safe things— his work, and her life in general.

It took him by surprise when she asked, "When did you first have feelings for me?"

Needing to distract himself with something, he patted the crabgrass and felt a rock. He picked it up and sent it skimming across the water's calm surface. A delayed response might have her changing the subject, but she playfully shoved him, waiting.

"As long as I can remember." It sounded vague, but he had no idea if he'd fallen in love with her when they played basketball that first day, or the Valentine's Day she'd shown up in his room while he was sick. "I think I've loved you since I met you."

"Oh." She tucked hair behind her ears again, shifting, and her shoulder brushed against his. So he suggested they rest their heads on the pillow big enough to fit the two of them.

"Remember when we used to lie here and look at the clouds?" she asked.

"And at night, we would stargaze whenever we camped," he added. Everything felt just right at his grandparent's house. "That's why I wanted us to be here... tonight."

He had no idea why he wanted to revisit their memories. But it seemed his past defined his present and future in some way.

"Look." Brit drew him back when he followed her pointer finger to the twinkling starry sky as she traced a crosslike formation. "There's the Cygnus."

And there it was. The Cygnus, the Swan forever floating on the Milky Way. "Good eye." While staring up, Lucas sighted another constellation. "Can you see another?"

"Hmm..." Brittney kept her gaze up to the sky, but after a few moments, Lucas closed the gap between them and took her finger, pointing to the small dots shaped like letter M. He did this all while schooling his features and struggling to breathe.

"I see it," she whispered, her warmth and proximity intoxicating. "I like that it's still visible on such a moonlit night."

"Yeah." He let go of her hand, hoping she didn't feel how shaky his hand suddenly became. He shifted to keep the gap between them, which didn't make sense while their heads touched as they shared a pillow and their feet tucked under the blanket. He wanted Brit more than his next breath, but it was no use putting himself out there like he did years ago.

A brief silence settled between them before she snuggled the quilt to her shoulders. "It feels so peaceful here." Her soft voice matched the pleasant night. "Can we stay a little longer?"

He didn't mind if they stayed there all night. "We can stay as long as you want."

"For the record," she said after a few moments of silence, "I love you... more than a friend."

A surge of warmth bloomed in his heart. He tried to open his mouth to ask what she meant, but his lips were unmoving. His ears needed to be checked because he must be hearing things.

Even though the silence should feel awkward, given the last few days, it felt just right, both of them comfortable together.

After several seconds or minutes, the rhythm of Brit's breathing was deep and even. He turned onto his side to look at her. She was asleep. He propped his elbow and rested his chin in his palm to study her. So peaceful and with the moon outlining her heart-shaped face, she was still the only girl who set his heart on fire.

It was cooler than earlier, but comfortable, so he pulled the cover all the way to her chin, leaving some to himself. He lay there for hours and watched her sleep. He couldn't help but press his nose close to her hair.

She looked like the sweet, vulnerable girl again, the one he'd sworn to protect and comfort since that brutally cold night. The night she'd waited for her mom to come back from the store, only to learn two hours later that she'd been shot during a gas station robbery.

This had happened a week before he was supposed to take Brit to the homecoming dance.

Although Brit's dad's caregiver switched to a live-in, Brit was terrified to sleep in her room and asked her dad if Lucas could stay with her.

Lucas's parents were fine with it too, as long as he and Brit slept in the main room. Even though they had their mattresses side by side, she would end up squeezing herself onto his bed.

Since that night, she never slept in a room without a night light, and she started being obsessed with checking locks.

Because Marjorie had given her power of attorney to Lucas's mom and dad, they took care of Brit and paid the caregiver and the insurance for Ronald's medical needs.

In the months that followed, Ronald ate dinner with Lucas's family daily. Brit and Lucas wheeled him for walks and brought him to Brit's volleyball games. Whenever he was feeling well, he would come to Lucas's football and basketball games, too.

A few months later, just as Brit was adapting to her new normal, her dad died—right before their junior prom. Her childhood home was sold to offset his medical bills, and she moved in with them.

Mom had set up a bed for her in Emery's room, but the first night, Brit asked if she could sleep in Lucas's room. Her eyes were swollen and red from hours of crying. With one look at her, Mom had squeezed Brit in a tight hug and agreed as long as Lucas moved into Emery's room with them.

There was nothing Lucas wouldn't give to erase her pain. That night, as he lay down and propped a pillow behind his back, he held out his arm, and Brit snuggled into the crook of it. He had no idea what to say except to be silent as she rested her head on his chest and closed her eyes. She shuddered and sobbed, but he just ran his fingers through her hair, which seemed to soothe her to sleep.

He stayed awake, aching and wishing he could take her pain instead. He didn't wish his parents to be dead, but he wished he could carry her burdens somehow.

"I'm so scared." She cried when she woke in the night. "I don't want to be alone."

"Shhh... hush." He wiped the tears from her face, assuring her. "As long as I live, I'll always be there for you. In fact, I'll be around so much you'll want to scream at me to leave you alone." Knowing his parents would take care of her too, he told her so. "You'll never be alone, okay?"

She nodded, and he meant it.

That had also been the night he decided to put off his desire to pursue her, choosing to wait until they were adults. Or until she fell for him on her own time. Even if she never fell for him, he wanted her to be happy, no matter what.

In their senior year as they talked about college, she said she wanted to be a caregiver and didn't want to waste several years in college while she knew what she wanted to do.

When Lucas heard from Harvard about his scholarship program, he fully intended to come back home and work at his hometown hospital so he could be with Brit. Until that single phone call from Adam, a call that changed everything.

An owl hooted, retracting Lucas from his stupor. Some creature, either a fox or a raccoon, slunk through the shadows across the pond, so he instinctively wrapped an arm around Brit. Not that it would protect them from a wild animal, but he intended to stay awake in case he had to fight a nocturnal beast of some sort.

His eyes were getting heavy, and he was struggling to keep his head still. He may have drifted on and off but when he opened his eyes, his arm was still wrapped around Brit. Her head was curled on his chest, her breathing steady. The blanket felt slightly damp with dew.

She must have been exhausted to sleep through all this. When he glanced up, it was still dark, but bright pink clouds were rising over the hills. It was breathtaking.... Brit needed to see this. He hated waking her up, but this may be the only time they saw a sunrise together, at least in this season of their lives. He removed her hair from her face, whispering her name. It felt like déjà vu, like he'd woken up several times with her at his side. Maybe that's what he dreamed of, still wished for.

CHAPTER 16

Brittney rolled Clarice's walker as she crossed the snaked line to the Ferris wheel. Clarice had been walking with her cane, but the ground was uneven, and Brittney decided to get the walker from the car.

The town was out in full, enjoying barbecue and games of ball and bucket toss, among the several carnival rides set out on the fairgrounds.

The overcast midmorning was perfect for the fair, especially after the night she'd had. A flush burned her cheeks. She'd woken up in Lucas's arms with the gentle brush of his hands to her forehead. They'd watched the sunrise while he'd yawned nonstop. Then, once she learned he'd barely slept, she insisted he take a nap as soon as they got back to the house.

Yesterday was perfect. Having him remember little things about her was amazing. No wonder she'd slept through the dampened blanket, needing to catch up from sleepless nights.

Now, there was no need to pretend she hadn't thought about him, thought of being more than friends. Her emotions had gotten the best of her and had her blurting her feelings for him. But Lucas never responded. Maybe she hadn't been very clear. Ouch, what if he thought she only wanted to reconcile their friendship?

She could get used to being around him, but he was leaving.

As she strolled through the crowd, she saw Clarice's shoulders shaking while she laughed at whatever Lucas was saying. Joy bloomed in Brittney's heart at the sight of Clarice's hand nestled in the crook of Lucas's arm.

If only he could stay, they could do this together. Take Clarice to her quilt shows and fairs.

As she approached them, Clint and Linda, who'd been in Soda Creek all their lives, stopped them. They'd also gone to school with Brittney and Lucas.

Lucas smiled in her direction, and her stomach fluttered. "There's Brit."

All heads turned to her.

"I can't believe you and Lucas have been friends this long." Clint extended his hand to shake Brittney's. His brown hair was trimmed short, much different from the mullet he'd sported during their senior year. "I could never just be friends with Linda." He looked at his wife affectionately, and Linda's face turned a dark shade of pink. "I wanted more."

"Maybe that's why Lucas and Brittney are still single." Linda winked, taking a turn to shake Brittney's hand. "They got so used to each other and couldn't settle for anyone else."

"We're...um," Lucas stammered, "still good friends."

"Best friends," Clarice added with a knowing look as she ambled to the walker and retrieved her camera to snap pictures.

Whatever Linda thought, Lucas could be engaged to someone in Denver by now, but Brittney hadn't asked him yet. That could very well be the reason he didn't say anything after she'd admitted her feelings last night. Even if he was still available, it didn't change the fact that they were friends... sort of, if her heart could stay intact when he left after the wedding.

Linda and Clint talked about their new catering business and their lives on the farm they'd inherited from Clint's parents. "We thought the fair would be a good place to spread the word."

As they talked, Brittney couldn't stop wondering if their former classmates weren't the perfect solution to Lucas's catering problem. As if having the same thoughts, he looked at her, his brows lifting, and she shrugged signaling he should go ahead and ask. At the very least they could add them to the list of catering contenders.

"We'll probably have lunch at your booth," Lucas said. "Brit and I are looking for food for my brother's wedding."

She nodded, hoping their food was tastier than the previous caterers he'd tried out.

"Don't eat any snacks. We'll have plenty of samples for you." Linda's eyes sparkled as she slid an arm around her husband's waist. "And if you hire us, you get a discount for the Soda Creek alumni."

Lucas touched his flat stomach beneath his blue shirt. "My mouth is starting to water. Can we come now?"

Clint laughed, and Brittney had to remind Lucas of the bumpy rides he was looking forward to.

"Our booth is right across from the roller coaster." With a light-hearted wave, Linda gestured toward the general area.

They said goodbye to their former schoolmates and promised to see them in a few hours.

At Brittney's signal, Clarice huffed and settled onto her walker's seat. Then Brittney fell in step with Lucas as he wheeled Clarice back to the quilter's booth.

"You're sure you don't want to come to the Ferris wheel with us?" Lucas asked his grandma.

Clarice stifled a chuckle. "If a carousel makes me this dizzy, how can I take a chance on any other ride? You kids go and have fun."

On the way to the entrance, they passed the funnel cakes booth, and Brittney's stomach growled as she breathed in the fried scent. "That smells so good."

"Maybe we should first eat lunch." Lucas glanced at her, his mouth curved up. "Funnel cakes for dessert."

Clarice patted her lap, searching for her handbag, and Brittney reminded her it was in the walker basket. "Stop, Luke, I need to buy you funnel cakes."

Lucas slowed the walker. "I think Brit is right. Eating anything before getting on a roller coaster, might get us sick."

Clarice stuffed her wallet back in her purse. "I'm glad you took Brit's advice."

"I'll get you a funnel cake, though." Brittney tapped the cross-body sling bag around her chest. "If you want one."

"Our guild is providing lunch," Clarice said, settling her purse on her lap. "I'm looking forward to having the turkey leg."

When they dropped her off, she told them to take their time, since she was one of the three people signed up to run the quilter's booth that afternoon until closing.

Riding the Tilt-a-Whirl, Ferris wheel, roller coaster, and all the spinny rides made Brittney's brain whirl, yet it felt so thrilling—something she'd not done for a long time. Even though she'd brought Clarice to the fair every year, Brittney didn't get on any rides. Everything about the fair was filled with memories, and she'd decided to shove some of those memories aside by steering away from things she and Lucas had done together.

"You're okay?" he asked, tucking her arm further in the crook of his.

She nodded, feeling more than okay with him holding her hand as they wove through the crowd toward the food truck. Now that she had her friend back and he knew how she felt—even though he'd not responded—she was at peace.

Or maybe that depended on the circumstances. She should be content with the way things were, but a hole deep within her wanted more, something beyond and forever.

She wanted this day to last forever. She wanted this moment with him to stretch on as she felt the heat of his skin through his light-blue shirt.

"I didn't think I'd make it through the scrambler." Lucas pulled her out of her thoughts.

"Whew, that ride was so cumbersome." Brittney laughed. She'd had to close her eyes to stop imagining their car was going to collide with the other ones.

"And that's what made it frighteningly fun," he added, planting a kiss on her cheek, igniting a certain level of temperature through her body.

Being the only food truck across from the roller coaster, Linda and Clint's booth was easy to find. Why did they call it a truck? It was more like a trailer.

When they joined the six to seven people in line, Linda beamed and waved to them from the window. Standing beside her husband, she whispered to him before disappearing from the window. Soon, she emerged toward the line. "I'll show you to your seats."

She ushered them toward the canopy, and they followed her to the side of their truck where they'd set up about five card tables with six chairs each. She grinned, rubbing her hands together. "Okay, we've never catered a wedding before."

That wasn't good. Brittney exchanged a look with Lucas, and as if Linda sensed their doubts, she continued, "Clint makes really good food. That's one reason I married him."

"I'm sure we'll like it," Brittney said to ease the tension.

"Good thing we are hungry," Lucas added.

Brittney had never had a business, but trying to please a customer must be terrifying.

"I'll have our helper bring you some food."

"You don't by chance have any fries do you?" Lucas asked.

Linda nodded. "Actually, we do, and burgers too. But that won't be a wedding dinner."

"You never know." He shrugged.

"I'll serve you five of our best dishes and add your fries to the side."

"Can we get some ranch, too?" Brittney asked, not just because she liked ranch with her fries, but because Lucas always liked to dip his fries in ranch, too.

With their drinks ordered, Linda left, and Lucas gave Brittney that boy-next-door grin. "You still dip your fries in ranch dressing?"

What could she say? It was among the many things she'd learned from him. "Some habits are hard to break."

With a wink, he gave a curt nod. "I find myself organizing my shirt drawer by color code. As strange as it is, I double-check the locks at night sometimes."

Pleased that he carried on some of her little habits, Brittney pressed her palms to her cheeks. But she needed to discuss her concerns about letting Linda and Clint down. Leaning forward, she braced her forearms on the chilly plastic table covering. "What if their food is awful and we can't hire them?"

He rested a hand on her arm. "It's hard for you to let someone down, but don't worry, I'll handle it. After all, I'll be leaving in less than ten days and won't run into Linda and Clint anytime soon. By the time they see me again, they'll have forgotten about this day."

Right, he was leaving. That was not comforting. She stood, reaching for the wipes from the table's edge, and started wiping down the plastic covering, ridding it of any dust the day had stirred. In fact, being so energetic, she needed to wipe the three vacant tables in the tent.

As if sensing her absurd reaction, he reached for her hand before she finished wiping the next table. His touch ignited a thrill through her body.

"Come on. Let's go wash our hands." He took the dirty wipe from her and led her to the portable sink at the tent entrance.

They were both silent when they returned to the table and a teen brought their Dr Peppers and two water glasses. Brittney learned the girl was Clint and Linda's daughter when Lucas asked her.

When Linda returned with a tray of kabobs and a basket of fries, one whiff of the delectable scent had Brittney's mouth watering.

"Is it okay if I pray over our food?"

With Lucas, everything was fine, and she'd do anything for him, even if she didn't grasp the prayer thing yet. "Sure."

He put out both hands for her, and she took them, loving the warm firmness of his grip. He eyed her, looking suddenly unsure. "I'm still new to this."

"I don't have a clue how to pray, so you're good."

With his eyes closed, he started to speak. "Thank You for bringing me back home to my family... to my best friend." His voice cracked at the word *friend*. "Bless this food, Lord. Amen." He squeezed her hand and gave her that bone-melting smile that made her heart squeeze.

"This is where you say amen."

Oh, she'd forgotten. "Amen."

When she took a piece of the garlic steak, it all but melted in her mouth. "Hmm... This is so good."

Lucas had his eyes closed as he ate the chicken as if savoring its deliciousness. When he opened his eyes, he pulled a piece of chicken from the skewer and held it closer to her mouth. "Wait until you taste the chicken."

She instinctively parted her lips. The sentiment felt romantic, yet it wasn't new. The savory juicy chicken melted into scrumptious deliciousness as she chewed. She agreed with Lucas—it was hard to determine whether the chicken or beef was better.

"Looks like we found our caterer." She spoke over a mouthful.

"We have to try the lamb first," he said, since each skewer had a sticker taped at the bottom, indicating what kind of meat it was.

Just like the steak and chicken, the lamb, the pork, and the boneless ribs were delicious. Even the grilled brussels sprouts and broccoli were delicious.

"I think brussels sprouts are not as bad as I thought," Lucas said, tossing another tiny cabbage in his mouth. He'd always hated brussels sprouts.

As they ate, she handed him a napkin when she caught a remnant of sauce at the corner of his mouth. "When did you become spiritual?"

"I wouldn't call it spiritual." He dabbed the napkin on his lips, skipping the corner with the sauce. "I'm far from perfect as you already know... just trying to pursue a perfect, righteous God and working at being a better person."

The last thing she wanted was to act as if she were accusing him about his newfound faith or have him get defensive in what he believed. "I mean, how did you learn the prayer thing? There's something different about you."

He used to struggle with apologies, and even if he'd been in the wrong, she'd always apologize so they could go back to normal.

"Ryan's wife introduced me to church."

"Ryan is a churchgoing person, too?"

"He didn't use to be. Then he met Destiny." He sipped water as if needing it before adding more. "Destiny and I sort of made a bet." He told her about asking Destiny out. "She would only go on a date with me if I went to church."

Something didn't add up. He asked his friend's wife on a date? What was wrong with him?

"Did Ryan know about this date bet you had with his wife? You guys still talk, right?"

His shoulders shook as he laughed. "Yikes, you think I'd go behind Ryan's back?" He shook his head. "That was before Ryan even noticed her."

A pang of jealousy coursed through her. All these years, she'd been stuck in the past, stuck thinking of him since his kiss. But what about *him*? Had he forgotten *her* completely? Suddenly hot with unwelcome fury, she needed water, so she gulped almost half a glass before setting it down.

As if sensing her inner thoughts, he continued to talk about Ryan's life turning upside down after his sister and brother-in-law died, his ex breaking up with him, and Destiny becoming the kids' nanny. "I wanted to make Ryan jealous. He and Destiny had chemistry, but he wouldn't make a move until I stepped up the game."

Whew! Did she just breathe? Good.

"I know you think I'm just a player or some sort of—"

"Please." She lifted a hand to stop him. "I was just upset, and I didn't mean it."

"I know."

Needing to stick to Ryan's dilemma, Brittney took a fry and dipped it in ranch, not surprised Lucas would play such a game. "Did this affect your friendship somehow?"

"If it did, Ryan didn't show it, but there was no reason for it to." He swirled a fry in the ranch too. "Destiny was crazy in love with him, and the few times she was with me, all she talked about was Ryan. After two dates, we both stopped playing, and I had to be direct with Ryan to go after her."

As he continued to talk about Destiny's personality, Brittney wanted to be friends with her. Her kindness and confidence was something she needed herself.

"This food, even the fries." Lucas changed the conversation as he chewed the french fry and spoke afterward. "Is exactly what we need for the wedding."

When Linda returned, they both told her how much they liked her food, and she handed them the menu and a form to fill out their options.

"Let me first pay you for our lunch." Lucas reached for his wallet, and so did Brittney.

"It's on the house." Linda waved him off. "Those were samples."

"You're running a business." Brittney said, pulling out her card, but Lucas told her to put it back.

"It's on me." He said.

Even though Linda tried to refuse payment, Lucas insisted, and in the end, he had to pay what he assumed was an honest price since she wouldn't tell them how much their food cost.

Brittney leaned in to study the paper menu in his hands, their heads almost touching. The smell of eucalyptus or whatever scent he had mixed with the tantalizing scent of Lucas sent her heart racing.

Breathless, she straightened her shoulders. "What about skewers?"

He ran his finger down the list. "There's chicken and steak."

It wasn't expensive for a wedding, but they probably needed to speak with Adam to determine what he could and couldn't afford. "Should we call and tell him how much it costs?"

"I'm paying." Lucas looked back at the paper. "Being a wedding, we'd better get the top five on the menu."

Helping his brother after the strain they had before was sweet. She'd heard Clarice on the phone whenever she spoke to Lucas and asked him to forgive his brother. Brittney didn't have to ask to know she'd been the reason for their conflict.

Lucas was always caring, always the glue in the family. Being the middle child, he'd stepped up to do what his siblings didn't want to do.

Although she'd told him this several times in the past, she still said it again. "You're a very kind person."

He shrugged. "Now that we have all the meat, we need to choose the sides."

"Broccoli and brussels sprouts."

He cringed. "Seriously, Brit, you choose brussels sprouts over fries?"

"Vegetables will compliment all this meat, don't you think?"

"It's a wedding... not a hospital meal."

She rolled her eyes, taking the menu from him and looking at the sides. "Next thing I know, you'll be ordering something as crazy as mac and cheese."

He yanked the menu from her. "Let's do roasted potatoes instead of brussels sprouts. And mac and cheese wouldn't be bad for the few kids who might be there."

She hadn't thought about that. She snuck a glance at his square jaw now covered in a few days' scruff. "I think Adam will be happy with your caterer."

"Our caterer," he corrected. "We worked together."

Even though they were so full when they left the tent, Brittney insisted they get a funnel cake for old times' sake. After eating two bites each, they decided to return the next day and buy another when they were hungry.

The stroll from one booth to another offered much-needed exercise as they stopped from time to time to play some of the games. They played balloon-and-dart as well as ball and bucket toss.

The afternoon sun was sinking down the horizon when Lucas suggested they go back to Clarice's booth.

Brittney tapped her forehead, feeling unprofessional. She'd had too much fun and didn't want the day to end. "I almost forgot my job."

"You're off duty. As long as I'm around, I'll help pitch in."

Around for less than ten days. He'd leave before she could get used to having him around. In fact, she felt like she was in a dream somewhere, that she had to pinch his strong forearm to double-check.

"What was that for?"

Just then, two kids, about ten or eleven, ran into their path. One almost spilled his popcorn, but Lucas let go of Brittney's hand and held the boy's popcorn box. "You better watch where you're going, buddy."

"Thanks." The kid flashed a toothy grin, and then joined the girl who was waiting.

Even if they were probably brother and sister, it reminded Brittney of her and Lucas about that age. It surprised her when Lucas said, "Remember my second summer in Soda Creek?"

It was like yesterday when his grandma had brought them to the fair for the first time. "You lost all your money because you wanted to keep playing bingo." She shook her head. "You wouldn't even congratulate me for winning."

He scrunched his face. "What twelve-year-old would be okay being beaten by his best friend?"

"You." She bumped her elbow into his ribs, her heart feeling light, and as they approached the quilter's booth, Lucas pointed out another booth close by.

"I have to play this game." He dragged her to a booth with the "game of skill" he'd played each time they came.

"You were terrible at target practice." Not that she was any better, but he'd never win any prizes. The game was like the claw machines that took your money, but gave no results. "Maybe you better not waste your money on this one."

He gently pinched her cheek. "I can't believe you've lost hope in me."

She was talking and laughing with him today—that was hope in itself. "Oh, I don't think I've lost hope." But she meant something else entirely.

A young man behind the counter greeted them. His purple hair matched his booth's vibrant colors.

"I'm not leaving until I win that sunflower bear." Lucas handed the man his credit card, but he only took cash. So Brittney dug in her wallet for a ten-dollar bill.

When the man gave Lucas the crossbow, he blew out a breath and winked at her. "Wish me luck."

"You've got this," she said, stepping further away since another customer was walking to the booth.

She had no idea how much Lucas would need, but she only had ten dollars left. She'd seen an ATM somewhere. Lifting onto tiptoe, she peered over a few heads toward the bumper cars. Was it behind the—

"I won!"

Lucas's voice had her turning as he tossed the bow on the red counter. "Several years of playing!" He punched a victorious high five to the young man before he walked toward her.

"In one shot." He flashed his contagious grin, catching her by surprise when he threw his arms around her and squeezed her in a warm embrace. "I finally won that stuffed animal for you."

Could he hear her thrumming heart against his? When he stepped out of the embrace, she managed to say, "I'm glad we didn't lose the ten dollars for nothing."

She tried to be light to offset her inner battle. But she was grateful when the man called Lucas to claim his prize and Lucas clasped her hand in his and led her back toward the booth.

"Congrats, man," the man said. As soon as the stuffed animal was in Lucas's possession, he handed it to her.

Before she could admire the stuffed bear, and despite the few people who were now lining up for the activity, Lucas bent down, startling her with the unexpectedness of a light brush of his lips, They were soft and warm as they caressed hers briefly and delicately, causing her to shiver to the core.

Her mind was spinning when he stilled. She looked at the people passing by minding their own business, but my, the tingle from that soft kiss left a mark on her mouth.

Just like Lucas, he took her arm in his and started walking toward Clarice's booth.

"I wish this day could last forever," he said, and she couldn't agree more.

CHAPTER 17

That night after Grams went to bed, Lucas worked on the puzzle with Brit, still energized from the fantastic day despite his lack of sleep these last two nights. Then they both walked down the lit hallway to their bedrooms.

"Good night," he told her when she stood outside her half-open door.

She smiled shyly, keeping one hand on the doorknob. "Thanks for making this day special."

She was the best part about this day. "The feeling is mutual."

Even though he was leaning against the wall across from her room, he felt like a live wire connected them as they stared at each other.

Her lips parted as if ready to say something, but she closed them. *Go. Get away while you can.* Ugh, why didn't his legs seem to get the message?

Starting something that couldn't go anywhere was a mistake. What if she only wanted him because she felt sorry for him?

"I don't want to pretend to be your friend," she said. For some odd reason, she was good at guessing what he was thinking. "I want to try..."

The door swung open wider, and her body went with it. He instinctively reached out before she could tumble. "You're okay?" When he steadied her and she nodded, the tender look in her eyes staggered him.

He reached out to caress her soft cheek, wanting to clarify if she knew what she was saying. "I'm broken." Because of her, but he didn't want her to like him for that reason. "But..." He shook his head. "I

181

don't want you to want me because you feel sorry for me. In that case, I'd rather not have you."

He wasn't injured like Troy, but she was the root of his shattered spirit.

She lifted his hand and pressed a kiss to his palm. A tremble zipped all the way through him. Nothing had ever electrified him the way her touch did.

"I'd like to try, too." His words were automatic.

As much as he wanted to pull her in his arms and kiss her senseless, he didn't trust himself to know how far that would go, not while in her bedroom doorway. With great reluctance, he withdrew his hand.

He couldn't leave like this. First, he had to know. Needing to confirm things, he framed her face and urged her to meet his gaze.

"What?" she asked breathlessly.

"I'm not a friend who needs rescuing."

"I'm the one who needs rescuing."

Hope thrummed through his heart, and he grinned, then planted a kiss on her forehead, lingering to smell the faint scent of vanilla and chocolate in her hair. "Nothing would make me happier than dating my best friend."

When he stepped back, he was rewarded by her deep dimples as her lips pulled back into that mile-wide smile he'd never forget. Lucas fought the urge to place a soft kiss on her lips. If he started with a simple kiss, she would kiss him back and they might never stop.

"Sweet dreams," he whispered and walked away, ignoring his inner voice screaming at him to look back, very aware of Brit's gaze on him, but proud of himself when he made it to the next room and closed the door.

He was breathing fast, and he was hot, really hot. As soon as he heard Brit's door close, he went to the bathroom to take another shower.

He yawned, his body exhausted, but he needed to update Adam.

It was ten fifteen when he put the call through. Since Adam wasn't fond of texting, it was no surprise when he answered on the second ring.

"We're set for the food." Lucas gave him a rundown of the meal choices he remembered, and Adam was grateful Lucas had gone for gourmet dishes, as he called it.

"We need to get your vows written." Lucas flopped onto his side on his bed, bracing his head on his arm, staring at the corner by the lamp. Not a fleck of dust on the hardwood floor. "I'll walk you through it, but you have to do it yourself."

"I have some time before work tomorrow," Adam said. "You want to meet at six?"

Lucas let out a groan through the phone. "I'm on vacation. Can't a guy sleep in?"

"You'd be at work in Denver if I wasn't getting married."

His brother had a point. Plus, he needed to get this done if he was going to spend time with Brit.

When he hung up, Lucas browsed through his phone for the Notes app, his thumb hovering over the blank area.

Hmm... He set his phone next to his pillow when he realized he had no clue what to write.

After the kind of day he'd had with Brittney—her waking up in his arms, watching the sunrise, spending time at the fair—the feeling was surreal, as if it were something normal, something they'd do together on any given day.

His lips tingled when he thought of the gentle kiss he'd pressed to her mouth. He'd wanted to win that sunflower teddy bear for her each year they went to the fair.

The excitement from the win, Brit's admission of her feelings for him last night, and her reverent smile all made him forget his insecurities of being rejected, and it was just natural to give her a peck. A peck that had made her eyes dilate, as if she wanted more.

He smiled at her bold confession tonight. *I'd like to try.*

That had been a big move on her end. He closed his eyes, picturing what she could be doing right now. Was she sleeping or staring at the ceiling? He shifted and reached for his phone. He needed to let her know of his early appointment so she didn't think he'd run off again.

Lucas: Hey, you.

His phone chimed in an immediate response.

Brit: Strange you have my number, and I don't have yours.

Unease hit him. He'd never given her his number, yet he'd kept hers all along.

Lucas: It doesn't seem you had a problem figuring out that it's me.

Brit: I got it from Clarice while you were still sleeping this morning. Just in case we got separated at the fair, I needed a way to get a hold of you.

The fight had its ups and downs, like Mom had said. It seemed after that they were off to a great start. A start where she didn't want to lose connection with him.

Lucas: I'll do my best to let you know my whereabouts from now on.

Brit: You barely slept last night. You should try to get some sleep.

Lucas: I'll blame you for my sleeplessness.

Brit: Go to sleep.

Lucas remembered his early appointment and why he texted.

Lucas: I'm meeting Adam at six. Don't wait for me for breakfast.

Brit: I'll wait for you as long as it takes.

Man. She meant breakfast, but somehow, Lucas's mind started spinning. Did she mean breakfast or waiting for him to get his act together?

Lucas: Nite

Brit: Sweet dreams

"As long as it takes..." As he whispered her text, it sounded like a good line to go in vows.

He typed that in his Notes app. His thumb hovered, his mind wandering to his life with Brit. He spun around to his back, closing his eyes as flashbacks filled his mind.

Organizing a strike in middle school so they could let girls play baseball since they only had a boys' team, laughing with her, crying and shouting at each other when necessary.

He was always himself around her.

Even before he developed romantic feelings for her, he'd never pictured a future without Brit in it.

If she hadn't figured out by now the extent of his love for her, he had no idea how to express himself.

As ideas popped into his mind, he sat up. Wide awake, he started typing all the reasons why he was in love with Brit, the reasons why he would want to spend the rest of his life with her, and why she should want to choose him as her husband.

He stayed up much later reflecting on his notes as if he were the one getting married.

When he got to Adam's on Friday morning, Adam opened the door with a steaming cup of coffee. "Would you like some?"

"Show me the cups, and I'll fix one." Lucas hadn't had time to fix coffee when he left Grams's house. After fixing his coffee in the one-cup Keurig, he joined Adam at the bistro-style dining table.

"I expected some kind of breakfast." Lucas nodded at the table setting for two. "But I get the impression you don't get company."

"Hey, I get company."

Lucas gave him a knowing look. "With just the two seats at your dining table?"

"I like to eat out." Adam shrugged, rocking back on the chair's metal legs—something he did often judging by the scuffed beige and green linoleum. "Thanks again for helping with the catering stuff."

"Brit helped." The food had been more enjoyable with her.

"You two worked together?" Adam's brows creased.

It seemed too good to be true, and Lucas didn't want to get his hopes too high. So he downplayed things. "We've sorted things out."

Adam's mouth parted as if he wanted to dig for details, but Lucas pulled out his phone since they needed to get things done right away. "You better get a phone or computer and take some notes, because I want you to write your own vows."

Adam stood and returned with a notepad and pen. He saluted Lucas with a pen to his forehead. "Yes, sir."

Lucas took a sip of his coffee, then stood to open the blinds, letting natural light into a room as cave-like as Adam's work garage. Honestly, to this day, Adam could stay holed up in a windowless room tinkering with mechanics. "Remember, you're dealing with someone who has no romantic experience whatsoever."

"Noted." Adam scribbled something on his pad.

"You don't have to write that." Lucas rolled his eyes and dropped back into his seat. Sure, Adam was playing with him somehow, but Lucas would rather not get embarrassed or fail at his job as best man. "So, why are you in love with Olivia?"

Adam sipped his coffee, then gripped his hands around his mug as if he didn't hear the question.

Maybe rephrasing would help. "What's the reason you were drawn to her enough to want her to be the first person you see when you wake up each morning and the last person you see before bedtime?"

"She's beautiful."

"That's good."

Adam ran a finger along the rim of his mug. "I love her."

Those were good reasons, but specifics would convey a better message to Olivia. "Let's get beyond two reasons why you want to spend the rest of your life with her."

Adam chuckled, shaking his head. "I don't need all the extra reasons. I have two big ones."

Lucas shifted in the metal chair. "You don't need to tell me. Just write it down for her."

Adam picked up his pen and scribbled on the pad. The reasons why he would want to spend the rest of his life with her and why she should want to choose him as her husband.

They seemed to be getting somewhere, so Lucas stirred his coffee. "Another way to spice up your vows, I'd think, would be writing something special—something on how you met, the little things she does that make her stand out above all the other girls."

He tried not to think of Brit and the way she put other people's needs above her own. Her tender spirit—

"Whoa... whoa. Wait." Adam tossed the pen on the table. "I need the whole poetic vibe to present those reasons, you know. Give me an example."

Lucas threw his head back. Seriously, his brother wasn't even putting any effort into his own vows. He huffed and narrowed his gaze at Adam. "I never thought I'd do this, but I'm tempted to talk to my lawyer."

Seeing through Lucas's joke, Adam offered a half-smile. "That ought to give our wedding free publicity."

At this point, he had to spoon-feed Adam so he didn't say things he shouldn't on his wedding day. Left with no alternative, it was time to tell him the script he ran through his mind last night. He didn't tell him he'd been imagining a future with Brit and what he'd say to her if he was getting married.

It seemed like a fantasy he hated exploring.

He opened his app and read the first line as if reading it to Brit. "From the moment I met you, I knew I wanted to spend every day of my life with you." That first summer in Soda Creek when she gave him that drawing, he knew then he wanted her in his life. "You've been my best friend and always the most beautiful person in the room. I could spend years looking for someone like you, but there's only you—you complete me."

He stretched his jaw as the words freely came out of his mouth without him reading anymore. "Today, I become accountable to someone other than myself. I give you my solemn vow, to love you unconditionally, to support you in your goals and dreams, to laugh with you and cry with you, to share my hopes and dreams with you. With God as my witness, I promise to lay my life down to protect you."

When he looked at Adam, his mouth was half-open, and he clapped his hands. "Wow, you gave me the perfect visual."

Lucas shrugged, clearing the small lump in his throat before he spoke. "It's just that simple."

"Did you memorize that overnight?" Adam stood and walked to the sink with his mug. "I gotta say I'm tempted to have you speak on my behalf."

Lucas stood with his half cup of coffee, giving his brother a sharp stare. "That's where we draw the line."

No way would he speak vows to Adam's wife.

"I'm surprised you didn't take poetry or something." Adam took Lucas's cup from him and set it in the sink with all the other cups.

Tempted to remind Adam to load all the dirty cups into the dishwasher, Lucas clamped his mouth shut. It wasn't his place, since he had enough to deal with. "The only job I have left now is to write the best-man speech and host a bachelor party."

"What for?" Adam frowned.

"In case you didn't know, the groom has to have a bachelor party."

"That's a waste of money."

"Afraid I'm doing one." He punched Adam on the shoulder. "We'll have the party at the beach on Friday, the day before the wedding, and I thought it'd be nice if the whole family came." When he checked the website that day when he hung out at Mom's shop, there was a whole wing still available for that weekend. "You always loved the beach. What better time to enjoy it than on your wedding weekend."

Adam blinked several times and inched toward Lucas, engulfing him in a hug. His voice heavy with emotion, he whispered, "I owe you big time."

"No, you don't. You're my brother." Lucas would do anything for his family, and he had some catching up to do.

When he left Adam's place, instead of driving home, he took the longer route to the sunflower field. The same land with the lake he and Brit had snuck onto. Perhaps he could bring Brit there later if he asked the owner. He'd have to make the trip there that afternoon to request permission.

His phone rang, and he glimpsed the screen—Olive Medical. He pulled off to the side of the country road and answered.

"Matthews!" A deep voice rang through the phone. "It's Fox from HR."

Anticipation tensed Lucas's nerves as the seconds ticked. He'd put up with a woman rejecting him. Now, did he have to be rejected at work too?

"Well, um, I just wanted to congratulate you as our new head anesthesiologist."

His heart soared as he squeezed the phone to his ear when a loud tractor clattered past.

"You're there?"

"What can I say?" Too stunned to form up his next sentence, he just listened while Fox told him the board's determining vote. With Fox's promise to email all the needed paperwork to review, Lucas hung up.

He grinned as he drove back to Grams's house so he could share the news with Brit. When he turned on another street with a few farmhouses spread apart, he stopped at a roadside tent someone set up. They were selling flowers. Not just any flowers—sunflowers among the many bouquets.

Grams considered cut flowers a waste, so she didn't care for bouquets. But Lucas bought three bouquets with three flowers each and asked for one more flower, needing ten today, hoping Brit wasn't tired of sunflowers yet. He'd bought her sunflowers each year for her birthday until these last ten years.

When he entered Grams's house, pots clanged, and dishes clattered in the kitchen.

Grams was working on her crossword puzzle with Midnight nestled nearby on the couch. Both girls smiled, greeting Lucas with knowing glints in their eyes as they stared at the flowers. While Midnight mewed and nodded at the flowers, Grams asked about his visit with Adam, thankfully not prying about the flowers.

After talking to Grams, he ambled toward the kitchen, a heavy warmth blooming in his heart at the sight of Brit flipping crepes on the griddle. He set the sunflowers on the island. "Need any help?"

"I'm almost done." Her smile, as wide and bright as the sunflowers, reached the core of his heart. "Clarice already ate. She had to take her medicine."

"You should've eaten too." He walked to the sink and washed his hands, then dried them with the washcloth she handed him.

"I prefer brunch to breakfast."

He caught a whiff of her sweet scent when he hung the washcloth back on the hook beside her. With the temptation of touching her, his mind struggled to reason when he inched behind her. He then leaned over and nuzzled her neck. "Brunch it is," he whispered and pressed his lips for another fleeting kiss, thrilled when she shivered.

Something clattered on the floor, and he stepped back.

Brit stooped to pick up the spatula she'd dropped and swung it toward him. Goose bumps covered her arms. "I don't think it's a good idea for you to be in the kitchen right now."

Giving her a sheepish smile, he took the spatula. "I'll wash this and finish cooking." Then he kissed her on the cheek. "If you can get the vase, I got you some flowers."

Her gaze darted to the island, and she put both hands on her heart. Then she walked toward the island and picked up the flowers. "Thank you." She tickled her finger across the seeded center. "These flowers are so big, I think they'll topple Clarice's vases."

She'd always had large, heavy vases for his sunflower bouquets. Had she not gotten sunflowers lately? "I needed to catch up on all the flowers I didn't send on your birthdays."

"I'm glad you're here now."

Not for long. But now wouldn't be a good time to share the news of his promotion. He needed to work out the details on how his relationship with her would go. Could he take her and Grams back to Denver? Could Grams's feet endure the long drive? She hated flying, so that wouldn't be an option. He'd have to think hard.

CHAPTER 18

B rittney winced at the powerful smell of rubbing alcohol when she wiped chipped nail polish from Clarice's fingernails.

Even though the sun was high in the sky, the mature trees in the back covered the porch with plenty of shade.

After breakfast, Brittney and Clarice had gone to the recreation center where she taught aerobics, and Lucas stayed behind replacing door knobs and working on random projects around the house, projects Brittney had been putting off.

When they came back, Clarice wanted her nails done after lunch. It didn't make sense that she wanted them done a week before the wedding, but Brittney wouldn't mind doing it again come Friday.

"This time I'll let you surprise me with the color." Clarice straightened her feet on the deck boards where Brittney was kneeling as she removed the polish from her toes.

Although all for the vibrant colors during the summer, Brittney also wanted a color that complemented the clothes Clarice wore often. So she picked up a soft purple from the basket and shook the bottle. "This will look nice on you."

"Perfect." Clarice waved off a bee from the sunflowers on the table. From the three bouquets she'd gotten from Lucas, Brittney put one outside and kept two inside.

"I'm glad you and Luke worked things out." Clarice might be prying, but Brittney didn't have much to tell, besides his pecks that left her breathless and desiring more.

She shivered as she could almost feel the tingle from his lips on her neck and her cheek. Polish dribbled to Clarice's toe. "Oops."

"Uh-huh," was all Clarice said. "I see."

What was Lucas still doing in the house anyway? Maybe if he were out here, Clarice wouldn't be talking about him, and Brittney could focus.

As if she'd conjured him up in her thoughts, the back door swung open. "What are you beautiful ladies doing?"

"Coloring." She kept her head down on her task. Was that even her voice?

"Brittney is painting my nails," Clarice said.

Did Brittney's word even register? Did she say coloring?

Lucas asked if Ryan's kids could camp in the backyard, and Clarice shrieked. "I'd love to hear kids laugh and scream on the street. Of course, of course."

Brittney was just listening and minding her business—painting—but the polish kept going over the nails. Lucas wasn't even touching her, but she was struggling to breathe. She dabbed the nail polish remover into a cotton ball and wiped all the polish off Clarice's feet. She needed to start over.

"May I?" Lucas picked up the small glass jar from the deck. "I want to see if my skills are still intact."

He used to help Brittney paint her right hand since it was hard for her to paint it on her own.

"Like I said, feel free to take on some of the work while you're here."

When he sank next to her and crisscrossed his legs, Brittney's body temperature went from normal to overheated. "I'll go get us some drinks."

She stood, needing air, needing space, needing time to compose herself.

Lucas responded with a knowing grin, saying something about not needing anything. Clarice didn't want anything either, but Brittney still left.

It's just Lucas. Nope, he wasn't "just Lucas" anymore. Things were very different between them. Should she be terrified to cross this line?

It was too late now.

Arms folded on the island, she rested her head over them, letting the marble cool her forehead as she took a few breaths before standing and pouring a glass of water. She gulped the entire glass without pausing for a breath. Then she let out the air and returned to the deck.

Lucas was already done with Clarice's toes and fingernails.

"That was fast!" Brittney said.

"It took you a long time to return, sweetheart." Clarice assessed her nails. "Now it's your turn to get pampered."

Lucas was rummaging through the basket, studying each bottle and putting them back. "Which color would you like, Brit?"

"Um... Anything is fine."

What did she just agree to?

He lifted a subtle pink and shook it, then pointed his chin to the empty chair next to Clarice. "You heard Grams."

No, no, no! Her mind screamed, but then she remembered her response. *That's* what she'd given him permission to do?

With no strength to argue in front of Clarice, Brittney did as told and sat.

She watched Lucas bend over her feet, and her stomach flipped at his touch when he brushed the polish along her nails in slow meticulous strokes. His tongue stuck out as he concentrated on one toe, then another. He then started on her fingernails with a teal color.

"Whew!" He brushed his hand in front of his nose. "I'd forgotten how stinky this stuff is."

"I'm impressed how skillful my grandson is, I tell you."

His lashes swept down, long and dark, and the sunlight cast a golden glow on his skin.

"You're pretty good at this."

He smiled briefly. "My career requires steady hands, so that figures." His hands brushed gentle strokes on her fingernails. "Do we still have any tents or sleeping bags around?"

As a thrill coursed through her, she did her best to answer. She'd thought of getting rid of the tent, but it was one of those things that held too many memories to part with. "Up in the attic. Yeah."

He capped the bottle. Then he talked about the church he'd discovered in the neighborhood and intended to go to on Sunday. It turned out to be the same church where she'd taken her counseling sessions.

Clarice wiggled her fingernails, inspecting the purple glaze. "I haven't been in church for a really long time."

That's when Brit remembered her promise to God that year in counseling. "I would like to go with you, if it's okay."

His head jerked up, surprise flaring his eyes. "Sure."

Even if she didn't know how to pray, she'd always known there was a higher power that could bring Lucas back to her.

When she went with Lucas to locate the camping items, Brittney offered to climb the ladder. With Lucas's height, he'd end up hitting his head on the ceiling.

"Who built the shelves in this closet?" he asked from below the ladder where he waited.

"I figured I could imitate some of your grandpa's skills."

"*You* built that?"

"The shelves are not that steady, so I wouldn't consider it much of a skill." She wiggled loose one of the sleeping bags from the top shelf, then passed it down to him. Cobwebs clung to her hand when she grabbed another sleeping bag.

"If I'd known about camping, I could have washed the sleeping bags ahead of time."

"We still have tomorrow. I'll wash them."

There wasn't much on the camping shelf. "The chairs are in the shed," she said, remembering they would need them.

"We can get those on Sunday when the kids come."

Reaching for the tent, Brittney let out a slight grunt at the weight of the bag containing it.

"Be careful." Lucas stood on tiptoes, stretched his hand up, and pulled the tent down from her.

"Careful, too."

"Will you and the kids sleep in the same tent?" She started to climb down, and by the time she took the final step to the floor, Lucas was steadying the ladder.

"I was hoping you could join us." He let go of the ladder and brushed his hands together to rid them of any dust. "You could stay with Ryan's daughter while I stay with the boys."

She'd thought of hanging out with them before bedtime, but no way could she turn down the invitation. "I can't wait."

His thumb swept across her cheek, leaving a trail of heat. Their gazes caught and held, and her heart stopped. Paralyzed with a strangely familiar need, completely captivated by him, she was staring at Lucas's mouth.

She couldn't have looked away if she tried. Not that she wanted to look away, not when he was looking down at her in a way she'd dreamed of ever since that kiss ten years ago. Or was she imagining things?

She probably was daydreaming, so she managed to bite the words over her tongue. "Anything else, um, I... we need?"

Lucas's breath hitched, reminding her how close he stood, and then he leaned closer. "This."

His lips brushed hers, soft and melting her insides. His hands cradled her face, his lips moving against hers as he deepened the kiss.

She barely suppressed a moan. He smelled so good. His scruff scraped the tender flesh of her palm when she moved her hands to his face, feeling like she was floating or dreaming.

She was kissing her best friend.... Everything about him seemed perfect; everything about them together was just right. She'd been so sure being together like this would feel awkward, yet it felt anything but—as though they were finally finding each other after all this time. But he was leaving soon.

"What if it changes things?" she asked on a gasp.

"It won't." He cupped her chin for her to meet his eyes. "I care about you too much to lose my best friend again." His thumb brushed her lower lip, and he let out a breath. "I've loved you for so long, wanted more for so long—and I think you now want the same."

"Yes." She did—with everything in her. "I'm just scared." Scared he was going to leave and never look back. Scared the moment the relationship didn't work they'd never salvage their friendship. Scared of going through life without him again.

"Hey." He brushed his lips over hers before pulling her into his warm embrace. "It's going to be okay. We'll figure it out."

There was comfort in being in his arms, comfort in his words. Her mind sprang a memory after her parents died, especially after Dad's death when she felt like her world was crashing down. But during that first month after his death, the only way she fell asleep was if she was lying next to Lucas as he soothed her.

His gentle words were the assurance she needed to be reminded she wasn't alone in the lonely world.

CHAPTER 19

Brittney breathed in the afternoon country air as she stretched her hand through the Sorento's passenger window. She and Clarice had spent the first part of their day at Olivia's bridal shower while Lucas ran errands for tomorrow's camping items.

By the time they returned home at two, Clarice was ready for a nap, and Lucas had a surprise trip for Brittney on an excursion down memory lane. Thrilled that her friend was back in her life, she'd showered and dressed in her knee-length jumpsuit.

"I like how relaxed you are," Lucas said, and she turned her gaze from the open field to stare at him through her sunglasses.

He looked relaxed, too, in his white T-shirt and navy shorts.

"You won't tell me where we're going. I've decided to trust you."

"Good." He glanced at her briefly before turning his gaze back to the road. His lips lifted into a mischievous grin, the one she remembered so well from whenever he had a crazy plan in motion.

Her curiosity piqued when he turned onto the bumpy road to the familiar expansive sunflower field. There weren't as many flowers as she remembered, but mid- to late-July the flowers would be in full bloom.

"Don't tell me we're going to run through this field again."

When he nodded, his smile wider, she shook her head. She'd do anything or go anywhere Lucas told her to, but this wouldn't end well.

"We're not teenagers anymore," she reminded him, in case he'd forgotten how they'd had to scurry out when the farm owner saw them strolling through his field and hollered at them.

"We have to go back in time." He spoke like he co-owned the field. "It's something I need to do before I go back."

Oh, thanks for constantly reminding me that you're leaving.

She peered through the open window. Sure, she knew he would leave, but part of her kept hoping—what? That he could consider coming back home. She held her anxious breath, listening to the relaxing mooing of cows in the distance.

Soon they reached the edge of the fields, and Lucas drove into an unpaved lot before a weathered barn. Her dejected feeling vanished at the sight of sunflowers.

"I don't remember this." Sitting up straighter, she gestured to the barn. The two times they'd snuck in, she hadn't seen any structure around. That must have been because they entered from a different side.

"I just discovered it yesterday afternoon."

She was baffled. He'd left after getting things out of the shed. "Is this what you meant when you said you had something to do?"

He stepped out and went around to the passenger side and opened her door. She crossed her arms, not ready to break rules. Lucas would be leaving, and she'd be left to face a mad farmer. "There's lots of places we can go, you know?" she suggested, hoping to convince him, but he kept his hand out.

"Look at me, Brit."

So she did.

"You have no reason to trust me, but I promise, we'll not get in trouble."

Staring at those bottomless brown eyes made it impossible to remember what she was or wasn't supposed to do. So she accepted the hand he offered.

When she stepped out and he closed the car door, he started sprinting, and she kept up as he led her toward the field.

"We're going to get in trouble." Her protests came out weakly, but Lucas's strong hold on her didn't make it easy to remain firm.

"Only if we get caught."

"It's a terrible... idea." Her last words were barely a whisper the moment her flat sandals set foot on the field's soft earth.

Lucas slowed his sprint, now almost jogging. "What were you saying?"

She could hear the smile in his voice.

It was her turn to kick up the speed. She was sixteen again, on her birthday. It was the last time she'd set foot in the field.

The breeze lifted her hair, and when she looked at Lucas, his dark-blond hair had risen off his forehead, the wind ruffling its silky strands.

"This is so magical!" she shouted, slowing her steps to match his as she flung out her free hand, breathing in the carefree smell of childhood, her spirit feeling light and lifted.

"I know, right?" He gave her a sideways glance, his face as vibrant as the bright-yellow petals carrying a warming early afternoon glow. "This way. Follow me." He finally let go of her hand and weaved into one of the rows in the tall stalks, and she followed slowly as she took in the outstretched field.

"Isn't it fascinating how every petal is stretched toward the sun?" She spread out both arms now, matching the flowers' posture.

He spun around, his hands brushing against the stalks when he outstretched them and took backward steps. "Whenever I see sun-flowers, I think of you."

The flowers bobbed their heads, nodding at his words, while his genuine confession squeezed her heart, leaving her speechless. But he didn't linger, instead turning and resuming his walk.

Twigs scraped her heels, but she couldn't care less. When they arrived in a clearing toward the end of the field, a wicker basket with a woven wooden lid waited on the thick picnic blanket.

"Stop," she whispered, balking, but Lucas, fearless as he was, reached for her hand and clasped it in his, then tugged her forward. Standing there, she shook her head. "Looks like we're crashing someone's party."

"It's our party. Come on."

How? "You're doing a terrible job explaining things."

She peered around to make sure they were not trespassing—okay, they were already trespassing by running through the farm, but a picnic blanket? And someone's food?

He stepped toward her and lifted a hand to her chin, his fingers trailing along her jaw, and a thrill ran through her body at the gentle trace of his touch. When he bent down and captured her mouth with his, there was no hesitancy in his kiss, and after yesterday's kiss, she felt bolder and more confident to grip his shirt in her hand. Lucas grazed his lips across hers, and her heart began beating again.

"I missed you," he said between gasping breaths, and although she'd missed him too, she couldn't speak while gasping for air.

When his hands raked through her hair and he deepened the kiss, her feet felt wobbly, like jelly. She mimicked him and moved her hands, traveling to his neck, to his jaw. His scruff scraped the tender flesh of her palm before her hands drifted into the hair at his nape. She was shaking by the time they ended the kiss and he rested his head on hers.

"I missed you so much," he repeated with a tremor in his voice. The genuineness in his confession brought such a thick lump to her throat, she had to clear it to speak. "I missed you, too." Apparently, she'd missed out on romancing her best friend.

After several minutes of silence and a comfortable embrace, he led her to the oversized blanket and picnic mat, and as she sat, her mind was whirling with questions. How did he do this? A picnic in the sunflower field. Did he remember her silly childhood wish? How did he get this picnic set up, anyway? Had he done all this while she was at the bridal shower this morning? She fidgeted with the sunflower earrings on her ears, the ones he'd given her.

"This one time, I asked for permission," he said. How did he know her unspoken question?

"Oh." She lowered her hands from her earrings. "So, does this basket belong to the farm owner?"

He opened the lid and retrieved a Dr Pepper, popping it open. "Yes."

"How did you find... talk to him?"

"I knocked on his door." He handed her the soda as he told her his confession to the farmer from years ago for sneaking into his field. "Thankfully, he didn't even remember chasing us off." Lucas popped open another Dr Pepper. "He was so thrilled that, after all these years, I wanted to bring you here. Anyway, he decided to throw in this surprise we didn't know existed."

Lucas pulled out a small container with cheese, then another with crackers, a Ziploc bag with mixed nuts and one with sunflower seeds, and another container with whole strawberries with the green tops nicely cut off. He then removed the sanitizer from the basket and squeezed some in his hands, then in hers.

"Did you pay for all this?"

He shrugged. "Just a little donation."

That was Lucas, her Lucas. The guy who'd ignored all the beautiful girls in school, especially at the senior homecoming, when he'd made a huge deal and asked her out in front of his football team after the game. Said he'd wanted it to be special, since they'd missed the sophomore dance after her mom died and she'd gotten the flu during the junior homecoming dance. Lucas had skipped the dance and stayed by her, pulling her hair to her back while she threw up. A strangled sound escaped her throat from the memories. How naive could anyone be? Couldn't she see he was in love with her then?

"What?" he asked, his brows squeezed together.

She took a steadying breath, doing her best to smile so he didn't worry about her. "You blow me away." Having no idea what else to say, she just gazed at his handsome face, deep-brown eyes that stared back at her so full of love and so many unexpected emotions. She gestured her hand around the display. "This is amazing."

"Soda doesn't go well with all this, but it's the idea of a picnic that counts."

She shook her head, her heart full with how romantic he was, how stunning that he would do this for her. "This is my best—*second best*—day ever."

"Is that so?" His eyebrows lifted inquiringly. "What's your first best day?"

"The first day we played together." Even though she hadn't known then.

He nodded. "That was my best day too. Sorry it took this many years before I could get you this picnic."

"You remembered," she whispered.

"Why wouldn't I?" He lifted the soda to his mouth and then put the can down on a patch of dead grass.

He passed her the snacks, but she wasn't hungry—the joy of the afternoon was filling enough. Still, she took a piece of cheese and popped it into her mouth.

Lucas ate some sunflower seeds and strawberries.

They munched their snacks while they talked about past plans and future plans, kids they went to school with, and kids who stayed in Soda Creek after high school. They talked about their struggles while apart and what their lives had been like those years.

"After you broke up with Adam, why didn't you date again?"

How did he even know she didn't date? Perhaps he'd kept tabs on her, or Clarice, of course, told him.

Why hadn't she dated? How could she, when she'd finally discovered what and who she wanted, but had no way to chase him?

Maybe she'd given up too easily, like she gave up on her quadriplegic care book. Lucas, however, had always been confident enough to go after his dreams.

She popped open sunflower seed shells. "One of the things I admire about you is that you know what you want and go for it."

"Look how long it took me to admit my feelings for you." He stacked the unfinished snacks back into the basket. "I'm still single, and I ran away from you... my best friend."

Single. How could he have stayed single this long? Especially after she rejected him. There had to be a detailed explanation for it. So she put one of her outstretched legs over the other and blew the sunflower shells from her palm, letting them float away to land on the grass. "I've asked you this before, but what took you so long to admit your feelings for me?"

He lay down, his stomach on the blanket, and tugged at the dead grass. "Timing was always a hindrance." He tossed the flimsy grass back and ran his fingers over the green stalks in front of him, then drew in a sharp breath.

"After your dad died, I promised to protect you, to be there for you. I didn't think it was a good time to pursue you while you were hurting. I didn't feel a need to rush things." He was silent for a beat. "As long as I spoke to you every day, I was cool waiting for the right time, but then you went out with Adam." His mouth pressed into a sharp line, and her stomach dropped at his anguish.

"It was just for—"

"To be a listening ear after his break-up," he finished for her, his voice terse.

She could be mad at him for sounding upset, but sympathy surged through her. After revisiting her past, with everything he'd done for her, she'd been foolish to betray him—at least, it seemed like she'd betrayed him.

But why didn't he say anything sooner? All those times he'd come home from college, and they went to the movies, strolled the beach, or caught up on a volleyball game, he'd harbored feelings for her and kept them to himself?

"When did you think it was ever going to be a good time to tell me?"

"I had this grand plan to surprise you. There were six weeks left in my residence at Olive Medical, and I was still waiting to hear from Virginia Medical for the private practice program."

The anguish in his voice engulfed her heart.

"But then you got engaged, and... I decided to stay for the fellowship program in Colorado."

If she didn't get engaged, he may have moved to Virginia. Maybe then she wouldn't have dealt with depression. Unwelcome tears were adhering to her eyes, and she blinked, hoping to clear them. She then took a sip of her soda, trying to ignore the random woodsy critters skittering back and forth.

After a few minutes of composing herself, she lay down on her stomach and faced him, needing to tell him more about her own feelings. "In eighth grade, I had a huge crush on you."

He arched his brow. "You had a terrible way of showing it. If I remember, you were busy crushing over all those boys who hung out at our house."

She brushed her hand to wave him off. "That was in tenth grade when I'd decided our friendship was more important than my crush. Dalia told me it was normal for me to feel attracted to you since you were the most handsome boy in school." A blush tingled up her neck over pointing that detail out, but she was relaying what her friend had said. She picked up a few more sunflower seeds and jiggled their shells in her hand. "She thought it would be awkward to mix romance with friendship since everyone saw us as brother and sister."

"Is that why you pushed me to go out with your friend?"

She cringed a bit. "Rochelle is not really my friend." Ever since he broke off with her that night at Darren's house, that friendship had stayed casual. Probably because Rochelle wanted Brittney to reconnect her to Lucas. "She was my buffer. I wanted to stop having fantasies about you."

"You did that to me?" He leaned forward, his voice light before he asked again. "Did you ever sense I had feelings for you too?"

With their heads tipped close together, he didn't break eye contact.

It had been confusing, especially when they had the best friends' kiss and he acted normal, but the day they had that practice kiss... She touched her lips. "After the practice kiss, I got a little bit scared. I never wanted to kiss anyone since." The way he'd looked at her with longing after the kiss had her thinking that if he wanted more from their friendship, he would make the first move. But the deaths of her parents within six months of each other left her downhearted, giving her no choice but to see Lucas as her brother, untouchable and off-limits. Because she needed him, she didn't dare mess things up.

Instead of answering his question, she said, "Without you, I don't know how I'd have made it through that first year after Mama's and Dad's deaths."

He cupped her chin. "I promised to never leave you then." Rubbing his thumb along her jaw, he kept his eyes downcast. "And I broke that promise, but I'm here now."

"I'm glad you are." And she meant it.

But the truth of it all was that she was still afraid to cross this line. He took off after they'd kissed last time, would he do it again? Forget about her the moment he returned to Denver?

"I'm not going to leave you," he said, tapping into her mind. His words were a pact, and the look in his eyes was the assurance she needed. "Not without letting you know, okay?"

She nodded.

"This is a do-over." He squeezed her hand, his eyes warm. "That's why I brought you here. I want to call you each night. I want to hear about your day. I want to laugh and cry with you again. All of it—like we used to."

His expression—full of promises, reverence, and so many emotions—made her chest tight. She shuddered and whispered, "Like we used to."

Where would his departure leave their romantic relationship? The unwanted thought surfaced, but she pushed it down. She didn't want to think about that, not now at least. He loved her as a friend and perhaps a girlfriend. At the moment, she was fine in her dream with the man of her dreams.

Yes, a dream was what she was in, and that was fine for today.

When they left the picnic area and the basket for the owner to pick up later, Brittney felt tempted to take off her sandals as Lucas clasped her hand in his while they sprinted through the tall stalks.

"My shoes." They kept getting stuck in gnarly twigs. "I can't go too fast." The way she wanted.

"There's no need to go too fast." He gave her a sideways glance, the adoration in his eyes making her heart swell.

The sunflowers were now facing west as the day's temperature dropped. Golden rays reflected a hue on Lucas's dark-blond hair. She didn't want to stop staring at him, and she was grateful he was holding her hand.

When they exited the field, the familiar lake, nestled beneath boulders and vegetation, was so serene and refreshing.

"Does the lake belong to the farmer, too?"

Ducks glided in the water. In the sky above, the geese flew in a pattern as if already calling it a day.

Adrenaline spiked, and an urge of recklessness, of doing something out of the ordinary, surged through her. Maybe being with Lucas made her feel this way.

"Ready for a swim?" She met his surprised gaze.

"You have a swimsuit somewhere?"

She was already bending and sliding off her sandals, then her earrings, and putting them on top of the sandals. "Who needs a swimsuit?"

Once, they'd swam in the same lake with their regular clothes.

She walked toward the boulders, climbing and wincing at the roughness of the rocks rubbing beneath her toes. She glanced back at Lucas, who was shaking his head, eyes aglow.

"This doesn't sound like you."

"You trained me well." She turned back to the water below her, pulling up her hands together, then springing off, squealing "Whee!" when she dove and the water splashed and her body sank in it. She popped her head above the surface, laughing. Refreshing coolness enveloped her as she pivoted to look at Lucas.

He was already leaping and shouting, "Cannonball!"

She touched her cheeks to keep them from hurting. She hadn't realized she'd been smiling most of the afternoon until the slight ache started in her cheeks.

"You got in after all!" she shouted, the echo of her voice vibrating around the lake.

"You can be very convincing, Brittney Young." He swam toward her, and she did the same, meeting him halfway. "What am I to do with you?" he asked, wrapping an arm around her waist and nuzzling her neck and her ear.

She was shivering, not from the cold water, but from his touch.

"I... don't know..." ...*what to do with you, either*. But her heart was beating too hard against his firm chest for her to finish. Could he feel it? Could be he did when his fleeting kisses brushed against her mouth and she greedily parted her lips, her hands darting into his damp hair. She was grateful when he lifted her up, her legs wrapping around his waist as he deepened the kiss.

Their breathing mingled, the cries of geese in the sky and the rhythm of their hearts creating the perfect beat for the sweet evening.

When they left the lake and walked back through the field, the sky was losing the last of its daylight, and one of her sandals came loose, tearing the straps.

Before she could say anything, Lucas lowered himself. "Get on my back."

She smirked, unbelieving of this man she adored. "I'm not as light as I was the last time you carried me." At the beach when she was seventeen. Did he realize how ridiculous this was?

"I'll not have you scrape your feet when we can barely see where we're going."

In protest, she put her hands on both shoulders to shimmy him out of the way, but he grasped her hands, secured them around his neck, and pulled her up to his back, then stood.

"Lucas, this is insane!" Laughter shook her chest.

"That's how you make me feel."

Her heart squeezed— there was such confidence in his words. Honestly, he'd driven her crazy. How could she not thank God for this, for Lucas, her best friend?

Today had been the best day ever.

She wrapped her arms around his shoulders and breathed in deeply of the sunflower scent and him. This excursion had started as childhood revisited, but now, with her arms around him and his kiss fresh on her lips, she wouldn't want to go back to childhood. She wouldn't want to be anywhere but here. "I don't want this day to be over."

"Well, it doesn't have to be." He was panting and breathing hard from carrying her. "We can stay up working the rest of the puzzle tonight."

Except... "There's church in the morning and a backyard camping trip in the evening."

If he slept that badly last time, who knew how he would sleep when the kids came over.

His sense of direction amazed her when they stepped out of the field and the Sorento came into view.

"Why did you say you wanted to come to church with me?"

Her arms tight around him, she peered at the last sunflowers they were passing, then tipped her face to the sun like the flowers were, but she was looking for Something brighter and bigger than the sun—Something that created it all. "Well, I told God"—or at least after listening to Lucas's prayer, that now made sense—"I *think* He's the one I was talking to when I cried out that I wanted a miracle for you to come home... to me and to restore our friendship." Going to church was the least she could do.

He stopped in front of the car and lowered himself for her to get down.

She'd been carried like a child. A blush crept up her neck. "Thanks."

"No." He stepped in front of her, placing his hands on her shoulders. Cold emanated from the dampness of her outfit, but Lucas's closeness and touch left her overheated. He then tucked a wet strand of hair from her face, his palm cupping her cheek when he finished. "Thank you for praying. I prayed for you, too, for God to give you peace and happiness."

She couldn't explain the swelling of her heart, a ball of something. This was pure joy. "I'm happy. When I'm with you."

CHAPTER 20

Sunday afternoon, Lucas drummed his hands on the home office table as he lip-synced to a Bon Jovi song from the CD that Brit had put together. Unfortunately, the CD didn't work, but using the list she'd saved on the computer, he'd downloaded the music to his iCloud library.

After church with her and Grams, they ate lunch, and then he sequestered himself in the office to continue reading through Brit's manuscript. She'd completed much of her book and underestimated herself. The draft seemed surprisingly clean, and the book just needed touch-ups and clarification from the experts on the medical terms.

He leaned back in the swivel chair, natural light streaming through the horizontal blinds. It didn't seem too late, but the computer screen said it was three p.m. Ryan would be dropping off the kids soon.

Lucas scooted forward and typed up the page to access his email for the video link. He and Ryan had agreed to use his time to drop off the kids. As he browsed his emails, he felt the air change in the room and his heart rate picking up. Just as his consciousness rarely let him down, he spun, and a grin lifted his face when he saw Brit.

He swallowed, almost biting his tongue while her lips spread wide and two deep dimples deepened in her cheeks as she leaned against the doorjamb. Even as casually as she was dressed in a peach-colored top tucked into olive-green shorts with a loose belt, she looked adorable.

She bit her lower lip. "I just wanted to see if you need anything."

I need you.

Even if he didn't need her help, he ushered her forward with a crook of a finger and patted his lap. "Yes, your computer is a bit hard to navigate."

"I'm not sitting on your lap!" Still, she inched forward. "We'll break the chair."

And I'll buy another.

The moment she bent and leaned to look at the computer, one whiff at her intoxicating scent had him curling his hand around her waist and settling her on his lap. As she predicted, the chair tipped and they fell. His back thudded to the carpet while his protective arm tightened around her and she landed on top of him.

They were both laughing.

"Where's Grams?" He tucked soft strands of hair behind her ear, plotting. He had to make up for all the fantasies he'd had of kissing her when he never could.

"She's on the porch." The words came out in a breathless rush. "She's so excited to see the kids."

"Really?" Their hearts were beating against each other, and he moved his hand to her neck, pulling her down closer to him. The moment their lips touched, he lost himself in her warmth, her sweet scent. Slowly, he explored her mouth. She tasted so good. Better than his wildest fantasies, better than he'd ever experienced. Brit sighed as they rolled around the carpet and he fought a moan when her fingers tangled through his hair.

There was so much to think about, so much unknown about their relationship. But right now, he was with the girl of his dreams, and something would eventually work out.

"How did you learn to kiss like that?" she asked when they pulled away facing each other. Her eyes were dreamy as she rubbed her fingers on his chin.

"It's easy when kissing the right person." Also, when it's two-sided. He tried to shove back the unwelcome memory of the rejected kiss. She was here now, in his arms, hopefully forever. She wanted him just as much. He curled a tress of her hair around his finger.

"It wasn't one-sided," she said as if she knew what he was thinking. "I kissed you back, remember?"

"Is that why you told Adam you kissed me?"

She nodded.

But, of course, she'd kissed him. Something tightened inside him, something that hadn't yet healed over that moment. "I left you no choice. I was whiny—you must have felt sorry for me."

After all, Brit was well known for her empathy.

She tsked. "You're not one for a pity party."

Her gentle hand caressed his stubble, and man, if their hearts beating against each other kept up that rhythm, someone might have a coronary. "I kissed you because you were irresistible."

Her breath tickled his neck when she shifted and rested her head on his beating heart. "You were the first person I kissed, the best friends' kiss, the practice kiss... and that final kiss before you disappeared." Her voice faltered as he rubbed her back. "I never wanted to kiss anyone but you."

Her confession staggered his mind, burning his chest. It was too hard to breathe, and instead, he squeezed her tight. After a few moments of comfortable silence, he managed, "I love you so much."

"I love you, too."

Adrenaline coursed through him, and when they finally stood and exited the office, he was grinning like a schoolboy.

"You're sure you will be okay hanging out with Destiny and the kids while I attend the video call?" He squeezed her hand, aware she was more introverted than he was.

"If Destiny is anything like you've told me, I can't wait to ask her all the gory details of your dates with her."

He pulled her arm toward him as she approached the front door, and his hand found the sensitive spot behind her ear, tickling her.

She squealed and wiggled and swatted at him. "Stop it!"

"Not stopping until you say you're not asking her anything of the sort."

Destiny had no dark secrets to reveal about him, but he liked tickling Brittney the way he'd done in the past. His hand went to another soft spot and tickled under her armpit.

She giggled so hard she probably couldn't breathe. "Okay"—she spoke between peals of laughter—"I'll not ask."

"Good." He pulled her to his side and swung open the door.

Grams grinned from ear to ear when she saw them, then shifted her gaze back to the road. She didn't say anything as she folded her hands on her lap.

What could he say? Grams was a character in her own way.

LESS THAN FIVE MINUTES later, Lucas shaded his eyes as Ryan's Highlander pulled up.

"They're here." Grams adjusted the bag of candy on her lap. Lucas had taken her to the grocery store, and she'd dedicated the shopping to all sorts of treats for the kids.

Eager to introduce her to his friend's family, he walked beside Brit toward the car as the three kids filed out, arguing about something.

"Your glitter is all over my telescope!" Pete, the middle child, wiped his hands on a telescope.

"Hello, if you cared so much about your precious telescope you would've put it in the back." Zoe, the youngest, stepped out with a hot-pink gift bag.

"You need to stop." Their older brother, Josh, scowled at them.

"Hey, guys!" Lucas shouted and the kids turned. Both boys sped toward him.

He high-fived the boys, and Zoe bounded in for her usual hug, her little curls tickling his chin.

"I want you to meet my friend Brit." He introduced the teens.

"I have something for you," Zoe told Brit after they shook hands. Then she reached for the sparkly purple handbag and handed it to Brit. Zoe folded her arms when Brit pulled out a canvas. "I drew it. Uncle Lucas said you love sunflowers."

Brit exchanged a look with him, her smile secretive and warm, before she studied the sunflower picture embossed with glittery seeds.

"Zoe, you're such a great artist." Brit set down the picture to engulf the child in a hug. The detailed sunflower drawing showed the promise of a burgeoning artist.

While Zoe chirped on about the drawing, Pete chatted about stargazing with his telescope, and Josh discussed some of the camping games he looked up online for them to play. Then Ryan and Destiny emerged, and Ryan asked the kids to grab their sleeping bags.

"This must be Brit." Destiny smiled. With her skin color slightly lighter than Brit's, they could pass as siblings except for her curly hair. Destiny hugged her like they'd known each other their whole lives, and her dear gesture warmed Lucas clear through. Then Destiny stepped out of the embrace, holding Brittney by the shoulders at arm's length. "I feel like I know you already."

"Lucas has told me so much about you, too." Brit tucked loose hair behind her ears, her shyness coming through, though she didn't appear uncomfortable.

Ryan took his wife's place and gave Brit a side hug. "It's been forever since I last saw you."

"I know." Brit grabbed his hands. "Lucas says you have six kids. Where are the other three?"

"You don't want to host troublemakers." Ryan winked, fondness rumbling in his voice.

"Send the kids over here!" Grams yelled.

So Ryan waved at her. "I better go say hello to Clarice."

When the kids returned, they walked toward the house. Grams greeted them by handing each one a huge Ziploc bag of treats, and Lucas chuckled. They'd be up all night if they ate all that. Good thing he'd finally gotten some sleep last night.

As the kids scrambled away to check out the tree house Lucas boasted about, Brit and Destiny offered to supervise in the backyard while Lucas and Ryan went inside for their meeting with Eric Stone, the CEO of a multibillion-dollar financial services company, who sponsored their hospital. Their friend Brady Sharp, who'd grown up next door to Ryan, had set up the meeting. Lucas shut the office door, the children's laughter still seeping in as Ryan booted up his laptop for the meeting.

"As you all know the purpose for this meeting..." Eric winced when he came on screen, his face pale, not the vibrancy Lucas remembered over the years they'd spoken at the annual hospital fundraisers. "Brady volunteered you both to help him with the Christmas fundraiser."

"I get to organize things, of course." Brady, also joining them online, rubbed at his tired eyes. For a moment, Lucas had forgotten the time difference between Uganda and Virginia. It was probably his bedtime. "Since you've both attended the event every year, I figured you could help show me the ropes."

"Not sure about the leadership part for me." Ryan rolled his chair near Lucas and slapped his shoulder. "But this guy just got chosen into a leadership role in his department. He will be a great asset in that area as I piggyback."

"I appreciate all you've done." Eric ran a hand over his hazel eyes. The dark circles around the rims made Lucas wonder when the guy had slept last. "Please pray for me..." Eric's voice faltered when he said they couldn't diagnose his lack of energy and ongoing fever.

Lucas's chest hurt for him. Eric had lost his wife and kids all in one year, yet he continued to be generous. With everything Eric had been through, he *still* talked about God's goodness and love.

I will never complain. Lucas had to remind himself because he had everything, while Eric was glorifying God and not blaming Him for the family he'd lost.

"I'm confident I'll be better by next year." Eric leaned back on the sofa, tilting his head back and putting a hand on his forehead. They didn't have to have Eric in the meeting, but he'd insisted on joining them to make sure Brady wasn't forcing Ryan and Lucas into doing something they weren't on board with.

"I think it's okay if you rest." Ryan voiced Lucas's thoughts.

Brady covered his mouth for a yawn. "The three of us can finish up."

"Thanks, guys." Sitting up, Eric logged off.

"Well... well..." Lucas rubbed his hands together ready to give Brady a hard time. "Just how are you going to organize this from clear across the globe?"

Ryan crossed his arms over his chest. "Exactly. I want to hear how you plan to make those meetings happen."

With a grin that seemed to shrug off his tiredness, Brady wagged a finger at them. "Ruth will be dealing with the organizational stuff. I'm sure she'll get better treatment from you troublemakers."

A successful entrepreneur from New York, Brady had fallen for Ruth on one of his business trips to Uganda, amazing Lucas by what love could do. It had turned Brady's life upside down, and he'd sold some of his properties to move to Uganda and help the underprivileged.

"So you volunteered your wife, too?" Leaning back, Lucas laced his hands behind his head.

"She's good at running charity events. In fact, you'll be glad she's involved rather than having me be in charge."

When Ryan asked about her, Brady told them about the two months they planned to stay when they came to the US in December. He asked about Ryan's wife, and the two went on acting like teenagers obsessed with their girlfriends. A twinge of something pierced Lucas. He wanted what his friends had. How close or how far was he from that perfect happily ever after?

For now, he and Brit were in some sort of a summer fling. He was leaving in less than eight days. They hadn't promised each other anything beyond whatever they had now, and he should be okay with it. But he wasn't.

"I gotta get going." Brady's farewell caused Lucas to focus on the screen where Brady stretched out his arms, yawning. "I have to wake up early for our village visit."

After they said goodbye, Ryan pushed his chair back and narrowed his gaze at Lucas. "So, what's going on with you and Brittney?"

"What do you mean?"

"You two seemed cozy when we pulled in."

It wasn't like they were holding hands or anything. But Lucas had always been transparent to Ryan. So he crossed one leg over the other. "We kissed."

Ryan arched his brow. "*And...?*"

So Lucas told him about their recent argument and how they'd finally talked about the past and reconciled.

"I know Brittney means more to you than a make-out situation." Ryan rubbed his shaven jaw. "Have you thought of the next steps?"

Next steps, right. "I got the promotion." Ryan knew that. Lucas texted him that night. "I have you guys. Colorado is... home." Even as he said the words, he felt like he was betraying someone.

Rocking back in his chair, Ryan crossed his arms again. "What is home to you?"

Hmm! Lucas drummed his hands on the desk, needing some time to think. "Home..." He thought of his apartment and the times he returned to an empty house, of ordering takeout, then of the feeling when he saw Brit, his family, and his grandparents' house.

"A happy place." Without Brit, it wouldn't be a happy place.

"And would that happy place be Soda Creek?"

He shrugged, ignoring the right response.

"Have you told Brittney about the promotion yet?"

"I will soon." They'd been so happy. He didn't want to make her sad by causing her to fret that he was walking out of her life again.

"Think through things, pray, and think again how long it's taken you to find the right person to replace Brittney."

He hadn't told Ryan he was on the prowl to replace Brit, but perhaps it's why they were such good friends. They understood each other. "I'm not looking for a replacement." He scowled. After all, how dare Ryan read his mind? "I could easily find anyone I want." *Yeah right.*

"I know." Looking smug, Ryan stood. "I also know your grandma is not commuting to Colorado if you plan to take Brittney with you."

"Wow, Dad, thanks for the heart-to-heart." Lucas stood and pushed the chair under the desk.

He had no idea what he was thinking. Obviously, he *hadn't* thought things through.

Why didn't Brit fall for him back then, before he got attached to Colorado, his job? He had a good thing going now, a promotion. Switching hospitals would mean a pay cut to a start-up salary. Good grief. He ran a hand over his face, not ready to make any changes, definitely not ready to start over and apply at a new hospital.

Soda Creek was his childhood home, not a place for him to stay as an adult. Why, oh why, were there so many whys and what-ifs?

CHAPTER 21

Brittney had enjoyed hanging out with Destiny as the kids, all fascinated by the tree house, spent most of the time climbing up and down as they role-played some game with Josh slaying Pete and Zoe. Clarice had joined them on the back porch later, while the boys kicked a soccer ball they'd brought with them. Zoe stayed by Clarice's side, asking all about sewing when Clarice showed off her quilts.

When Destiny talked about her upbringing in foster care, Brittney shared about her parents' deaths. Destiny told Brit how her faith in God had carried her through her pain and loss, saying, "Someday we all die, but what happens after we die? Where do we end up?" She'd emphasized the many blessings she credited God for, like the kids and Ryan.

All those things left Brittney thinking about her life while she fixed more lemonade for her guests. Lucas and his family were the biggest blessings in her life. The preacher's words from that morning rang through her mind, teaching about faith and believing in what you didn't see or know.

That's how she felt with God. He was invisible, yet signs of His power were everywhere.

She wasn't angry at Him for taking her parents because she hadn't thought of God's hand over who died and who lived. It now sounded foolish that she'd never thought that deeply about Who created her.

If Destiny wasn't angry after the life she'd had, it was probably good that Brittney didn't have to blame God for anything, while she'd never asked Him to save her parents' lives. She'd already had her share of anger after Lucas left, and that had only taken her to a dark place, a place she'd rather not go to again.

When she set the glass dispenser on the table, Destiny poured herself a glass and glanced at her phone.

"Ryan and I have reservations at five," she apologized, leading everyone back to the house.

Destiny and Ryan said their goodbyes while the kids rubbed Midnight's back. She'd come out of hiding after the guests walked in and out of the house.

By their vehicle, Destiny embraced Brittney in a tight warm hug, and Brittney fell into her embrace. Destiny's hair smelled of coconut and vanilla.

"When you come visit Colorado, we should go dancing for fun." Destiny spoke with such enthusiasm.

Even if she'd only danced with Lucas, Brittney could see herself going dancing with her new friend. But going to Colorado was not an option, not any time soon. She couldn't leave Clarice. Still, she said, "That will be fun."

Destiny's vibrant curls bounced over her shoulders as she wrapped her arms around Zoe and kissed her forehead with motherly affection.

Then the boys gave her tender side hugs, saying they loved her, and she responded with the same affection. To their uncle Ryan, they gave high fives as he reminded them to behave and be helpful. Then they were off to the tree house.

With the way Destiny portrayed her love for the kids and their close resemblance to her, it would be easy to assume they were her biological kids. She'd said she and Ryan now had two biological kids.

"Thanks so much for having the kids come camping." Destiny grinned at both Lucas and Brittney. "We owe you two big time."

You two. She said it like she knew Brittney and Lucas were a couple.

"Don't worry." Brittney waved her off, already looking forward to revisiting her babysitting skills of long ago, even if Zoe looked about the age Brittney had been when she'd been a babysitter.

"It's unfortunate for you, Brittney"—Ryan punched Lucas's shoulder—"but this guy has to pay back for all the cookies he eats at our house."

Lucas winced dramatically, shaking his head. "I knew someday it'd all come back to bite me. I'll have to be careful next time."

When Ryan and Destiny got into their vehicle, Brittney stood back while Lucas engaged in casual banter, leaning his head into the car window.

She understood why her best friend had asked Destiny out even if it was fake. Destiny and Lucas had a few things in common. Animation, adventure, and dancing. Lucas always loved to dance, and would get Brittney to dance with him in the backyard or wherever they'd been hanging out when he brought along a cassette player. He'd even snuck her into a dance hall on her sixteenth birthday. One of his friends' brothers was a DJ and got them in.

"What are you smiling about?" Lucas nudged her shoulder.

A thrill coursed through her at the sight of him. With his smile so deep, her heart bounded as he took her hand and squeezed it.

"Destiny's nice," was all she admitted as they walked back to the house.

"I'll take it you two had a good visit?"

She was looking forward to seeing her new friend again. Lately, she rarely spoke to her friend, Dalia, who now lived in Poland. That, and having elderly people as her friends had its benefits, but it was nice to know more people close to her age. Destiny was a few years younger—Brit had done the math when Destiny told her how old she was when her dad died. "Did you say they're coming to the wedding?"

"Only for the wedding eve. They have to go back on Saturday."

"At least we'll have enough people playing volleyball." She hoped Destiny played.

"Exactly why I twisted Ryan's arm into coming."

Instead of grilling, the kids wanted pizza. Clarice was just as happy, since Brittney hadn't let her eat pizza in a long time. Clarice said good night at six and handed Zoe her camera, insisting she take everyone's pictures. Zoe, obviously the right person for the task, responded with enthusiasm.

She took pictures while Lucas and the boys set up the two tents, and snapped pictures during their games of horseshoes and football, which Zoe didn't want to be a part of. "I don't want to be tackled," she'd insisted while capturing a picture of the sunset.

They were all sweating when they finished playing, and Brittney and Zoe went back to the house to shower. When they returned, Lucas took the boys to shower. Those showers were all pointless, though, once smoke billowed after they started a bonfire by the pond.

As the day lost its light, Brittney breathed in the smell of smoke, bug spray, and firewood, making for the perfect summer. The kids' excited chatter rang out while they roasted marshmallows in their camp chairs. Lucas's excitement as he kept up with the kids' energy made Brittney's heart squeeze. She wished she could start a family of her own. He'd be a great dad and husband.

Their gazes collided from across the fire, and the glow danced in his handsome face when he smiled before responding to Zoe's question about bears.

"We don't live so deep in the mountains." Then, his voice soothing, he told a bear tale his grandpa had shared with him.

"Miss Brittney?" Zoe tapped her shoulder after Lucas's story. "How long have you known Uncle Lucas?"

Brittney smacked a whizzing mosquito from her neck. "We grew up next door to each other."

"Oh." But the girl's bright eyes shone as if Brittney had said something else entirely.

The air was getting crisp, cooler when Lucas suggested they get ready for bed.

"We have to see the stars," Pete reminded them as he bounded to his propped-up telescope.

They all took turns spotting constellations they could see.

When they headed for their designated tents, Brittney lay down in the dark to be peppered by Zoe's curious questions.

"Do you and Uncle Lucas like each other?"

"We're best friends."

"How did you become besties?"

Brittney shifted in the sleeping bag. "We played together most of the time."

Zoe let out a loud yawn. "Will you marry him?"

Oh my, this child! So sweet and smart. Warmth filled Brittney at the thought of marrying Lucas. But how did Zoe know something was brewing between them? It wasn't as if they'd made out in front of the kids. Perhaps she'd done a terrible job schooling her features earlier. "What made you think of that?"

"You look at each other the same way Uncle and Destiny look at each other."

What was the right age to talk about romance? By twelve, Brittney'd had their best friends' kiss with Lucas, but no adult spoke to her about marriage. So it might not be the best topic. She rolled onto her side, tucking her hands under her cheek as she faced Zoe. "How did you learn to draw like that?"

"I've always been into art, but then Destiny signed me up in a drawing camp last summer. That took it to a whole new level!" Zoe nearly bounced as she flopped onto her side to face Brittney. "I learned so much about technique, and I'm going back again this year—so just you wait until I finish!"

Zoe switched onto her tummy, tucked her face against her arm, and kicked up her legs behind her, the sleeping bag staying firmly zipped around them. "Summer's so great. We're going to some summer concerts in the parks and the art walk...." Her voice was slowing.

"I love Destiny." She trailed off about how she came to be their uncle's wife, her words going softer and her breathing getting heavy.

As Zoe fell asleep, Brittney listened for sounds from the boys' tent, but could only hear the crickets.

Between the uncomfortable sleep pad and Zoe's proactive questions, Brit didn't count on sleeping for a while. Perhaps if she sat outside, the cool air would tire her out. Or maybe, by some miracle, Lucas would join her. She slid on a sweatshirt and cozy slippers, then wiggled out of the sleeping bag, not unzipping it, afraid to wake Zoe.

When she stepped out, Lucas's silhouette was outlined in the chair as he stared at the fire he'd relit. He turned at her footsteps. "Brit."

Lucas. Sweet anticipation was hot in her belly, leaving her glad she'd come out of the tent.

He stood and pulled another chair right next to his. As she plopped into the seat, he sat and spread his quilt over her legs, too, tucking them both into its coziness.

"I was hoping you'd come." Their shoulders brushed when he shifted, and she savored the warmth of his closeness.

"When did you get here?" she asked.

"As soon as the boys fell asleep."

"They must have been more tired than Zoe."

"Once I told them the legend of the tree house, they were out in no time."

"The Superman and Wonder Woman legend?"

"Yep. I told them the two heroes are still finding their happily ever after." He took her hand in his underneath the blanket. "At some point my fairy tale got them to sleep."

Easygoing Lucas. He could hang out with anyone and enlighten them without much effort. "You were always great with kids."

"If I remember, you were the one who took on the nanny job." Her first job at fourteen. She'd only done it for one year before the family moved.

"If it weren't for you always coming and entertaining the kids, I'd have been fired after one month."

He slid her hand from the blanket and lifted it to his mouth. His soft kiss sent shivers running up and down her spine. "You were great at feeding and sitting with them while you read. That's something I wasn't good at."

"Let's say we're a great team."

"That I can agree with."

They spoke about spontaneous topics. She asked more about his life in Denver in comparison to Soda Creek.

"It's a big city...." He told her the ups and downs of his job. "But I golf and mountain bike sometimes with Ryan. Now that I go to church on Sundays, I hang out with Ryan's family after church.... Not every week, of course."

Speaking of church brought to mind all her questions since her conversation with Destiny, then the church service itself.

"What is it like to believe in God?"

He was silent for a beat. "For me, it changed how I view things." He wrapped a strong arm around her shoulders. "That started when I felt something within, like a presence of contentment, peace, and joy.... It drove the desire for me to do the right thing, a desire to stay the course so I don't ever lose that feeling again."

Was she content? Probably not. She was still hoping her life would turn out different, still wishing she could have a family—so many things she wished to be, things she didn't have. She stared at the pond where soft ripples of water reflected the almost dying fire.

She wriggled in her chair. "Besides going to church, how did you come to a point of having faith and believing in God?"

With the fire dying, the night's chill stalked them, so he pulled the blanket up to their chests. He cleared his throat. "Emptiness... Brokenness... I could see how happy Destiny was. Then, when Ryan made a change in his life, he spoke about God in ways I hadn't known before. The way they trusted God when they'd experienced such loss had me curious. If I could believe in anything, why not give this God a chance?"

As she pondered, something howled in the distance, the sound lonely and aching as if it, too, was crying out to God. *Emptiness, brokenness.* "What kind of brokenness?"

"Huh?"

"I mean, I wouldn't take you for someone who's broken or empty." He was always cheerful.

He drew out a breath, his hand still strong on her shoulder. "If only you knew how I love you." His hoarse voice ruffled her hair. "Always loved you. When I thought I couldn't have you as my forever, my life went from hope to despair, just like that."

A sudden heaviness gripped her heart. Why, oh why, had she accepted Adam's proposal? Why hadn't Lucas told her he was in love with her much earlier? Why had she made all those decisions without consulting her friend?

When Lucas left after the wedding, would she still be happy? Would she have the kind of contentment he had?

"Hey, it's okay." He kissed her cheek and tightened his arm around her.

"Faith," she whispered, unsure of how it all blended into her mistakes and consequences. "I don't know."

"You don't have to understand. It's believing in what you can't see, and only God can give you the grace to believe." Speaking so gently, he said words similar to what the preacher had taught earlier. "If you tell God you want to know, He will give you the answers."

Somehow, his assurance made her hopeful she could talk to God. She had before, and He'd answered her prayer. Maybe—just maybe—she might dig deeper to find out what brought contentment.

CHAPTER 22

Lucas patted Midnight's back in gentle strokes after she polished off the meaty food in her ceramic bowl. "Now you should drink some of your water." He spoke to the cat, then stood, taking the bowl to the sink and cleaning it. After washing his hands, he reached for the washcloth on the fridge to dry them.

The time on the stove showed six fifteen. Still fifteen minutes before the designated time to meet Brit for their morning run, like they'd done so far this week.

Things between them had taken a major leap, and since the night they'd camped with the kids, she'd had further—and deeper—questions about God, faith, and how one can acquire faith in God. Not being as knowledgeable, Lucas had taken her to a Christian bookstore on Main Street and let her choose a Bible, telling her to start from the beginning, and sharing his own slow process of learning how the world came into existence.

Besides talking about God and running each morning, they walked Grams around the block, and he and Brit went ballroom dancing on Monday. Lucas watched her teach her aerobics class on Tuesday, and yesterday, he'd gone with her to the disability center, where her tenderness amazed him as she interacted with the residents, played board games with some, and read stories to others.

Best of all, he kissed Brit every day. Morning kisses, spontaneous lingering kisses whenever they were alone by the pond, and goodnight kisses that stirred a kind of desire he'd never experienced... a desire that kept him tossing and turning at night. He'd never loved her more.

But what was he going to do? He'd said yes to the job without thinking or praying about it.

When he'd come to Soda Creek, he hadn't expected Brit to fall in love with him.

He spun toward muffled footsteps as she emerged from the hall. He could scarcely breathe when she smiled at him shyly.

With her hair pulled back in a high ponytail and a turquoise top over mid-calf tights, she was still the gorgeous athletic girl he remembered. She'd been the fastest runner among the girls' track team in school, and she'd beat him several times whenever they'd raced.

"Hey, beautiful," he whispered when she was within reach, his hands sliding around her waist.

"Hello, yourself." She tiptoed and pressed a soft kiss on his lips. It was supposed to be a fleeting kiss when he kissed her back, but when she parted her mouth in an invitation for more, what was a man in his state supposed to do?

The roar of a motorcycle outside interfered with their moment, and they tore apart.

Peering toward the noise, she pursed her lips. "I've never heard of a motorcycle on our street."

"Have you forgotten I once had a motorcycle that we drove on Oak Lane a few times?"

She shrugged as they walked toward the front door. "You know what I mean. But your motorcycle was centuries ago."

When he opened the door, he blinked, then exchanged a look with Brit. Her eyes had widened, perhaps just as surprised to see Adam walking toward the house, a motorcycle helmet in hand.

"Good morning to you, too," Adam said sarcastically. "Where are you headed this early?"

"That's what I should ask you." Lucas waved to the motorcycle, still surprised to see his brother here this early and riding a motorcycle. "Tomorrow is the bachelor party, wedding eve night, you know."

Instead of responding, Adam handed Lucas a key. "I'll be in debt for the first six months of marriage. But I crashed your bike, and I wanted to make things right."

Lucas gaped at the key dangling from a familiar key ring as it danced in the morning light. He didn't need a motorcycle. "Adam, I know you're—"

"Spontaneous, yes, but this is something I've thought through." He beckoned them. "Come see. You may not even like it."

Lucas was still frozen in place when Brit tugged at his hand. "Let's go see."

And wow. Lucas trailed a hand over the olive-green fenders. "This is way fancier than my motorcycle."

"You went all in for a BMW?" Brit walked around, assessing the dirt bike as she touched the slide panels.

"The R 1200 GS." Adam nodded approvingly, his chest puffing up.

Adam had chosen an enduro—an adventure bike, yet street legal, too. Lucas gripped the leather handlebars, his hands itching to take it for a spin. But how could he accept this from Adam? "Don't hold me accountable for your debt."

Brit tapped the front fender. "This is the same green shade your old bike had."

"I switched out a few pieces to add some personal touches."

He'd probably added some pieces from Lucas's old bike. Wanting to take it for a spin, Lucas asked, "Are you off today?"

"Yes, even Livy is, for a change." Adam peered at the road. "She's picking me up. She wants to go to the art museum, of all places."

While they were admiring the motorcycle, Adam told them his plans with his fiancée that day. They were taking a slow day to themselves before the big family event at the beach tomorrow.

Soon, Olivia's Fiesta pulled up. Lucas and Brit walked over to say hello, and said their goodbyes when Adam stepped into the passenger seat.

"I left your title with Mom and Dad."

"Thanks." Lucas was still taking all this in, unsure of whether he liked the idea of his brother going into debt on his account. He didn't need a motorcycle—but if he was going to get one, Adam couldn't have chosen a better one for Lucas's adventuresome spirit.

Spending unnecessary funds shipping it to Denver wasn't wise either.

"Adam will be okay. If you give back the bike, he will feel guilty." Brit read Lucas's thoughts. How did she know what he was thinking? Perhaps Adam was growing up and owning up to his mistakes.

Lucas shook his head, amused as he met with her glowing smile. She took the helmet from the motorcycle. Lucas hadn't even seen Adam put it there. "Are you going to test-drive it?"

"After we get you a helmet." Perhaps they could run all the way to town and buy one.

"I still have the one you got me years ago," she said. "Your old one is still there, too. Not sure how up-to-date it is...."

He handed her the keys. "Let's postpone the run. We're going for a ride."

With a frazzled look, she eyed the keys.

"You should wear the new helmet if you can help me find my old one. You're driving."

But she was shaking her head. "It's your motorcycle."

Holding her hand, he led her back to the house. "You didn't have a problem being the first to test-drive my first car or my first motorbike. Why should this be any different?"

She didn't argue, and while she looked for his helmet, he wrote a note for Grams and left it on top of her magazine stash in case they stayed longer than expected.

After Brit brought their helmets, she said, "I just remembered that you need a license to ride a motorcycle on the road. Unless you have one, I don't think we can bike."

Lucas slapped his forehead and threw his head back. His heart sank. "I'd forgotten about the license."

But while they had their helmets, going around the block shouldn't be complicated. And he told Brit.

Hesitant, she eyed the lane. "It's a quiet street." She then shook her head, the corners of her lips lifting. "What am I going to do with you, troublemaker?"

"You're the source of my troublemaking." He strapped his helmet on.

In less than twenty minutes, they were riding on the wide street and on to the next. With homes spread apart, they only saw one neighbor, Zebadiah, who was sipping coffee on his front porch, and he waved at them.

When they returned and parked the bike in the driveway, Lucas let Brit decide their plans for the day.

Seeming energized after their ride, she wanted to drive them into town before breakfast. Lucas sat in the passenger seat of her car as she drove through the quiet neighborhood. As they arrived in town, a few shops were just opening their doors.

Brit parked in front of an old store with a big flag flapping past the rooftops of the shops. Since the store sold antique toy classic cars, she bought a Mercedes 300SL Gullwing, her dad's favorite car. She ran a finger over the little roadster and kept her chin tucked down. "I thought it would be a good time to visit the cemetery."

Lucas couldn't agree more.

After another stop at the flower shop to get a daisy bouquet for her mom's grave, Lucas suggested they stop at the game shop on Main Street. He bought a board game of checkers.

"I always hated board games until that day we played with your dad." Even though it hadn't been as fun, the game of checkers held a special memory of Brit's dad, a memory of the first day he met Brit, the day he was feeling downhearted when Brit and her family lifted his spirits.

She slid her hand into his. "Playing checkers is a great idea."

At the cemetery, they sat on the soft grass in front of the two tombstones as they paid their tributes with things they remembered about Brit's parents. Lucas beat her at a game of checkers.

"You taught him well, Dad." Brit smiled, taking Lucas's hand in hers. Her eyes were shiny, and she let out a shuddered breath, then asked him to pray.

They'd never been church-goers, but that could be because Marjorie dreaded the process it took to get Ronald in the car. Lucas clasped Brit's hand and closed his eyes.

"Thank You, God, for their time on earth and the impact they made in Brit's life, my life...." Watching Ronald's inability to move had helped Lucas appreciate his own good health, made him feel compassion for people with disabilities whenever he came across them.

"And, God"—Brit's voice trembled—"tell them that I miss them."

Lucas wrapped his arms around her, his throat thick with emotion. They stayed there in silence as he held her, not ever wanting to let go.

THE NEXT DAY, LUCAS was panting, sweat dripping down his forehead when he leaped to slam the volleyball back over the net.

"Great job!" Rochelle squealed right behind his ear before springing in front of him for a high five like she'd done for the last

THE PHYSICIAN'S HELPER 235

fifteen minutes or so, when she'd asked if she could join his side since they were one player short.

Brit was the best player in the group, and everyone agreed it wouldn't be fair for Lucas to be on her team. Adam claimed Lucas was just as good as Brit. It wasn't true, unless Rochelle's constant high fives distracted Brit. She'd given sloppy serves and dropped the ball three times. Not that Lucas was keeping track, or anything—maybe he was.

The family and wedding party had checked into the resort earlier that day, and he'd spent most of the midmorning and early afternoon swimming and surfing with Adam and the two men in the wedding party. Lucas was surprised to still be standing and, of all things, playing volleyball.

Ryan served and scored another point. Their team was ahead by five, yet they'd been behind by seven before Rochelle showed up. Lucas glanced at the side where the parents and grandparents sat in a semicircle of canvas chairs, talking as they watched the game.

Panting and grunting rebounded over the sound as the ball bounced to Brit's side before it flew over to Lucas's side. Adam leaped for the ball and hit it before Rochelle reached for it. But she missed, and the ball landed on the soft sand instead.

Lucas served again and scored another point, sending Rochelle rushing over for another round of high fives. His gaze instinctively darted across to Brit. Their gazes caught, and she rolled her eyes—their brown depths ablaze.

He bit back a smile at her jealousy. There was comfort in knowing he wasn't alone in this love dilemma, and she wanted him as much as he wanted her. He shrugged as Rochelle dove for the ball in front of him.

When they took a break, warm sand squeaked beneath his feet as he crossed over to seek out Brit, but Rochelle fell in step behind him. Ignoring her and the crowd, he shuffled through while maintaining a steady gaze on Brit. She was talking to Destiny, but he needed to talk to her before their final round.

"I can't catch up," Rochelle's breathless and squeaky voice called out.

"See you in a few." He didn't glance back.

Brit and Destiny turned when he approached, and suddenly self-conscious, he wiped sweat from his forehead with his palm.

Destiny looked over his shoulder, probably at his pursuer. Before he could politely interfere to ask for Brit, Destiny was putting out a hand, and he realized it was not intended for him.

"You're the wedding organizer." She introduced herself to Rochelle.

He'd have to thank Destiny in the future. He whisked Brit away, taking her hand in the crook of his arm, and led her from the onlookers.

"Where are we going?" she asked breathlessly.

He didn't respond until they arrived at a cluster of palm trees on the beach. She let go of his hand, leaned against one trunk, and crossed her arms. She was so adorable, tempting him with those round lips she tried to put in a pout.

Leaning closer, he braced both hands on the trunk just above her head.

Her breath hitched, and her tantalizing scent, mixed with the ocean's brine, sent a rush of adrenaline down his spine. He bent and captured her mouth with his, kissing her senseless, and she slid her arms around his neck, kissing him back until they were both breathless.

"Lucas." Her soft voice swirled through his senses when they eased out of the kiss.

"You're distracted, and your team is losing."

"Why do you care if my team loses?" She bit her lower lip.

"Because I'm nice." He ran a hand over the tress of hair that escaped from the ponytail, then took her hand, putting her palm to his beating heart. "Don't be jealous of Rochelle. It's always you. Always."

The tension left her shoulders. "I—It's annoying when she flirts with you." Brit stared at the gentle lap of water sweeping to the sand. "I'll try not to."

"That's my girl." He wrapped her in his arms for an embrace and gave her a fleeting kiss on the lips before he broke away and started sprinting. "First one back!"

"What?" Laughter rang in her voice as she sprinted behind him. "You cheated!"

Lucas made it to the volleyball area just as she caught up to him.

After another forty or so minutes, her team ended up beating his by two points. He'd said goodbye to Ryan and his family, then Dad took his parents back to the hotel room, and Brit went with Emery and the rest of the girls in the bridal party to have massages. Most people, also seeming to need a break, had left.

While Lucas stayed with Grams and Mom, Mom shuffled her feet in the sand. "You and Brittney had a battle going on during the game."

"That girl has been the happiest I've seen in such a long time." Grams's pale blue eyes seeped into him like water on the shore. "I sure hope you don't leave her behind."

"Grams, I leave on Monday." Not that Grams wasn't aware. Even if it didn't make sense, he still asked, "What if you and Brit came to live with me?"

Letting out a mirthless laugh, Grams looked down at her scruffy hands. "My dearest child, even if I make it through the drive, I'm too old to start in a new place. A city worst of all."

He understood.

"But you should take Brittney."

Not when Grams felt comfortable with her. "I can't do that to you. Who will take care of you?"

"Right here." Mom pointed a finger to her chest. "That's if your grandma doesn't fire me before I start."

Grams dismissed Mom with a wave. "I'm too old to put up with you barking orders at me."

Eyes aglow and lips twitching, Mom shook her head. "I still think that coffee isn't good for you."

"See what I'm talking about?" Grams cocked her head. No way would she let her daughter give her any form of instruction. "I'll be fine, though. I read in the church pamphlet that they help widows and seniors."

When he'd taken Grams to church, she'd picked up a couple of pamphlets.

"You should invite your mother and your father to go with us on Sunday," she added.

A thrill swept through Lucas. Grams wanted to go back to church! But staying at the beach tomorrow would make it a challenge for her. "It'll be an early start. Maybe you could go with them next week."

"I want to go this Sunday." She shifted in the chair. "If possible, I would also like to go back home tomorrow night."

"I'll talk to your dad." Mom patted Lucas's forearm. "Maybe we can join you for church, too."

It wasn't definite, but it *was* a glimpse of hope that could turn into something. Even though he'd paid for two nights, he wouldn't consider it a loss by not staying the second night. He'd paid a flat group rate for the rooms.

He gave Grams an assuring nod. "I'd like to go to church, too."

"Good." She ran her hands over her floral skirt, eyeing him before she asked, "Have you thought about staying?"

Oops. He hadn't been able to tell Grams about his new commitment. He lowered himself and sat in the sand, drawing a heart as he delayed his response.

"I just accepted a position as chief anesthesiologist." His heart felt heavy at the confession. Could he have asked HR to give him some time to think about it?

Mom's eyes lit up, and she scooted to the edge of her chair, leaning toward him and stretching her hand to touch his cheek. "Honey, I'm so proud of you."

"I'm always proud, you know." Her gaze distant, Grams peered at the ocean. "What did Brittney say?"

Lucas winced, gripping his neck—Ryan, now Mom and Grams knew. But he hadn't told Brit.

"Oh, child." Low and soft, Grams's voice washed over him. "She doesn't know?"

Her obvious distress heightened his guilt. But he couldn't say anything yet. Not until... "Tomorrow. I don't want to ruin the wedding."

Grams nodded. "Whatever happens, just don't disappear like you did last time."

He still couldn't believe he'd done that. "I won't." No way would he do that to her or himself.

"By the way, your brother told me what you did." Mom changed the topic. "I'm so so proud of you." The last words were hoarse, and Lucas pulled in a deep breath.

"You," he said, tilting his head to Mom, then Grams, "and Dad are the teachers of my actions."

Mom laughed, and Grams shook her head and said, "That's my Luke."

He still had tonight, tomorrow, and Sunday to make his time with Brit count.

CHAPTER 23

After the rehearsal dinner, Brittney sat on the leather bench in the hotel lobby. Over the fountain, the chandelier lights refracted on its spewing water drops, haloing it in a rainbow of prisms. She twisted, leaning her side against the back of the bench and draping her arm atop the backrest, her mind wandering to the filet mignon dinner she'd barely tasted. She'd been too distracted by Lucas's shoulder brushing against hers, and Adam and Olivia staring at each other with simmering looks. How could she help thinking about her future with Lucas?

How soon—and *if*—they'd make it to their happily ever after occupied her thoughts. He was leaving, that she was aware of, but she wanted a long-term plan. Of course, it was too soon to know such details when they'd been sort of a couple for less than two weeks.

"Hello, stranger."

A thrill ran through her at the sound of his deep voice. She didn't need to turn to know he'd sunk down on the bench behind her, and soon, the top of his back touched hers. So he'd mirrored her position, sideways on the bench and back to back.

She craned her neck, and nearly at the same time, he did, too. Their heads were almost touching when she spoke. "Shouldn't the best man be tending to the groom?"

"The groom is doing just fine with his bride sitting next to him."

Oh my. She tried not to read too much into his response. He meant Adam and Olivia, not Lucas and Brit, but goodness! He looked so handsome with the new look. Instead of having a clean shave, he'd groomed the stubble so perfectly. Her fingers itched to touch his strong jaw.

She remembered she was in a public place when the phone rang and the woman behind the counter answered it. Although they were a few yards away from the receptionist, it would still be quite a scene if she caressed his jaw.

"A penny for your thoughts?" His warm breath against her cheek ignited a trail of goose bumps down to her arms. Good thing her long-sleeved top hid everything.

Her gaze darted to his mouth, and her heart raced when his eyebrow lifted in question.

"Swimming," was the first word that came out of her mouth. Huh? Swimming? "I mean..." What did he ask her again?

"You're up to no good, Brittney Young." Laughing, he stood and walked around to her side. He put out his hand for her. "Come with me."

To where? Anticipation rose as she accepted his offered hand. "And now who's up to no good?"

"As long as we don't get caught, I don't plan to break the law."

"That would be something if the best man gets in trouble before the wedding."

Soft, welcoming lights illuminated the rest of the lobby. Natural plants, nestled in big decorative pots in the two corners toward the entrance, lent a cozy feeling. The door split open as they approached, and they stood aside to let a middle-aged couple haul their luggage through.

Outside, the evening air was slightly cool, but they were both dressed in long sleeves. Lucas looked handsome in his gray sweater.

Between the hotel's security lights and the different buildings they passed, plenty of light showed their way to the building closest to the beach. "This is where the reception will take place." Lucas spread out his arms. "If weather permits, the ceremony will be outside."

"That will be beautiful." The summer they'd worked here, the beach weddings had looked so romantic.

"Adam and Olivia seem to like the place." Lucas pried open the door as if he owned the place.

"Shouldn't this be locked?"

"Rochelle made an exception."

Rochelle! Her heart twisted, but it bounced back when he grinned that boyish grin that melted her insides. *He's here with me and not Rochelle.*

"If it's of any comfort, I told her that you and I are a couple."

A couple. Brittney felt her chest thrust out at the confident way he'd said *couple.* From friends to being a couple. She liked that even more.

Lucas closed the door when they entered and flipped on the switch, illuminating the glistening festive lights strung across the ceiling.

"Wow." She had to spin around to get a better look at the white silk fabric draped over the beams and woven through the twinkling lights.

All the tables were set with cream table linens, and the room smelled of the fresh roses centered in decorative vases on each table. It made the place feel intimate and romantic.

"It looks nice, doesn't it?" he asked.

When she turned to him, he was pulling his phone out of his jeans pocket and walking to one of the front tables where he set it down.

As much as she hated to admit it... "Rochelle did a great job."

"She used to have a team in charge of decorating. Remember that time?" Lucas was bending bending as he scrolled through his phone. "We stayed up late cleaning one of the reception rooms?"

Brittney nodded, remembering the night the two of them had been assigned to disassemble the furniture after a wedding. "You asked the DJ to play 'Oh, What a Night.'"

He craned his neck, nodding with mischief dancing on his lips before he pressed his phone and the strings of a familiar tune sounded. He walked back to her, his eyes alight when he took her in his arms and started to move.

"Are you serious?" she said, although she didn't have it in her to protest. Unlike last time when the DJ had been their audience, today it was just her and Lucas.

With his free movement, he sure could dance, and it made following him so effortless—the way it had always been. She smiled to match his as he whirled her to what must be the dance floor. As she put her free hand on his shoulder, she felt light, already caught in his infectiously playful mood.

They covered the floor from the center to the left, and then back to the right, whirling and turning in tune to the music. Then they glided around the corner table and danced their way toward the panoramic window.

Outside, lights reflected over the water, adding to the night's tranquility.

She couldn't help her carefree laugh. Lucas grinned, staring down at her as the song faded.

Before they could still, the phone played another song, a slow song, one of the songs she'd added to the list she'd put together for him.

"This is good practice for tomorrow," he murmured as he fit his hands around her waist. "It's perfect for us to calm down after that fast-paced song."

Her heart was racing now, more from the closeness than the fast carefree tune they'd danced to earlier. She slid her hands toward his shoulders as they shifted from one foot to another.

"You were always a great dance partner." His breath fogged over her, his hands burning against her back as he moved them. Had she known about tonight's plans, she may have opted for a different outfit rather than the long-sleeved top. She was hot and now sweating.

She looked up into his brown eyes. "You're the only person I've ever danced with." That should tell him something. "You make it easy for me to feel the music."

"Well then, we can dance each night... when we video chat." His face turned serious, his hands tense around her waist before he pressed his lips together and pulled her tight against him, resting her head on his chest.

"You're okay?"

He buried his head in her hair, inhaling deeply. "Yeah."

Something was wrong. And as if to confirm her thoughts, he'd stopped moving by the time the song wound down.

She eased out of their embrace, wanting to meet his gaze, to know he was okay. "Talk to me." The last thing she needed was a redo of that awful loss ten years ago.

He cupped a hand on her cheek in a slow movement that weakened her knees. His eyes shone beneath the twinkling lights, and the look in them made her swallow. Love, reverence, and so much more poured from his soul, and her heart bloomed when he spoke in a low voice. "You mean the world to me."

How could he love her this much? What did she do to deserve him? If anything, he'd always been her knight in shining armor. He loved her without expecting anything. Tears clogged her throat, and she tightened her arms around his waist, squeezing him tight and swallowing against the lump. "You mean... the world to me, too."

WARM AFTERNOON AIR drifted around them, and the sun shone high in the sky when Brittney and the other guests gathered in the canvas tent. All focused on the preacher addressing Olivia and Adam about the gift of marriage.

Two days ago, the resort's motivational speaker had come down with shingles, so Lucas asked the preacher from the church, who was thankfully available, to conduct the wedding.

Brittney's gaze shifted from the preacher to the best man, who lit her heart, only to find him looking at her. Her stomach somersaulted. He looked so handsome in the navy suit and bow tie he was now fidgeting with.

The preacher went on about bearing each other's burdens....

From the corner seats in the same front row as Brittney, Clarice, Emery, Sandra, and Gary looked on.

The flowers and bows tied to the tent poles and the decorations hanging inside the tent made for a romantic and intimate feel. Olivia looked beautiful in her white dress and bouquet of red roses splashed with white flower fillers.

The preacher asked Adam and Olivia to face each other as he continued with his thoughts of a marriage founded with God at the core. The adoration as Olivia stared into Adam's eyes and the blush on Adam's face evidenced how they both felt for each other.

Brittney's heart squeezed with a mix of joy and envy. She was happy for the couple but wished it were her and Lucas. If only she'd not made that wrong choice to go out with Adam, perhaps it would be hers and Lucas's wedding. That was in the past, and she couldn't fix what was already done. But she could do something today. So, she shifted her eyes to Lucas, who was looking at her, his eyes a little glassy as if he'd read her thoughts. Her lips tilted upward. A moment of sweet internal communication washed between them like the gentle sway of water against sand. Would anyone else ever understand her or love her the way Lucas did?

"Olivia"—the preacher's voice sounded against the breeze—"repeat after me."

Brittney tore her gaze from Lucas as Olivia repeated her vows, her gaze planted firmly on her groom. She then took the ring from Lucas and slid it onto Adam's ring finger.

Adam said the same: "To have and to hold, from this day forward, for better, for worse." His voice came low and unwavering. "Till death do us part."

The preacher then asked them to share their written vows and handed Olivia his microphone for her to read hers first.

"Adam." Her eyes were so deep as she looked into his. "You make me laugh...."

Funny, Brittney never laughed much around Adam. Love was interesting that way. Some people just clicked in different ways.

Now that she liked Lucas, what were the next steps?

People clapped, and Olivia passed the microphone to her groom. Brittney was attentive, more curious as to what Adam wrote since Lucas had insisted he write his own vows.

"Liv." Adam cleared his throat, holding Olivia's hands as he looked at her with such tenderness—a softness Brittney didn't remember noticing when they dated. "I'm not poetic."

As guests laughed, he continued, "I'm a man without a plan. That's why I didn't even write anything down. I disassemble metal, then put it together. A mechanic who fixes cars, but sometimes I can't even fix them." He swallowed. "When it comes to matters of the heart, I know one thing. I can't fix the hole in my heart—only you can."

Olivia eased her hand out of his and wiped at her eyes.

As the crowd oohed and aahed, Brittney's eyes tingled at the simplicity of his vows, yet so genuine. Just typical Adam.

"You may now kiss your bride."

People applauded while the couple shared their official kiss. The preacher then announced that Adam had one more thing to say.

Adam adjusted his bow tie and cleared his voice. "I wanted to thank my brother, Lucas. Without him..." He acknowledged Lucas for all the effort he'd put through for them to have a perfect wedding.

When Adam finished, Olivia embraced Lucas and so did Adam before he spoke through the cordless microphone. "My brother had helped me write vows that I didn't want to go to waste."

Lucas's face took on a certain shade of pink when he gave Adam a don't-you-dare look.

But Adam continued, "So I humbly ask please..." Lucas's eyes were wide as Adam added that innocent plea to his expression. "You had the vows memorized last time. Can you recite whatever you remember for me?"

Lucas's mouth slid open, his eyes widening. "Now?"

Adam nodded.

And people clapped, urging Lucas and leaving him no choice but to do as asked.

"Is it illegal to press charges against the groom?"

Laughter erupted from the tent, and the tension eased from Lucas's shoulders.

Although he didn't have a microphone, his voice was loud enough over the breeze and the sound of water carrying through the tent.

"I didn't expect this, but... I'm..." His face serious, he glanced at Brittney before continuing. "I'll do my best to remember what I wrote down. Of course, I'm not one for words, either, not this type, so I apologize in advance."

Brittney winked at him, hinting he had this down.

He gave a curt nod and surveyed the crowd. "Love is when you love someone so much that you'll give your life for them."

His gaze flickered back to Brittney. "When you are over-whelmed by that feeling, the words just flow, the vows and commit-ment to them are automatic. You promise and mean it when you say that you will love them unconditionally."

His face turned serious, eyes intent on Brittney still. "You'll be there to cry with them when they fall, to laugh with them when they achieve their dreams, and you'll support them in everything, even if you don't feel like it...."

Just like he'd supported her and loved her, even if they were not married. He'd held her when she cried, rejoiced with her when she was happy. Forget the last ten years, but the many years before then.

She shuddered, swallowing the tightening of her chest as a pow-erful feeling swept over her. With her heart racing and her stomach fluttering, she had no idea what to do with herself.

Lucas continued, "More importantly, you love them uncondi-tionally. The way Christ loves His church—loves us."

The chair was suddenly uncomfortable, and even if she wanted to, she couldn't tear her gaze away from him. Not only was he hand-some, but he was also kind and compassionate, and he loved her... *loved her!*

Warmth flooded her while applause erupted after Lucas's vows. Her lips parted and she mouthed, "I love you."

Lucas touched his heart and mouthed back, not seeming to care that he was standing in front of an audience, "I love you, too."

With that, he craned his neck to the couple after the applause died down. "Olivia, welcome to the family." Lucas faced the audience and spread his hands. "I hope I don't have to give a best-man speech anymore."

Loud cheers joined the clapping, and soon, they informed peo-ple where to go to the reception while family members stayed behind for photographs.

As the wedding march played for the happy couple to exit the tent, Brittney had a march in her own heart while her mind replayed the vows Lucas shared. She needed to be alone to savor and almost meditate on each word.

CHAPTER 24

Lucas rubbed at his aching jaw once the photographer announced she was done taking the photos. After smiling throughout the ceremony, the receiving line, and the photo shoot, he might never smile again if he didn't have to. Except smiling for Brit. His smile for her came automatically from deep within.

Thankfully, having her in the front row helped him maintain his smile through the ceremony. She'd also been an inspiration when Adam put him on the spot. Despite himself, he couldn't stop staring into those brown eyes, couldn't look away because he wanted her to know how he felt and what he'd do if she agreed to marry him someday.

Someday—when was that going to be? Swept by a longing for her, he drew in a deep breath to fill the hollow in his chest. She'd mouthed "I love you" to him, boldly doing it in public, but Grams had looked at Brit before staring at him. Nothing got past Grams where they were concerned.

At the reception hall, a pop song played while the wedding party entered. Lucas held the maid of honor's hand in the crook of his arm, following the two couples in front of him as people applauded over the music.

His eyes scanned the room for Brit, but she wasn't in sight. Where could she be?

He remained standing by his seat, like the rest of the room, as the DJ announced the bride and groom.

The chords of "You're My Light" strummed. Everyone turned to the entrance, and as soon as the happy couple emerged, people clapped and cheered until the bride and groom took their seats.

Lucas still didn't see Brit. She was hard to miss in her green dress. Grams would know. He made his way through the crowd, stopping and chatting with family members and Adam's friends. By the time he reached Grams at the family's table, his heart was racing from anxiety more than anything else.

She lifted her hand as if to embrace him when he bent down. Instead of the hug, her scratchy fingers touched his chin, and she whispered, "She went to get my medicine."

This woman was something else. He whispered his thanks, then headed out of the door.

Lucas welcomed the breeze, even if the sun was slowly making its way west and wasn't as warm as it had been earlier.

When he raised his gaze to the paved path leading to the hotel, his breath left his lungs at the sight of Brit headed toward him and the reception hall.

He pulled at his stifling bow tie. Adrenaline spiked. She was stunning—always—but today, with her dark hair in waves dancing over her shoulders and that scoop-neck dress gracing her lithe form... He swallowed. It hit just above the knee and fit her in all the right places.

"Hi." She waved as their gap narrowed. Her leg got off balance, and she straightened herself. "I'm not used to high heels."

When he reached her, he caressed a tress of her hair. "You're doing just fine in those shoes."

Golden specks shone in her dilated eyes.

He was so dehydrated, he realized when he tried to swallow. He should've gulped a glass of water from his family's table before he left.

"I liked your vows." She bit her lower lip, drawing him to give her luscious lips the attention they deserved, but an "excuse me" behind him interrupted him. Brit peered over his shoulder and rested a hand on his arm as they stepped to the side, in the sand.

She then lifted the tiny sparkly bag that fit in her palm. "I need to take Clarice her medicine."

"Of course." Lots in his eyes, he'd forgotten. "Can you meet me over by the palm trees?" He gestured to the clustered trees where he'd kissed her yesterday during the volleyball game.

"Sure."

Moments later, he eased out of his jacket and spread it on the sand next to him as Brit returned. He kissed her in greeting, grateful when she gripped his shirt collar and kissed him back with such urgency.

"Sorry." She touched her lips when she pulled back, her smile shy. "I didn't mean to go all out on you like that."

"When did you learn to kiss like that?" He tucked back her hair, remembering her saying she hadn't kissed anyone other than him, besides her chaste kiss with Adam.

"You." She playfully poked at his chest as she sat down on the jacket. "I guess it comes naturally when kissing the right person." She used his words from when he kissed her.

Whew. He took a seat next to her, part of his bottom sitting in the warm sand. They had a reception dinner, and he had a speech to give at some point. Good thing the dinner was buffet-style. They wouldn't be looking for him until after the first dance when he'd give the best-man speech.

Taking Brit's hand, he entwined his fingers through her softer ones, and they fit so perfectly. "I was thinking about you. When I came up with those vows."

"I know." Her words were barely a whisper. "You're... everything to me, Lucas." She shuddered as she rested her head on his shoulder. "I also know there are long-term plans—"

"About that," he interrupted, needing to be as honest as possible. "When I came home, I didn't expect things to be like this between us."

"I know."

He stared at the expansive ocean, taking in the deep breath he'd need before uttering the next words. "I wanted you and Grams to come with me—"

She shoved from his shoulder with downcast eyes. "Oh, Lucas, you know Clarice would never leave Soda Creek."

"I know." He then pressed his lips together, unsure of what to do. He'd prayed the last few days about it, but he still had no definite answer to the puzzle. "I got promoted to chief anesthesiologist, and I volunteered to help with the charity fundraiser in December."

She let out a shuddered breath and unclasped her hands from his. "I'm happy for you."

She looked anything but with her sagging shoulders as she pulled her knees up and hugged her legs. "As long as we can stay friends, I'll be okay."

"Brit." He touched her bare shoulder. "I want more than just friends."

Ignoring his touch, she stood. "I do, too. But we both know that won't work when we're far apart."

He opened his mouth to remind her about his friends, Brady and his wife, and how they'd dated long distance, but then he clamped it closed. In the end, Brady had to move to Uganda.

"If you knew you wouldn't stay, I don't even know what we were thinking to start a relationship like this." She threw her hand up, her brows creasing. "You can't move here, and I can't relocate there."

She was right.

As she gave him one long hard look, something shifted in her eyes and hardened the corners of her lips. "I'm headed back to see if Clarice needs my help." She started walking, her steps unsteady in the sand. She bent and took off the strappy heels, carrying them without a glance back.

His mind screamed for him to stand and go after her, but his feet were too weak to move.

Feeling sucker punched by the situation's hopelessness, Lucas turned back to the wide sea. With hands dangling over his knees, he spoke, hoping God could hear him.

"You created this huge ocean, and You command when a storm should come and when it shouldn't." He remembered the story he'd read in the Bible about creation, and in the New Testament about Jesus calming the storm. The ache in his heart raged like a storm in itself.

"Please, God, help me out." He ran a hand over his face and rubbed his burning eyes. "What can I do?"

He'd read about God speaking to people in the Bible, but he was probably too far from knowing and hearing His voice. The pain dug deep, claiming residence as it passed against his lungs, making his breaths shallow. He scrambled to his feet, not caring that the seat of his pants was full of sand. He gripped the back of his neck. "God, can't I have both the girl of my dreams and a career? Is that too much to ask?"

A gentle breeze and the soft sway of the palm trees met his question.

Breathe. He had to get his act together. He had a best-man speech to give. He could only hope to get through the evening.

HOURS LATER, LUCAS drove on the highway that would take him back home. Traffic wasn't bad, except for the few cars that whizzed past them, exceeding the speed limit. With Grams in the passenger seat and Brit in the back, the car was uncomfortably silent, and the tension too intense to bear.

He'd endured the night, surprised he'd managed to give a speech that had people laughing. As for dancing, he'd not dared ask Brit.

While she'd kept herself busy wiping down and handing used plates to the servers like she was one of the hired staff, he'd made himself available to dance with his mom and Grams.

"It's a shame you two never danced together." Clarice spoke, just the way she'd tried to break the awkwardness over the last twenty minutes. "Maybe at your wedding."

Brit snorted from the back.

Rejection again. No, it wasn't. It was on him this time. He was leaving, for Pete's sake. Could he blame Brit for being upset and ending things between them?

"Brittney." Clarice craned to look in the back where Brittney was sitting behind him. "In case Luke forgot to tell you, we're going to church tomorrow."

"You guys have fun."

There was only one day with his grandma before he returned to his busy life. He intended tomorrow to count, at least with the one person who wasn't mad at him. "Brit should have the day off tomorrow. I'll take care of you, Grams." Brit needed a break.

Grams resettled in her seat, arms across her lap, fingers twitching as if needing her sewing to occupy them. "After church, we should go to Mount Vernon."

In fourth grade, before Lucas moved to Soda Creek, he'd gone with Grams and Grandpa. "I still remember the George Washington plantation." Vaguely.

"Good," Grams said.

Brit remained silent in the back, even as he parked in the garage. She stepped out of the back seat before he could pull out the keys, and she dashed to Clarice's door, opening it and taking Clarice's hand.

Lucas walked behind them toward the kitchen as he carried Grams's heavy handbag. Did she have rocks in this thing or what?

"Wait." Grams held one hand to her chest, wincing.

"Grams, what's wrong?"

"You okay?"

Lucas asked at the same time as Brit.

"I just need a moment to sit."

Lucas dropped the handbag on the hardwood floor and was at Grams's side in no time, taking one hand while Brit held onto Grams's other hand as they led her to the dining table.

"Let me get you some water," Brit said, and he grasped both of Grams's hands, needing to assess any signs of a heart attack.

"Is your chest hurting?"

Grams brushed his hands away and touched her forehead. "I feel—"

"This is serious. Grams, can you just answer me?" His tone came out sharper than he intended. "Brit, has this happened since I left?"

"No." Brit set the water in front of Grams and knelt at her feet.

Lucas pressed his palm to Grams's forehead, his heart racing. She wasn't breaking out in sweat, but that could change. "Are you dizzy? Do your arms hurt? Your back or jaw?"

Grams put her hands on her stomach and bent, letting out a groan. Adrenaline spiked as he shouted at Brit to call 911.

The phone clattered on the kitchen tile, and Brit picked it up. Her hands must be just as shaky as his when he rested one on Grams's shoulders.

What if anything happened to Grams? No... *No, God, no!*

Melancholy swept over him. Even if he was an anesthesiologist, a physician trained to treat patients, he was never trained to stay calm when taking care of a loved one. Hence his frozen mind as he scrambled for what to do.

"Stop!" Grams shouted, and Brit jumped, the phone falling out of her hand. "Don't call 911."

Was she crazy? Lucas scooped the phone from the floor, just as someone answered.

"What's your emergency?"

"It's my—"

"There's no emergency. You two need to talk!" Grams straightened, wagging her finger between Lucas and Brit.

Lucas's words died in his mouth as he stared at the more-than-fine old woman who happened to be his grandma. He breathed into the phone as the tension eased from his shoulders. The relief over having her be fine was more powerful than the anger over the stupid game she played.

"Hello, are you still there?" the voice sounded through the phone.

"I'm sorry." Lucas spoke. "She seems to be doing better.... Um, we will drive her to the emergency room." The home emergency talk they need to have about her playing such pranks.

He ended the call with an apology, grateful the woman on dispatch wasn't angry.

When he turned to the table, Brit was sitting in a chair across from Grams, her mouth pressed in a hard thin line, her chin quivering. "That was not your best joke, Clarice."

"I have to agree with Brit, Grams." Lucas crossed his arms and let out a long breath, needing it after the last few minutes they'd endured.

He couldn't even imagine how Brit felt, since she'd experienced major losses.

Grams shrugged, unapologetic. "You two are going to give me a heart attack if you don't talk to each other."

Lucas closed his eyes, not sure how to handle this, before opening them only to find that Brit had both her hands over her face.

"Grams, I leave the day after tomorrow. I don't intend to leave without talking to Brit." *If* she was up for discussing and hearing him out. Even if she was set on just being friends, as much as it stung not to have more, he'd have to be okay with it.

Grams nodded, then squeezed Brit's shoulder. "I'm sorry, I scared you."

Brit opened her eyes. They were red with unshed tears as she shuddered. "I'm glad you're okay." Then she stood and wished them a good night.

Well aware he'd be up all night, he responded with a good night.

CHAPTER 25

Parked on the side of the road, Brittney sat in her car, staring at the expansive sunflower field. With the sun already heading into the west, it was fascinating how all the sunflowers faced it and would follow its direction all day. Seeing this made it easier for her to relate to the creation story she'd read with Lucas one of the days they'd read Genesis together. *God commanded the plants to exist.* If the farmer planted the seeds, God sent the rain to make those seeds grow.

Speaking of growth, her heart needed a lot of growing up. Despite Clarice's stunt almost sending Brittney into a coronary, the woman was right. She and Lucas needed to talk.

Like a pouty child, Brittney had gone to her room last night, and that morning she'd cowered and stayed in her room until they left for church. Ugh. Guilt gnawed at her. She still wanted things to work out as friends with Lucas, but she was acting as if she didn't want him in her life anymore.

She swung open the car door closest to the field and shifted to look at its expanse. With the yellow so refreshing, a smile tugged the corners of her mouth as memories of her and Lucas running through here sprang to life.

"It was good to feel loved." Her ache slowly faded as she remembered their kiss in her favorite place, their picnic, and everything they'd done during the last days. It was now a memory.

"Is that what life is?" Enjoy one day, and when you move to the next, it's like yesterday's joy never existed?

Lucas was leaving. She didn't expect him to turn down a promotion. *"I wanted you and Grams to come with me."*

He'd at least thought about her. But not just for Clarice, Brittney had those dear friends at the disability center who she would miss and who would miss her, no doubt. They looked forward to their game days on Wednesdays, and she looked forward to their happy smiles.

Going with Lucas wasn't a possibility. Her heart ached, but he had responsibilities in Denver. The volunteer hospital counted on him too.

"What now?" She placed her hands on both cheeks. She was happy when Lucas was around, but maybe he was right. She needed that everlasting joy that didn't depend on a person or circumstance. A joy that came from within, contentment that surpassed any emptiness her heart clung to.

Random cars drove past now and then as she peered back at the field, and God came to mind. The God Lucas believed in, the God Destiny and Ryan believed in.

"If I could believe in anything, why couldn't I give God a chance?" Lucas's words rang loud and clear.

Yes.

Why couldn't I take the chance to believe? Faith. Believing in something I don't see.

"I can see sunflowers, and they make me happy." She tilted her face to the sun, copying her favorite flowers. Blue sky peered back with a puffy cloud. "If You made such beautiful flowers and You coordinate how they follow the sun, then surely You can direct me to do the right thing." She'd made terrible choices by running her own life, but having someone in charge of her life would be nice. "I want to believe in You."

Her lips trembled when she said the words, her eyes blurring as she continued with what must be a prayer.

"Like the endless field, fill my heart with everlasting joy.... Like the gentle breeze swaying the stalks, let Your peace sway freely in my heart. When Lucas is gone, help me to remain content and find fulfillment in what You would have me do."

She closed her eyes, tears flowing freely. The melancholy feeling was suddenly replaced by something, something that bloomed like the sunflowers as she let out a breath.

It's going to be okay. She let Lucas's words echo in her mind. And honestly, everything was more than okay. Clarice was alive and healthy. Lucas's family was strong and fine. She had a family, even if they weren't her biological one.

Lucas loved her. As a friend or otherwise. He still loved her, and she wanted him to be happy. He'd given her more than she ever deserved, loved her unconditionally without expecting anything from her.

She closed her door and fired the engine. Her heart ignited with adrenaline she hadn't had when she woke up that morning. It was only two, and she didn't want to go home and be by herself.

Lucas and Clarice had gone to the George Washington house quite a ways away. Brittney could join them, but Clarice needed to enjoy time with her grandson.

Instead, Brittney drove into town to the gift shop where Lucas had bought her Bible and spent a few hours browsing books about how to read the Bible and what God did for mankind. She read the first three chapters of the summarized book.

Her lips whispered the words she read from a devotional book: "God made a sacrifice when He sent His son Jesus to die on the cross for our sins. Whoever believes in Him will never perish but have eternal life."

Did God die for me too?

She added the book to her shopping cart and pulled another one from the shelf.

"How to spend five minutes with God every day." She added that to her cart and moved to the gift section displaying chains, bracelets, and random items.

Knowing Lucas was a simple guy, she chose a ceramic travel mug with the Bible verse: *Trust in the Lord with all your heart...* for him. She then selected two identical black rubber bracelets with the words *What Would Jesus Do?* stamped on them, choosing them in reference to the vows he'd said at the wedding, something about laying his life down for her, then supporting her in pursuing her dream. Was he thinking about Jesus when he said that? To sacrifice things for Brittney? He'd done that even before he changed his faith.

So the bracelet would remind her to let him pursue his dreams, to support him as a friend would.

It was now her turn to encourage him. She needed to congratulate him, too, so she intended to celebrate tonight when he came home.

AS THE GIANT BALL OF sun sank below the horizon, Brittney sat on the patio enjoying some cake with cream cheese and lemon frosting. Her heart bloomed with what she assumed to be joyous contentment.

Forks clanked against porcelain as Lucas and Grams polished off their last bites of cake. Then Clarice set her fork on her empty plate and dabbed a napkin to her lips. "You should've baked the wedding cake."

"If I knew she could bake serious cakes, I would've hired her." Lucas eyed her with questions in his quizzical brows.

She didn't blame him after her sudden change in mood. She shrugged.

"I thought it would be nice to try something new, something that I've never cooked before." She cooked the same things they normally ate. Even for Lucas's visit, she'd only cooked meals familiar to him, his favorite ones.

"Now that we finished dinner and cake..." Clarice put both hands on the table and narrowed her gaze at Brittney. "It's time to hear what has you in such a jolly mood."

When they'd come home at five, Brittney had dinner almost ready and welcomed them with a smile, apologizing for not going with them. Clarice wanted to take a bath before eating, and while Brittney helped her, Lucas opted to get himself showered, too.

Brittney stacked the plates and looked at Clarice, then at Lucas, focusing on his eyes, so warm and expectant for what she had to say.

"I'm sorry for how I behaved last night." She eyed both of her favorite people in the world. "I had a good day today. And I did a lot of thinking." She pushed the chair back and stood. Knowing she had plenty of time to talk to Clarice, she asked, "Will it be okay if, after I clean up here, I talk to Lucas?" She inclined her head to the oak tree. "Maybe we can go to the tree house?"

"As long as you're talking to each other—yes. Go now." Clarice gripped the table to stand. "I have lots of crosswords to catch up on."

While Lucas saw Clarice safely inside the house, Brittney followed them. After setting the dishes in the sink, she went to her room and grabbed the brown gift bag.

Soon they were walking out through the back and crossing the grass to the tree house.

The wooden bed in the tree house creaked when Brittney sat on its flat pad, then patted next to her for him to sit.

He hesitated, raking a hand through his hair before sitting. "Everything okay?"

She traced her fingers over the bed. "Ever since you kissed me ten years ago, I've never sat in here."

He blinked. "Really? Why?"

She'd come in to dust the cobwebs and left as soon as she finished. "It was never the same without you." It saddened her whenever she thought of the memories they had.

"For the record, I'm still nervous being here." He looked up at the unplugged string of lights that didn't work anymore. "The last time I was here—"

"Our friendship was put to the test." She finished the sentence. "But not this time."

She took her hand in his, and warmth filled her as she squeezed it. She would miss him so much, but she was here to let him go. "I made peace with God today."

"You did?" His eyes lit up, and his face crinkled in a sweet smile.

Brittney nodded, a lump forming in her throat. "Thank you for coming back to me, for sharing your faith."

He shifted on the rickety bed and tugged her into his warm embrace. "I'm so happy for you."

At the tremor in his voice, she fought back the tears. Instead, she wrapped her arms tight around him and pressed her words into his hair. "I'm happy about your promotion. I now understand God has put you in this job to help people, the way you've always helped me."

He eased out of the embrace and cupped her chin. "Brit."

Despite the unbearable agony on his face, she composed herself. She. Would. Not. Cry.

She never said what her vows would be, but now might be a good time. "You've always believed in me, and that has helped bring focus to my dreams. From this day on, your dreams are my dreams, and I want to support you, to believe in you." She had no idea what plans God had for their relationship, but... "It doesn't matter how far apart we are from each other, as long as I can hear from you once a week...." Her voice wavered. He was the love of her life, and she told him so.

"You make me happier than I could ever imagine and more loved than I ever felt possible."

Her heart ached, overpowered by this feeling of love for him.

"Brit," he whispered, but she kept her focus beyond the window, on the oak's swaying leaves. She wanted him to know all the things she didn't tell him while she thought of him during the ten years they were apart.

"You've made me a better person, and I'm so lucky to be a part of your life, your friend...."

His hand curled around the back of her neck, and he pulled her head to touch his forehead, closing his eyes. "I want to have a future with you."

"I want that, too," she whispered, aching and wishing they could start their future together now, but it wasn't the right time. She cleared her throat to get rid of the lump. "I'll wait for you, as long as it takes."

"As long as it takes." He shuddered. "I wish I didn't have to—"

"Everything's going to be okay." She used his words against him and then pressed a soft kiss on his moist lips. "A best friends' kiss," she said before easing away and reaching for the bag on the floor. She retrieved the black rubber bracelets, slid hers on first, then took his hand, and eased his onto his wrist.

He smiled, lifting his wrist and reading the words written in white text. "What would Jesus do?"

She lifted hers to him.

"I love it. Thank you." He took her hand.

She then handed him the insulated coffee travel cup.

He read the words about trusting in God, grinning, appreciating. "This could be the perfect reminder of how I need to lean on God for wisdom." He turned it in his hand, then asked, "How did you find peace with God?"

So she told him about her panic from Clarice's stunt, and her drive to the sunflower field.

He scrambled to his feet, retrieving something from his shorts pockets. "I almost forgot. I got you something. I was going to slide it under your door if you didn't talk to me, but…"

A small bag.

It contained a necklace with a sunflower pendant.

She smiled when she realized the pendant was a locket. When she opened it, the message inside left her heart beyond words.

"You are my sunshine," she whispered those words before leaping at him in an embrace. Blushing, she eased out of the hug. "You leave me speechless. Thank you."

He slipped the necklace from her grasp and unclasped it. "I think that's the last sunflower-related gift I'm giving you," he said, urging her to turn around. When he slid the necklace over her head, goosebumps blossomed throughout her arms, shuddering her spine as his fingers brushed her skin.

They stayed in the tree house and discussed their plans for the new chapter in their lives. He was looking forward to starting his new position. She was looking forward to going to church consistently.

"You should also finish that book," he encouraged.

"I intend to." She gave a firm nod, motivated to do everything she'd ever hoped to try but never stepped up to.

"I can help you find an agent."

He'd helped her do so many things. She rested her hand atop his. "I'll do some research. You're going to be busy enough with work."

"Don't hesitate to let me know if you need help."

"I will." She meant to do so.

As they headed out of the tree house, she asked how he was getting to the airport. "Dad and Mom are driving me. I'd like you to come if possible."

"I'm counting on it."

She was finally at peace, letting him go pursue his dream, knowing she had her best friend back. Whether their relationship took off to marriage or not, she would have to be fine with the outcome. Perhaps now she could start trying to reach her unfinished goals.

CHAPTER 26

Lucas went through the following week with his heart dampened, as if he'd lost someone or something. His new responsibilities were to manage a staff of anesthesia doctors, technicians and nurses, to make sure the anesthesia department ran a smooth operation. He'd also had to work with several hospital staff and department directors to ensure the highest services.

All the extra work didn't catch him off guard. He just hadn't expected to dive right in. He'd hoped to have a few days to ease into the routine while he replayed his moments with the girl he left behind. Technically, she came with him, if her domination of his heart counted.

Grateful for a slow Saturday morning with no work-related plans, he headed to Josh's three-on-three basketball game. With his insulated mug in hand—the one Brit had given him—he reached for his keys by the door before stepping out of his apartment and heading for the garage. Since he'd returned from Soda Creek, his apartment felt more foreign and empty, and despite the busy week, he dreaded staying home and catching up on laundry.

There had been a few tears at the airport when he said goodbye to his family. Grams rarely shed a tear, but even her eyes had been glossy when she squeezed him in a tight embrace.

As promised, he'd texted, twice, very late-night texts because he'd barely had time to breathe during the daytime. Brit had called him, too, but again, he'd missed her calls. Even the two-hour time difference made it hard to find a time when each of them were available.

The parking lot was packed when Lucas pulled into the complex, so he drove around and parked on the street, then took a moment to sip the rest of his coffee and reflect on the words. *Trust in the Lord with all your heart and lean not on your own understanding.*

I really need You, God, to direct me. How did Brit fit into Lucas's plans? Lucas stepped out and closed the door.

The smell of coffee and different body scents along with leather drifted through the room as Lucas peered over people's heads in search of Ryan's family. Since the warehouse-style building hosted several courts, multiple games were already in progress with basketballs bouncing off the surface in different horizontal waves.

Arms flung around Lucas, catching him off balance, and he steadied himself as he looked down at Zoe.

"We're over there in the far court." She spoke over the dribbling thud, and he hugged her before they walked toward Josh's team.

Ryan sat on a bleacher, nestled between his two toddlers, keeping one hand around the boys' shoulders and another hand around the girl's. Lucas ruffled four-year-old Carter's hair, who sat next to the girl.

Ryan nodded his greeting, and Pete gave Lucas a high five, then sat next to him.

Zoe joined Destiny, who was standing intent on the game, while she cheered Josh's jersey number. "Go Number 3!"

Josh played hard and was a fast player when it came to stealing the ball from the other team. They played nonstop, except for a quick intermission at halftime, when Lucas waved and gave him a thumbs-up. During the second half, Josh's team won by two points, so Destiny suggested they go celebrate the win.

Josh wanted to go to a Mexican restaurant. Even though Lucas wasn't hungry, he didn't mind the company. He also didn't mind holding toddlers on his lap when they wiggled out of their high chairs and smothered his shirt with salsa.

"You're such a great uncle." Ryan rolled his eyes as he stacked several napkins on the table in an attempt to wipe the water one of the toddlers had spilled.

Destiny was busy on the floor, cleaning up the beans. "It will save the workers some time."

Their life seemed chaotic, but they looked happy. Could he and Brit start a family, or was it too late at their age to have kids?

"Are you coming with us to the fireworks on Wednesday?" Zoe's voice pulled him out of his thoughts, as she bounced to his side after the mess was cleaned up.

"Ahh... Oww!" Lucas winced when the little guy in his arms tugged his hair.

"We're having a barbecue at three." Destiny scooped one of the kids from him.

"Sounds fun." Lucas's voice emerged weak. Grams had pleaded with him to stay and celebrate the Fourth of July.

He had everything he wanted, a career, a promotion.... But where did Brit fit in God's plan for him? Something was still missing, and being around Ryan's family reminded him how much he needed to be a part of his own family.

The kids talked over the Latino music playing in the background, chattering about their Fourth of July decorations and the glow sticks they needed. When they left the restaurant, Lucas walked Ryan and his family to their car and said goodbye to the kids.

Then Ryan followed him to his car. "Dude, why don't you go home?"

Lucas blinked at the sudden words. Folding his arms across his chest, he leaned against his Jeep. "What do you mean?"

Ryan gave him a you-know-exactly-what-I-mean look. "You walked around the hospital like you were in mourning all week."

"Try managing a bunch of adults and see if you'll stay the same."

"You were barely present in the restaurant."

"How was I supposed to hold a conversation when the littles were pulling my ears and spilling everything?" It wasn't the first time he'd sat through it, but he'd always managed to be chatty with the kids.

Ryan just raised one eyebrow. "You can tell yourself anything you want." Like the family man Ryan was, he stared Lucas in the eye. "Tell me you don't go to your apartment each night feeling empty without Brittney, regretting not proposing to her."

Lucas's face burned. Ryan was right, no denying it.

Lucas shrugged. "I can't quit when I just accepted a position."

"They can find another candidate."

"I have to help organize the charity event."

"Brady is running it from clear across the world."

Why did Ryan have all the answers? Lucas fidgeted with the rubber bracelet. "It will take a while to get back to the top if I start at a new hospital."

"Priorities." The look Ryan gave him seared clear through him. "How important is money to you over Brit?"

Did he have to say Brit, instead of Brittney? He sure knew how to hit the right chords.

Ugh. Lucas's jaw clenched. He thrust his hands in his jean pockets and yanked one out when something sharp pierced his nail bed.

"Ouch." He blew on his nail. It wasn't bleeding, thank goodness.

"You're okay?" Ryan clamped a hand on Lucas's shoulder.

"As long as a spinal needle didn't accidentally end up in my pocket." He slid his hand in his pocket and probed a rough cardboard surface. He chuckled. It was the missing puzzle piece.

"What's that?" Laughter shook Ryan's voice. And Lucas told him about the puzzle Grams had him and Brit do the moment he'd arrived.

Ryan lifted both hands. "Well, there's your answer." He then gave Lucas a curt nod and left him standing there, looking at the scratched cardboard, rippled from running through the washer.

"My answer," he repeated as he flipped the piece over in his hand. He'd left home and taken the piece with him. Either he was the missing piece to the puzzle or Brit was the missing piece in his heart.

As he drove home, his mind was spinning, and instead of heading to his lonely apartment, he drove to a jewelry shop. He was going to buy a ring. Not just that, he had a proposal to plan. He had no idea how things would fall in place, but he didn't want to wait or make Brit wait for him as she'd promised.

CHAPTER 27

When the doorbell rang, Brittney opened the door to the mailman.

"Hi, Brittney." His face colored as he sheepishly handed over the
mail.

"Hi." She gave him a curt smile, not wanting to encourage him
any further than she may have in an effort to be polite. She lifted the
magazine and a couple of envelopes, likely bills. "Thanks."

"I... I was wondering. Um, waiting for your call."

She'd never had the courage to do this, but after what she'd put
herself and Adam through, she could still be polite and say no. "Listen, um..." She focused on the big flag swaying off the porch in honor
of the upcoming Fourth of July as she tried to remember his name.
Oh no! Why didn't she remember? Looking him straight in the eye,
she put on her apologetic smile. "You're a very nice man, but I... My
heart belongs to someone else."

The color left his face. "Oh..."

"I know Clarice gave you the impression I was single and searching, but—"

"That's okay." Sounding breathless, he took a step back, wincing
and probably uncomfortable. "Sorry... um, to bother you."

Her heart ached for him, and she couldn't bear to look at him
scrambling down the path, so she closed the door and sank onto
the couch. Thankfully, Clarice, in the backyard, couldn't hear the exchange. She felt energetic, pulling weeds from the pumpkin garden
she'd planted on the other side of the house.

It was for the best, Brittney told herself as she stared at the puzzle
on the table. A tiny funny-shaped hole was missing from the fire-

works. That's how she felt in her heart—like Lucas was the fireworks that blasted in her heart. The times they'd spoken on the phone or texted were minimal, but they always left her bursting with fireworks of joy.

Her reasoning that they stay best friends hadn't worked since she never imagined or pictured him as just best friends. She lay down each night and pictured him as a best friend and the love of her life.

During the week—surely, it was more than a week?—since he'd left, she'd stayed busy enough. Despite Clarice's schedule, Brittney had had time to flesh out her draft, research agents, and contact three of them. She'd received a response from one who seemed most enthusiastic about her story, but she still needed to pray before deciding.

Although a ways from finishing the book, she felt confident researching an agent at this point. She'd also met with a couple of people at the disability center. They had quadriplegic family members and agreed to an interview about their experience having a loved one who was wheelchair-bound.

Plus, with her visits to church last Wednesday and then on Sunday, she was figuring out how church life worked, and she signed up to join a small group of people her age.

Clarice liked going to church, as well, and wanted to join the senior's small group. Not that she needed any more engagements, but as long as she didn't mind it, Brit was more than okay taking her.

The timer went off, and she walked to the kitchen to check on her spinach-sausage soup. Steam rose when she lifted the lid and stirred the contents. The smell of garlic permeated the kitchen.

She turned down the heat. The time on the stove showed 12:07—time for their lunch.

While they ate, Clarice talked about their Fourth of July, her eyes flashing with her typical animation, and Brit couldn't help smiling with her. Clarice looked forward to the Fourth every year. "Tomorrow we're spending the day at Gary and Sandra's."

"I thought they're joining us for the fireworks?" Lucas's parents always joined them. Brittney shoved the sausages to the side, saving them for later.

"Not this time." Clarice dabbed a napkin on her lips. "Sandra wants everyone there by eleven for the barbecue."

That would make for a long day for Clarice, but she'd need a nap before the fireworks anyway. "Do we come back here before heading to the park?"

Clarice shook her head. "Let's just plan on drinking a lot of coffee tomorrow."

And several bathroom trips. "Which means more water for you." Brittney eyed Clarice for a defiant reaction.

"I'm planning on that, too." Clarice waved a hand, then clinked her spoon against the bowl when she ladled the soup then lifted it to her mouth.

As long as Brittney packed all the medicine and anything else Clarice needed to be comfortable, eleven hours away from home should be tolerable.

That night, after Clarice went to bed, Brittney lay on her stomach as she typed Lucas a message as she'd done each night. Although he responded every time, it wasn't usually right away.

Brittney: Are you working tomorrow?

Lucas: Maybe.

Brittney: You're the head of your department, and you don't even know your schedule?

Lucas: It seems when you're in leadership you don't have a definite schedule.

That would make sense if he had to fill in for anyone who wasn't around.

Brittney: Are you watching fireworks tomorrow?

Lucas: I hope so. Wish I was there with you and Grams.

Her heart longed for him. But she'd promised to let him go, and acting needy would only make him feel guilty for doing what he was supposed to do. So she typed instead,

Brittney: There's always next time. Shouldn't you be sleeping anyway?

Lucas: Working. You? Shouldn't you be sleeping?

She grinned that he was using her words against her.

Brittney: Yes. Especially since your grandma and I will be gone for 11 hours tomorrow.

Lucas: Yikes. Why?

Brittney: Barbecue with your family during the day. And then fireworks at the end of the day.

Lucas: Playing with your phone is the worst way to get yourself to sleep.

What a stinker. Her heart was full. She'd better let him be, since she had a long day tomorrow, too.

Brittney: I miss you.

Lucas: I miss you, too.

AT A LITTLE PAST NINE p.m., the first rocket soared into the air, exploding with a bang. Patriotic music played from the stage where the musicians had been performing before the fireworks. More rockets fired into the air, lighting a canopy of sparkling orange and white glitters.

People cheered from time to time, and Clarice, sitting beside Brittney, snapped one picture after another, her eyes fixated on the firework fountains. On Clarice's other side, Sandra and her husband linked arms where they sat, Sandra leaning against his side as they whispered about the fireworks while, standing behind them, Olivia and Adam wrapped their arms around each other's waists. Something about the couples sharing this moment left Brittney lonely, so she edged closer to Emery, who was also alone sitting close by.

Bang after bang and light after light, the crowd oohed and aahed, others gasping in appreciation. "Wow!" Clarice lowered the camera as if taking so many pictures was wearing her out. "This year's fireworks are much better than last year's."

With it so breathtaking, an ache hollowed out Brittney's chest. Lucas should be here to enjoy the explosion of radiant colors.

The smell of fireworks replaced the popcorn and hot dog scents as the song ended and the first notes of "America the Beautiful" began from the onstage sound system.

She pulled the light blanket to her shoulders, chilling from the fascination when more silver fountains shot up, colors changing through red, orange, and blue, then back to silver again.

As the music wound down, a massive ball shot up and exploded, compelling people to erupt in applause.

Joining in the excitement, Brittney clapped until her palms hurt. Then, like the fireworks fizzling out, so did her excitement, leaving her downhearted when the light in the sky vanished, the stage lights lit up, and the microphone crackled. The DJ thanked everyone for coming and wished them a good night. "See you next year."

Next year seemed too far, but hopefully, Lucas would be home for the Fourth of July then.

"This is when sitting in the back pays off." Gary rubbed his hands together, then helped his mother-in-law to her feet while his wife and daughter folded their picnic blanket. "We don't have to shuffle through the crowd to exit the park." He and his family walked Brittney and Clarice to the handicap lot, which was closer to the park than the main parking.

"That was quite the show!" Clarice said as she buckled herself in, while Brittney started the car and pulled out of their parking space.

Brittney kept her gaze on the man in the yellow vest, waiting for his hand signal for her to drive further. "The city must have had some extra funding," she said in response to Clarice's comment about the fireworks show.

"It's all through donations this year." Clarice smoothed her fancy red-and-white-striped blouse with its blue collar under her seat belt. Not that Brittney didn't read the paper to keep up, but Clarice still always knew the town more.

"I'll have to donate something next year." Brittney let her foot off the brake and pushed the gas when she was given the signal.

The dashboard showed 11:10 as she pulled into the garage and Clarice let out a yawn, covering it with her palm. Brittney pressed the small remote in her car to close the garage door. When she stepped out of the car, her gaze went to the motorcycle parked on the other side. The light from the bulb above reflected against its fuel tank cover.

After the heat of the long day, Brittney needed to take a shower.

"Would you like to take your bath tonight?" she asked as she held the door for Clarice to step out.

Clarice fumbled with her cane and pushed herself from her seat, then smoothed down her top again. "Luke should be home by now."

Huh? Her heart rate shooting up, Brittney blinked and eyed Clarice, who seemed unfazed by her statement. Had the day been too much for her? Was she losing track of what was going on?

Eyes aglow, Clarice patted Brittney's hand. "I just don't want you to panic if we walk in and he's there."

Sure, Lucas knew where they kept the spare key, but he was in Denver. Brittney had texted with him yesterday—not today, of course, but still. Why would he miss the fireworks and show up when everything was over?

Appearing to have all her wits about her, Clarice clicked her cane against the cement garage floor while Brittney hobbled from behind.

Right now, it should be Clarice walking behind her since she seemed steadier than Brittney.

She patted her stars and striped tank top. Then her hair. She hadn't even looked in the mirror to know if her hair was messy. If it were possible, shouldn't Clarice have warned her about Lucas's arrival much earlier?

Brittney could've showered at Sandra and Gary's house, and perhaps carried a change of clothes. Wait, when did Clarice find out about—?

"There you are!" Lucas's voice sounded from the hallway to the bedrooms the moment they walked into the kitchen. Dressed in jeans and a black T-shirt that defined his broad chest, he stood there, his mischievous expression teasing her.

She could hear the air conditioner whirring, so it shouldn't be warm. But her body felt more heated than when she'd been in the afternoon sun.

"Hello, my dearest Luke." Clarice stepped into his open arms, and he planted a soft kiss on his grandma's cheek.

Brittney knew how warm and soft those lips were, and oh, her mouth tingled.

When he stepped away from Clarice and walked toward Brittney, her feet somehow locked in place. And unlike his greeting when he'd come home last time, his smile was so warm as he closed the gap between them and swept her off her feet.

Brittney wrapped her arms around his shoulders and squeezed him. "You missed the fireworks." Of all the things she could've said, those were the words that flew out of her mouth.

"I tried to make it, but..." He set her down and hugged her tight against him. She felt even warmer, but this different kind of warmth created a fuzzy feeling in her stomach. He then kissed her head, breathing into her hair before planting a soft kiss on her mouth. "I missed you."

She opened her mouth to respond, but when her gaze darted to the dining table, Clarice was sitting there, her lips lifted in amusement.

Brittney closed her mouth, holding in her breath.

Lucas eased out of the embrace and patted his jeans, his hand sliding into one of his pockets. He retrieved a flimsy piece of paper, cardboard, she realized when she inched closer.

"It's the puzzle piece. I must have put it in my pants without thinking."

Her mind rushed back to that night when he'd come home. He'd been wearing the same jeans and had decided to go to bed. "I saw you put it in your pocket, but I forgot." After they'd gotten past the tension, Lucas had been too distracting for her to remember her own name.

"You both better go fill in that puzzle." Excitement glinted in Clarice's tired eyes.

Brittney fell in step with Lucas as they walked to the living room and he turned on the lamp by the table, then knelt. She knelt beside him while he fit the piece in the tiny round ball to the sparkling firework fountain.

"Now it's complete." His eyes were so vibrant beneath the light when he stood, taking her hand with him. "That's what I've been missing."

She shook her head, amazed he had the same analogy as she did. "So have I," she whispered, and hoped Clarice couldn't hear much of their exchange. They were just supposed to be friends now. But he wasn't looking at her as a friend, and maybe she wasn't looking at him that way, either.

He's only here for a night or maybe two. She needed to remind him of their place.

As if tapping into her mind, he said, "I have something to show you."

"Okay." They'd be up much later, trying to catch up on their time apart. "Let me first see Clarice to bed."

"She's coming, too."

She tipped her head to the side to read Lucas's eyes for a hint of what he had in mind. But the chair scraped the kitchen floor, and her gaze flitted to Clarice instead. She was gripping the table to stand.

When Lucas asked Clarice to lead the way to the backyard, she shuffled her feet, and Brittney followed, her curiosity piqued. On the deck, Brittney paused, blinking at the abundant lights spread throughout the yard. Lanterns were hanging from the oak trees and the tree house and the rest of the trees. She spun to Lucas. "What's going on?"

He shrugged, displaying that mischievous grin he had whenever he was up to some adventure.

"Clarice?" she called as Lucas hurried to help his grandma down the deck step.

"All I know is Luke has a fireworks show of his own."

Yeah, it sure was a fireworks show when she followed the pair down the path toward the lit pond. They strolled through clear straw LED lamps that looked like they were shooting out fireworks from the ground.

"Here's your chair, Grams," Lucas said, halfway toward the pond. This was something he'd planned. Was he proposing? No. They had barely shared I love yous during their over-a-week separation.

Brittney wiped her sweating palms on her shorts as he returned and draped an arm over her shoulders. "Feeling cold?"

She hadn't realized she was shaking. He ran his hand over her bare shoulder, electrifying her body with instant heat. "I'm..." She was anything but cold. Her shaking had nothing to do with the breeze.

Lucas took a step forward, shifting her hand to the crook of his arm. They continued a slow stroll, his voice coming out gravely. "Remember the words on your necklace?"

Her other hand flew to the sunflower pendant. "You are my sunshine." She bumped into him with her hip. "You have it the other way around."

"The backyard is usually dark. But I put all these lights on, and it's not dark at all."

"When did all this happen?" She stopped walking, and he did the same.

"I had professional help."

No wonder Clarice wanted them to be gone for eleven hours.

"This is the brightest I've ever seen it back here."

She slid her arms around his waist and stared up at him. The lights hanging from the trees and swaying around the pond illuminated his handsome face. Her tongue was too heavy to move. Otherwise, she wanted to ask why she deserved him being so nice to her. It wasn't a proposal, but it felt like something she'd see in a movie when someone rich was asking a girl they loved to marry them.

He cleared his throat, and she ran her hand over his firm jaw.

"About the sunshine," he said, "when I look into your eyes..." He peered at the pond, then to the lit trees. "I see a reflection of light and happiness. When I think of you, I know no one else will ever hold my heart the way you do."

Streams of tears unleashed down her cheeks. She couldn't stop them even if she wanted to.

Lucas continued his poetic words. "I want to spend each day, for the rest of my life, laughing with you, smiling with you, because you, Brit, are the light God has used, the light that will continue to bring sunshine into my cloudy days."

She sniffled as he wiped at her eyes. "I... love... you." She could barely speak the words—she was such a wreck today. Thankfully, Lucas clasped her hand and led her forward, and they stopped in front of the pond.

Her breath left her lungs. *Floating candles* spread out through the pond, and the light reflected the yellow petals in between. She eased her hand out of his hold, needing to use both of them to hold her chest. Perhaps it would contain her rapid breaths.

"Sunflower... petals..." Her voice unsteady, she blinked away the tears to read the sparks forming the letters in the center of the pond—*Marry Me, Brit*.

Sparkling and shimmering, the words illuminated the water—and something in her heart.

She gasped and clamped both her hands over her mouth as she turned to gape at him while nodding and sobbing. *I will. I want to marry you.* The words echoed in her head, vibrated in her heart, whispered in her soul, but wouldn't come to her lips. How she hated her tongue for failing her at such a time!

Lucas lowered himself, kneeling on one knee and retrieving something from his pocket.

"Yes... Yes!" Finally, she managed.

He removed what must be a ring from the fancy dark-red bag.

"Brittney Young..."

"I will... Yes." She spoke over his words while she knelt beside him and put her hand out.

She savored the feel of his steady fingers against hers as he slid the cool sparkly diamond on her ring finger. Swirly diamond accents lit up the ring like fireworks forever frozen.

As she looked at the center of the swirl, the accents sparkled brighter than all the lights around them, brighter than all the fireworks at the show. Words failed her, but she did her best to take her eyes off their joined hands and look into his deep eyes—their love-light the brightest of all. "This ring is perfect."

"You"—he spoke with such reverence, his voice held a tremor—"are perfect."

She leaned to him, their lips almost touching. "You are more perfect."

He buried her lips with his and kissed her deeply with passion and purpose. They ended up on the cool grass eventually.

"I gotta get to bed, kids." Clarice's voice carried to them in laughter. "You have until forever to kiss."

They chuckled as they tore apart and stood.

"Until forever," Brittney whispered the promise.

"I still have a job I haven't quit yet, but I intend to." He pulled her closer to him as they ambled back to Clarice.

Her limbs felt as light as the floating candles. He'd done this for them. "Are you sure?"

"Yes." No hesitancy slowed his response.

Heat radiating through her chest, she felt like breaking out in their favorite song—"Oh, What a Night." Her chest was burning, full to the brim. Is this the kind of happiness God offered? That kind and more. She felt her own response. She'd already found peace with God, and now Lucas was hers forever. What more could she ask for?

EPILOGUE

Six months later...

Spontaneous applause erupted from the disability center's main room after Lucas's wife had given a summary of what *The Joy of Caregiving* entailed.

Lucas stood, clapping, and next to him, Grams shifted, trying to pull up. He held out his hand to help her up. Dad and Mom also stood next to Grams. When Lucas glanced over his shoulder, more than half the room was standing, except for those who couldn't because they were bound in their wheelchairs.

"Thank you." Brit's voice sounded from the stage, and he faced her as she put her hand to her chest.

With the two big glass windows radiating natural afternoon light in the room, he could see her eyes shiny with tears—tears of joy—and his chest puffed. He was so proud of her and the work she'd put into meeting her deadline with her enthusiastic agent.

As the clapping died down, her focus moved from the crowd to him, and their gazes held. Her hair, styled in waves, cascaded down her shoulders against her teal silk blouse tucked into flowy designer pants. The designer belt showcased her slender waist.

His heart quickened, and he winked. She winked back as her agent stepped on the stage and whispered something in her ear.

All business, Primrose ran a dark-skinned hand over the blazer matching her navy pencil skirt. Although the launch was two months away, she'd set up tours for Brit to talk in nursing homes and disability centers.

"If you'd like to stay and ask Brittney extra questions"—Primrose spoke over the crowd's humming voices—"you can join us for refreshments and snacks in the café."

As soon as Brit stepped off the stage, Lucas was at the stage threshold in one long stride, taking her hand, then pulling her into his arms for an embrace.

"I'm so proud of you." He pressed his face into her hair, inhaling that tantalizing conditioner of hers, the happy smell of home—the smell of Brit.

"How did I do?" Her soft breath tickled his ear, warming him inside and out.

He couldn't get enough of her. "You did great," he whispered over the chatting crowd. "Better than the last three times."

He drew away and clasped her hand in his, leading her back to their front seats. His family congratulated her with hugs, telling her how proud they were that her book had hit the bestseller list before its launch.

In honor of her dad, Brit had arranged for all of the proceeds from the book to go to the Quadriplegic Foundation to assist individuals in becoming healthier and more independent, and aid their families in providing care. The things they bought changed the quality of life for people like her dad and mom, who'd had to limit their outings because it was so hard to get her father in the car.

"I give the glory to God," she said, bending down to embrace Dad, and her deep dimple flashed as she answered Dad's question about why she assumed God was behind her book's success.

Lucas had to whisper a prayer of thanks for himself, too. For the last five months, he'd been able to wake up every morning to that captivating smile before he left for work.

He'd run out of patience, and once he proposed, he was ready to talk about their wedding. They'd both agreed to marry at the beginning of August.

They'd had a small ceremony in Grams's backyard with close friends and family. Adam had laughed at him for his spontaneity, saying, "You thought I was crazy for getting married with one-month notice. Now, you're doing it!"

Lucas understood then how love didn't have a schedule or routine.

He'd paid for a wedding planner to deal with extra details. Even though he'd had to commute between Soda Creek and Denver for six weeks while they found his replacement, he'd had time on weekends to come home and test the wedding cakes with Brit before they hired one of the bakers. Food had been easy, since they'd stuck with their old schoolmates' catering services.

Saying goodbye to Ryan's family was bittersweet, and although Zoe had cried, she'd felt better when Lucas reminded her they'd see each other every Christmas and in the summer when Ryan brought them to visit their grandparents. He could understand how parting with anyone was particularly hard for her and her brothers after they'd lost their parents.

Lucas was pleased that Eric Stone had another charity hospital in Virginia. Lucas now volunteered there once a week and worked four days at the new job he'd started two months ago.

It was a bigger change than he'd expected when he applied at the hospital in Soda Creek. As a much smaller hospital, the salary it offered was a huge pay cut after Olive Medical, but he wouldn't trade money for the life he had.

He and Brit lived with Grams in Brit's bedroom since it was bigger than his old room. They had no intention of moving out unless God made that clear.

Grams had legally transferred the house to them and joked that she was homeless and at their mercy, because they let her stay with them.

As Lucas glanced over the dispersing group to the glass window, it was a cloudy January day. But when his eyes flickered back to Brit, who was finally turning toward him, her smile warmed him. She was the sunshine he needed to get through the long winter, with a smile that brightened any gloomy day.

-THE END-

If you've enjoyed The Physician's Helper, please leave your review on Amazon, Goodreads and Bookbub

Next in the Series is The CEO's Companion. You can order your copy on Amazon

Feel free to connect with me on Facebook[1] in my Reader's group, where I usually chat with my readers on a regular basis.

---

1.   https://www.facebook.com/groups/243932449976110/?ref=pages_pro-
file_groups_tab&source_id=435344610252020

COMING January, 25 2022

THE CEO's COMPANION

Despair held him captive. Can her love break his chains?

After a deadly fire robbed him of his wife and children, billionaire Eric Stone clings to God and buries himself in work to distract himself from his grief. But when a mysterious illness takes away his ability to work, Eric must retreat to his childhood home to rest and recover. Grief-stricken and hopeless, he is irritated by his new caretaker's enthusiasm for life. But against his will, her sunny outlook makes inroads.

Joy Musana got a new lease on life after beating cancer four years ago. Now, she lives every day to serve God and others. In her opinion, the grumpy CEO she is caring for doesn't need her sympathy—but making him smile is her priority.

When she asks him to attend a wedding with her to avoid the matchmaking efforts of her roommate, Eric surprises himself by agreeing to pose as her fake date to shield her from a pushy suitor. As unexpected sparks fly, Eric's and Joy's hearts are trapped between what's fake and what's real. Could this weekend be their chance for a new beginning?

Order your copy on Amazon.

A NOTE FROM THE AUTHOR

Thank you for reading *The Physician's Helper* It's always a blessing to meet new readers. And to those who have read all my stories, thanks for giving me another chance and for your reviews and notes of encouragement.

I can never forget to thank God who enables me to create these stories. Thank you Lord!

You can connect with Rose on Facebook or email her at rjfresquez@gmail.com

ABOUT THE AUTHOR

Rose Fresquez is the author of the Buchanan -Firefighter series, Romance in the Rockies, The caregiver series, two short stories and two family devotionals.

She's married and is the proud mother of four amazing kids. She loves to sing praises to God. When she's not busy taking care of her family, she's writing.

Printed in Great Britain
by Amazon